KENNY BOYLE was born on the I
an actor at the Royal Conservatoire
an honours degree from the Unive

the star, alongside Natalie Clark, of the multi-award-winning
short film *Perfect Strangers* (2015) and of the feature-film follow-
up, *Lost at Christmas* (2020). His plays include *Playthrough* and
An Isolated Incident, and in 2021 he received a New Playwrights
Award from the Playwrights' Studio, Scotland. *The Tick and the
Tock of the Crocodile Clock* is his debut novel.

Praise for *The Tick and the Tock of the Crocodile Clock*

'Very different and engagingly unique. Kenny Boyle is bristling with talent, and this may well be the best book I've read in years'
Peter May

'A charming, funny and unique story that tackles tough issues with a gentleness and poignancy that really resonated with me'
Clare Grogan

'Funny, intelligent and insightful. Kenny Boyle is a singular voice'
Sanjeev Kohli

'A brilliant, big-hearted book about art, friendship, mental illness and the power of poetry and storytelling'
Maggie Haggith

'From the first line, *The Tick and the Tock of the Crocodile Clock* has a kind of gleeful playfulness at its heart, a light sense of humour applied even to heavy material. Immediate and engaging, it will resonate with anyone who ever wanted to escape everyday life'
Rodge Glass

A bittersweet paean to friendship, art and making your mark, with a sharp line in patter and a big heart'
Alan Bissett

'Funny, heart-breaking and compassionate. Kenny Boyle deals with difficult subjects with great insight and a light touch. If you have ever dreamed of escape and of living life with no safety harness, this is the book for you'
Catherine Simpson

THE TICK AND THE TOCK
OF THE CROCODILE CLOCK

KENNY BOYLE

Lightning
Books

Published in 2022
by Lightning Books
Imprint of Eye Books Ltd
29A Barrow Street
Much Wenlock
Shropshire
TF13 6EN

www.lightning-books.com

Cover design by Nell Wood

Typeset in Dante MT Std and Emmascript MVB Std

British Library Cataloguing in Publication Data
A catalogue record for this book is available from the British Library.

ISBN: 9781785633027

Dedicated to everyone who has ever stood
at the top of the mountain,
or seen that dark figure
in the corner of their eye.

I taught you to fight and to fly.
What more could there be?
from J.M. Barrie's *Peter Pan*

1

attic

Sometimes I worry my mind isn't on my side.

Ugh. No. Start over.

If you're reading this, I'm already dead.

Sorry. No. Worst start ever. Cliché. I just always thought if I were going to write something like this then that's how I'd start. Now that I've written it, it sounds a little insensitive given the circumstances.

Then again, she'd probably have laughed.

If you're reading this then the chances are I'm probably not dead.

Although that depends on *when* you're reading this. Maybe you've found this in an archaeological dig in the year 3020. Just a wad of ancient fossilised paper that survived after all the hard drives and supercomputers of the early twenty-first century were destroyed by an apocalyptic electro-magnetic pulse that ended social media forever.

Focus. Sorry. I've got a lot of adrenaline just now.

Start over.

I'm wasting too much time.
We only have so much.
Tick-tock, tick-tock.

My name is Wendy.

Yes. That's much better.

I'm writing this from my grandmother's attic in Giffnock, where I'm hiding. I'm frightened, I'm angry, I've still got dried blood on my cuff and collar, and mostly, behind all the adrenaline, I'm sad.

Sadness is tingling all over my skin and poking my eyes.

'Sad' is such a pathetic-sounding word, there are so many other words for this feeling. I know a lot of them – knowing stupid unnecessary words is a bit of a hobby of mine – but 'sad' seems the truest.

You're probably asking yourself some questions.

'Why is she hiding? Is she being hunted by someone?'

Yes. And they'll probably find me.

'Why is she being hunted?'

I stole a painting. A priceless work of art. I know that doesn't really show me in the best light, but I had a good reason, I swear.

'Does she really think she'll be safe hiding in the attic of her grandmother's house?'

I live with my gran. It would be ridiculous to steal a priceless painting and go hide in the attic of your own home – so ridiculous that it'd be the last place people would look.

So that probably buys me some time.

Oh God, what am I doing?

On windy nights in my gran's house ghosts chap the letter box. They sing through the windows, and run on clawed feet over the slates on our roof. They're up there just now, over my head, rattling the stones, asking to get in. We don't answer the door when it chaps on windy nights, or open the windows when we hear the phantom carols. They're just ghosts.

But it's hard to ignore them tonight, because I don't know whose ghosts they are.

Oh, I'm in trouble. I really am. I'm in trouble.

It's easy to judge people; we do it every day. People say, 'never judge by appearances,' and I agree with that, but we still do it, don't we? It's a survival instinct hardwired into us all.

You might have judged me already. You might think I'm crazy.

I hate that word.

I really, really hate it.

But maybe you'd be right.

All I can do is tell you what happened, from the start.

Okay. Deep breath. Here's the story.

2

Revolution

There are loads of different visions of purgatory. Lots of different religions have this idea that before you get to paradise you have to go through a period of cleaning out all the sins, like a spiritual detox diet. When this all started I worked in a call centre. Lots of big banks like to have call centres in Glasgow or other parts of Scotland. Studies have shown that deep-rooted cultural stereotypes mean that when people hear a Scottish accent they associate it with the old trope of Scots being frugal, so they trust us with their money. It's ironic really, because I'm awful with money.

You've probably heard people saying that working in a call centre is hellish. Honestly, I don't think call centres have the strength of character to be hell. In call centres even bright things or bright people get washed out and individuality is smothered by customer service. Every call is recorded for 'quality and training purposes', and every toilet break is timed to the second. Call centres aren't hell – they're too bland – but they might be purgatory. I think, compared to hell, purgatory would involve a lot more paperwork.

I finish a call and another comes in immediately.

'Thank you for calling Chay Turley Telephone Banking. How may I dissuade you from truculence?' I say into my silly little 90s popstar headset microphone.

I'm fascinated by words. I think of them like beautiful, endangered wild animals. They're incredible but I have a healthy fear and respect for them. I know that might sound a bit strange, and that it's not how most people think about words, if they think about them at all. I do. I think about words a lot.

There are words that are still around but hardly ever get said: taciturnity, which means to be quiet or shy; loquacity, which means the opposite: to be outgoing and conversational; acquiescence: to accept something; ubiquitous; abnegation; naïveté, you get the point. They're mostly useless in conversation, because people look at you like you've just flown in from some fantasy land if you say them. Having to explain the meaning of a word every time you use it goes against the whole point of having words in the first place. I like them anyway; their uselessness adds to their mystique.

Some words are so ancient they don't even get to stay in the dictionary. They're so unloved they got kicked out of the book of all words.

Words like daedalist.

Daedalist just means anyone who flies. Pilots, airline passengers, chickens with something to prove. I think it's a magical word. Daedalist.

The customer I'm speaking to is Mr Robert Mullins, and

I've strayed from the company's carefully crafted script. I'm playing a game. It's called 'Sneak as many unusual words as possible into a call.' The rules are in the name.

When I come across new words I can't just drop them into a casual conversation with someone I might have to speak with again, but a call with a faceless stranger is a pretty low-risk opportunity to try them out. Usually the people on the other end of the phone aren't really listening anyway.

'I have a charge I'd like reversed,' Mr Mullins' voice grumbles into my ear.

I can see from the call log that has popped up on my screen that Mr Robert Mullins has charges quite often.

'You have a charge? Well I shall endeavour not to be too ultracrepidarian regarding that, sir,' I reply.

Ultracrepidarian means to give advice about things you know nothing about.

'Right. Good. I hope you do.'

Well done Robert. Not many people let a word like ultracrepidarian just go by unchallenged.

'I got a text from Chay Turley just now, saying you were taking an unauthorised overdraft fee,' he goes on.

I'd usually lose my nerve after scoring as long a word as ultracrepidarian, but Robert really seemed to understand what I meant. I might be able to beat my own top score with Robert on board. I try another.

'How curglaffic,' I gasp.

'Aye, you're telling me,' Robert replies. Do I detect a hint of a laugh? I'm not sure.

Either he knows the word curglaffic, which is the feeling of shock when you come into contact with cold water, or he's just one of these bigger-pictures types who can get it from the context.

I'm getting carried away. It's been a fun ten seconds or so – probably the best I've had in work all week – but I should stop messing around now.

Maybe just one more.

'Sir, I would ecstatically indulge in retrogressing your account to an earlier state, would you like that?' I offer.

'What?' he asks.

'Retrogressing your account?' Maybe he just didn't hear me the first time.

'I'm sorry, what's that mean?' comes the response.

I'm disappointed. I'd hoped that Mr Robert Mullins had been a kindred spirit. I thought I'd found someone with the same niche interest as me. It *was* a bit of a weird turn of phrase I guess.

I want to give Robert another chance to share with me in the joy of having a bloated vocabulary. I want him to prove he understands words so old they only really belong in sentences that have 'thou' or 'art' in them.

'I apologise, sir. I'm being obtuse. I'm just asking if a volte-face would be a favourable figurative baisemain?' I say.

No.

Sorry.

I don't say that.

I'm lying.

I want to say that, but I don't.

All Mr Mullins wants is for charges on his account to be reversed. He might deserve the charges; he might not. I don't know. I've wasted too much of the call being silly and I have targets to meet. I also don't really care if he deserves them. I can see his accounts; they're overdrawn and unhealthy. I can see that some of the transactions leaving are going to a nursery, and others to a pay-day loan company. I'm in a position to help Mr Mullins. It's the right thing to do.

'I'll reverse the charges for you, sir,' I say.

'Thank you,' Mr Mullins says.

'Sure thing, sir. Have a good day. Thanks for calling CTB.'

'You've been great,' he says. 'I liked the lexiphanicism.'

I grin in delight.

Robert hangs up – the small human connection we had, severed with a click.

The aftercall notes form pops up on my screen. I know the moment I hit the 'next' button another call will be shoved into my tired ears. I hover my mouse cursor lazily over the button, drawing little infinity signs with it like a sparkler on Bonfire Night. I try building up the willpower to take the next complaint. Robert is probably going to be the highlight of my day, which means it's all downhill from here. I write down the word 'lexiphanicism' in a notepad I carry with me; I can look it up later.

'Wendy.'

The voice doesn't come from my headset. It comes from behind me. It's Lindsay, my manager, a tyrant of a woman with delusions of adequacy.

'Wendy,' she says again. It won't be the last time she uses my name in the next two minutes. At some point, some middle-management training course must have taught her that using staff's names builds rapport and helps maintain control of a conversation. If only I'd kept Robert on the phone longer.

'Yup. Here. What's up?' I enthuse. It never hurts to be upbeat when dealing with a superior.

'Everything okay, Wendy?' Lindsay raises an eyebrow.

'Yeah. Certainly,' I say. Certainly is a good word. Very professional. It's a word that suggests you're willing to give one hundred and ten percent even though that's mathematically impossible.

Lindsay has a trick, or a natural gift, because I don't think she does it deliberately: her mind is ponderous, like an iguana. When you say something to her it takes her a good two seconds to process it – two whole seconds of silent glaring as the words take root. When someone like that meets someone like me it doesn't ever turn out well. I can't bear those two seconds of silence, so I have to fill the gap. A lot of the time I fill it with incriminating evidence to my detriment.

'Why wouldn't it be?' I go on, about one and a half seconds into Lindsay's processing cycle.

'I've just had a call from a very upset old dear, Wendy,' Lindsay says. 'She claims you called her a foul name.'

'What?' I'm genuinely shocked. I'd never. 'I didn't. I wouldn't swear on the phone. I try not to even swear in the building.'

'She didn't say you swore, Wendy, but that you called her a name.'

'What?' I say, with less confidence; a memory is bubbling up. 'What name? What did I say?'

Lindsay, after the necessary two seconds of accusatory staring, pulls a folded Post-it note out of her pocket. She peers down her nose at it, with the air of someone reading through varifocals, but she lacks the decency to actually be wearing any glasses. She utters the word 'Slackumtrance.'

'Slackumtrance?' I giggle dismissively. 'That's not a nasty name.'

It is.

Lindsay glares dimly into my soul. The giggle dies and is

eaten by the ennui that lingers in the call centre air. Lindsay looks down on me literally and figuratively and says, 'Wendy, I'm not some ignorant fool.'

She is.

'That lady knew she was being insulted.'

She didn't.

'It took only a brief internet search to confirm her fear.'

Oh no.

'You called that lady a dirty harlot, didn't you Wendy?'

What can I possibly say? She's spot on. That's the exact meaning of the word. It's hard to argue with a dictionary definition. I hadn't realised when I said it. I jot down words I like in my notepad when I hear them. I'd thought I was calling the lady something endearing. I'd read the wrong line. I felt awful when I found out. I was so worried about it I'd stopped playing my game for weeks. This is exactly the reason I don't use new words in the real world.

I can't believe the lady would have thought to look the word up so long after I'd used it.

I stammer hopelessly.

'I don't really think that your behaviour is becoming of the Chay Turley group, Wendy,' Lindsay goes on. 'You seem to think you're too good for us. Us. One of the biggest banks in the world.'

She's beginning to pick up speed, like a juggernaut of discipline ready to smash through me with sheer momentum. I'm curling up inside, rolling into a ball. Why does she have to do this here? Why in front of everyone? They're all looking. They're all watching me withering in front of them.

'And let me tell you another thing, my girl,' she goes on, 'you're certainly not as clever as you think you are. Not so clever that you can afford to just ignore my instructions for generating leads and creating sales.'

I can't hear anyone else talking now, which is unusual in a call centre. I wish that overture of employees on calls would return, but everyone near me has put their calls on hold. It's schadenfreude – that's another word from my notepad. They're miserable here, but at least they aren't getting their heads bitten off by the boss, so It could be worse for them. I'm an example to them all. My stomach is eating itself.

'You're lucky to be here, Wendy, because the life and energy that I used to see in you on your first week has quickly turned into dour-faced stupidity,' Lindsay finishes.

Dour-faced stupidity.

'Well? Do you have anything to say for yourself?' she prompts.

Dour-faced stupidity?

Yes. I do have something to say for myself. 'My behaviour? *My* behaviour? The chief exec is all over the newspapers this week after being caught out having a string of affairs; I don't think that me accidentally using an old insult will add much tarnish to the CTB name. This is one of the banks whose dodgy dealings and greed led to the total economic downfall of the entire country. It's not exactly got the best of reputations as it is. And Lindsay, listen up, this is important: I'm not your "girl". Don't ever, *ever*, call me that again.'

No.

Sorry.

I'm lying.

I just want you to like me. I don't even know who you are, but I want you to like me. I'm going to try to be honest from now on, I promise.

I don't say that. I don't say any of that. I just open and close my mouth and try not to cry.

'Well then,' Lindsay concludes pompously, after watching me struggle for the prerequisite two full seconds, 'this doesn't look good for you at all, Wendy. Follow me to my office. We'll be filling in an incident report and then I'll be passing it further up the chain. I imagine they'll take a dim view.'

She turns and starts walking to her office with the same joy she'd probably have if she were ushering me to the guillotine.

My limbs are stuck in rigor mortis. I can't be marched out in front of all these people; I just can't. If I get to my feet, I'll break down. If I do anything I'll break down. I've got rubber bands wrapped around me and they're getting tighter and smaller every second. I can't move.

'Wendy,' Lindsay says, pointing at a spot on the floor next to her, calling me like a naughty dog.

I'm not trying to be nasty, I'm in fight or flight survival mode. I want to teleport out of the building and never be seen again. I'm not in any fit state to be deliberately picking a fight. I've never picked a fight in my life, but some part of me notices something, and some other part of me that would usually stop me from saying anything out loud must be on annual leave.

'You've got lipstick on your teeth,' I say quietly.

The whole call centre draws in a breath.

Lindsay stares at me a lot longer than two seconds this time. Finally, she speaks. 'You insolent little girl.'

'I quit,' I blubber suddenly. Something in my subconscious has pulled out a half-remembered fact about how it's better to quit than be fired. I can't recall the specifics.

'Pardon?' Lindsay bears down on me like an angry shark.

She's going to tear me apart. This isn't how this should go.

I've quit now; she has no power over me. She's no one. I can just leave.

But I don't. I'm powerless before her. All I can do is brace for the tirade. It's incredible when you think about it – all of this has happened because I said a single, solitary, mostly forgotten word.

'If she's leaving, so am I,' comes a voice from the other side of the washed-out blue cubicle divider wall.

I have no idea who this person is.

Whoever she is, she stands up, so her head is visible over the top of the divider.

'Who are you?' Lindsay demands. I'm surprised to learn that not only do I not recognise this person, but the manager doesn't either.

'Doesn't matter who I am. She stood up to you, I'm standing with her.'

She does, physically. She walks around the sad little divider and joins me in my cramped cubicle. I feel the elastic bands tied around my limbs and stomach loosen off a little.

'Wait.' Recognition dawns on Lindsay's face. 'It's Catriona, isn't it?'

Catriona doesn't answer. Instead she turns to me, showing her back to Lindsay.

'Ignore her,' Catriona says. I notice her voice is shaking, but it's not fear. She's angry. She's absolutely furious.

'You only started taking calls this morning,' Lindsay blurts, incredulous.

Catriona keeps on ignoring Lindsay. 'Do you want to leave?'

'Yes,' I reply, confused and still not totally sure if I'm being supported or elaborately teased.

'Then let's leave.'

Lindsay rallies. 'Now listen here, young lady, if you leave on your first shift on the floor you better not expect to be paid for the month of training we've given you.'

Catriona spins on her heel, her clenched fists shaking by her side. I honestly think for a second she's about to hit Lindsay.

'I don't expect anything from you,' Catriona says.

She turns back to me and she winks, assuring me I'm complicit, then she marches past Lindsay and straight out of the call centre.

'And you *do* have lipstick on your teeth,' she shouts back, giving Lindsay the finger over her shoulder as the door swings closed behind her.

I watch her go. I see Lindsay, standing next to me, mouth dangling down by her collar bone. I can't help but smile. Robert Mullins wasn't the highlight of the day, after all.

Then it starts to happen. A guy three desks down tosses down his headset and marches to the door. Then another. Then another. I see other people watch them go with a hungry longing in their eyes. Those dominoes will fall soon. Maybe not today, maybe not tomorrow, but soon.

This must be what it would feel like to start a revolution.

3

Cavalier

When I get home my gran is waiting for me. She's made fairy cakes. Not for any special reason – just because she thought I might like some. She asks me how my day was, and I tell her I don't have a job any more. She still gives me a cake. I feel like a monster.

I go to my room. I lie on my bed. I write off the rest of the day. There's plenty of time to do something, to make something of today rather than let it just be the day I lost my job. I could try to find another one, I could write a new poem, I could do anything.

But none of it seems important enough to move. I lie in bed with the spectres of all the things I could be doing, or ought to be doing, peering over me, willed into being as promising ideas, starved to death by lack of motivation, decaying into niggles, then to worries, then to black clouds of failure. I'm surrounded by the corpses of possibilities. I try to ignore them.

There must be a name for this. There must be a word.

I get caught off guard by a memory from a long time ago. I hop into the memory like a time machine.

When I was young, I had a cat who thought she was a dog. She was brought up with two dogs and I guess when you're surrounded by dogs and people, and you're pretty sure you're not one of the bald things that walk on two legs, then it stands to reason you're a small one of the other hairy four-legged things. She was called Cavalier.

She didn't have the snootiness you might think of when you think of your stereotypical cat. She was boisterous.

The first poem I ever wrote was about her. I spent all day on it, carefully picking words that rhymed. I became the first person to ever rhyme the word 'cat' with 'hat'…as far as I knew, anyway. I illustrated it all with felt tip pens and hung it on my gran's wall. It's still there, but the ink has mostly faded.

I found out one day she that she was as protective as any dog, too. I was about seven, and I was out walking Cavalier. Not on a lead or anything – I guess I should say we were out on a walk together. It was one of those balmy long days that we all remember happening when we were kids but that don't seem to exist now. I don't know if climate change has messed up the world so much since I was seven that our whole experience of weather is different or if those days are actually just warmed by the heat of nostalgia. An hour of nice weather becomes a day, a day a whole summer. What's time to a seven-year-old?

I had this toy with me, a little plastic blue bone. I was working on a game called 'Can a cat play fetch?' The rules are in the name.

Isn't it funny that in primary school you always call people by their full name, and you never really get out of the habit?

You're in your twenties and you meet someone from primary school in the supermarket and you don't think 'there's George', you think 'There's George Scourie who wet himself in class once.'

God, George, if you're reading this, I'm sorry for bringing that up.

The full name of the girl I met that day was Felicia Malcolm. Like me, she was seven. Unlike me, she was a little shit.

I saw Felicia Malcolm a long time before she saw me, but I also saw that I couldn't avoid her – there was only one way to go and it was towards Felicia Malcolm. I put my head down. I remember I blushed just seeing her. I can't remember exactly what brought that blush on – I don't know if I was ashamed to be afraid of her, as though my fear of her conflicted with the brave little girl I knew I ought to be, or if I knew that whatever was about to happen would be embarrassing or demeaning, or maybe it was anger, a blush of pure, bottled-up, child rage. I don't remember why I blushed, but I remember the feeling, the warmth tightening the skin on my cheeks. I looked at the pavement.

Felicia Malcolm didn't care that I wasn't looking at her. I could sense when she finally noticed me, and I could feel her eyes sweeping over me looking for something to make fun of. Before I passed her completely and she missed her chance, Felicia Malcolm, all curls and cuteness, marched across the road. When they first met Felicia Malcolm, teachers would often think she was a little angel. Soon they learned that if she was an angel, she'd been on the losing side of the war. You know, the ones that fell?

I stopped walking. It seemed rude to keep going, given I knew she was coming towards me. I kept looking at the ground, still hoping she might not see me. Looking back now it was a major faux pas to approach me outside of school. Back then, generally bullying was confined to school hours, as though we'd all agreed to some weird code of honour. I'd have said that to her, but I didn't know the term 'faux pas'.

Felicia Malcolm had been waiting for a chance to get me alone. She'd tried a few times to tease me at school. I don't know what I'd done to annoy her – maybe she just saw an easy target – but at school my teachers were there to stop her. There weren't any teachers there that day. She was bigger than me. It wasn't fair at all.

'What's that?' Felicia Malcolm pointed at the dog-chewed little blue bone.

'Just a toy,' I said, retreating into my own hair.

'It's not like any sort of toy I've ever seen.' Felicia Malcolm wrinkled her turned-up little nose.

I couldn't see how I was to blame for how many toys Felicia Malcolm had or hadn't seen. I shrugged. I hoped that that would be the end of it.

'I have better toys,' she pointed out with lazy superiority. I imagine Felicia Malcolm's parents were little shits in their own right when they were young. That meant that by breeding they had birthed a multiplication of their own little shittiness. A little shit squared.

'It's a dog toy,' I said, as politely as I could.

'What do you mean by that?' Felicia Malcolm replied.

I had no idea how to answer that question. I hadn't said anything complicated, it was just a fact.

'Why would I play with dog toys?' Felicia Malcolm poked my chest.

Now I see where the confusion came from, but at the time

I thought she was genuinely asking me if we were in some parallel world where she, Felicia Malcolm, liked to play with dog toys, then what could that mean. I thought it was a test, to see how logical I was.

'If you were a dog?' I said, demurely.

Wrath flared in Felicia Malcolm's nasty little eyes.

'Touché,' Felicia Malcolm said.

She probably didn't say that actually; she was seven. I don't know.

I do know, though, that with the sudden viciousness and speed you'd expect from a king cobra, Felicia Malcolm grabbed my hair.

She hadn't expected a cheeky reply from me. She hadn't expected any reply at all, really. I suppose her plan had just been to tease me and make me cry. I think Felicia Malcolm was the sort of kid who would get some sort of satisfaction from that.

I struggled, but I could tell straight away that she was stronger than me and I wasn't going to get loose. My hands and feet were free but I didn't want to punch or kick her. I couldn't imagine doing something like that. What if I hurt her?

That's when Cavalier happened.

Yeah, I know a cat can't 'happen', but at this point Cavalier wasn't just a cat, she was an event. She was a thing that happened to Felicia Malcolm and I don't think Felicia Malcom would disagree. Cavalier sailed majestically down from the wall above us. I watched her drop in slow motion, forgetting entirely about the pain of my hair being yanked. I was terrified for Cavalier, It was a long way down, even if cats do always land on their feet, and there was nothing below but hard concrete.

But I didn't know that Cavalier wasn't planning on landing on the concrete. She landed right on Felicia Malcolm's face. That was the day Felicia Malcolm learned that loyalty was a lot more effective than fear, that picking on people smaller than you has consequences, and that cats have sharp claws. Felicia Malcolm ran for Felicia Malcolm's life.

I told my gran everything. When Felicia Malcolm's mum came to my door later that afternoon, I spied on the conversation she had with my gran as I hid on the stairs.

'Your brat granddaughter set her cat on my girl,' came the indignant cry of the scorned Mother Malcolm.

'Who?' my gran asked innocently.

'My daughter,' Mother Malcolm repeated.

'Yes dear, of course your daughter,' my gran said with soothing patronisation. 'I mean, who did it?'

'Your brat granddaughter,' Mother Malcolm spat.

'I don't have one of those,' gran explained.

'A granddaughter?' Mother Malcolm railed. 'Oh yes you do.'

'No,' my gran said, 'a brat.'

Mother Malcolm looked taken aback for a moment, then recovered.

'Your grandchild,' she complained, 'ordered her cat to mutilate my daughter.'

'Do you mean this cat, love?' my gran pointed at Cavalier, sitting next to her blamelessly licking a paw.

Mother Malcolm didn't seem sure how to answer that.

'It would be quite the trick really, wouldn't it?' my gran mused. 'Training a cat to attack people, without me knowing, when she's only seven.'

Mother Malcolm eyed Cavalier suspiciously.

'Perhaps you've got the wrong house, dear?' my gran

suggested, giving Mother Malcolm a chance to save face while also giving her a chance to go directly to hell.

After that I knew that, with Cavalier at my side, I was safe. She spent her whole life protecting me. She is my archetype of a cat – the perfect cat that all other cats wish they were but will never be.

But one day Cavalier died.

One day my Gran will too.

4

Lost Shadow

The next few days, or maybe even weeks, are a void. I watch whatever old, brainless action or adventure movies I can find to stream. Nothing too thought provoking – I don't need to think just now, I'd far rather not.

My gran asks me a few times if I want to come downstairs and watch TV with her – reality shows where people sing, or dance, or skate, or do all of those things at once. I tell her I think I'd rather just stay in my room for a wee while.

She keeps saying, 'Just enjoy the break. You'll find something.'

But it's not a break. I'm not on holiday.

Imagine you're on a bus and the person sitting next to you turns in their seat and stares at you. They just turn and stare. You don't want to acknowledge them or look back at them, in case they're dangerous, so you just keep looking straight ahead, out of the bus window. You can see them from the corner of your eye. You certainly aren't relaxed.

Sitting on the battered couch in my room, day after day, I'm not sitting there alone. There's something sitting next to me, intangible and dark, and it's just staring at me. I look like I'm watching TV but actually I'm trying not to look at it. It's just there. Staring. I'm certainly not relaxed.

The wallpaper asphyxiates me. The couch consumes me. It's too cold without the heating on, but with it on the hot air gets in behind my eyeballs and dries them out. It feels like my eyelids are blinking over sand.

There's so much I should do, or could do. I always feel like I have no time to do the things I want to; now I have nothing but time, but I can't do anything. I'm just letting it pass.

Tick-tock, tick-tock.

I think a lot about Catriona. I keep on trying to write off the whole walkout thing as just a strange experience, and not something I really have to think much more about, but whenever I do manage to move on and focus on just watching those old movies, or the necessities like helping my gran with the cleaning, I find my thoughts tiptoeing back to it.

It was her first day.

It's as though my head is only big enough to hold one feeling at a time, and this persistent curiosity is pushing everything else out. It's not a bad feeling to be preoccupied with – it's a lot better than acknowledging that dark thing on the couch with me.

I decide I have to get out of the house. My limbs agree a few hours later.

I pop down to the shop to buy essentials – a loaf of bread, a tin of beans, and a pack of instant noodles. I have a nagging craving for beans on toast, and a spooky premonition that, once I satisfy that one, a craving for noodles is patiently waiting its turn. It's amazing how, even after you leave university, it takes a wee while to shake the student dietary patterns, isn't it?

The supermarket I'm going to isn't the closest one to my house. In fact I've walked past two just to get to it, but now that I'm outside I'm enjoying the fresh air, so I've decided to prolong the walk. I'm headed to Shawlands. Half of everyone who lives in Glasgow will tell you Shawlands is up-and-coming, and the other half will tell you it's going rapidly downhill. It's such a reputational yoyo. Personally, I've always liked it.

My gran makes dinner every night; healthy, wholesome stuff. I keep turning it down in favour of blowing the last of my money on takeaways. I'd absolutely love to keep on just ordering pizza every night but I'm unemployed now, so I guess I have to eat like it. Gran says that ordering food is bad for the environment, which I instantly bristle against and deny without wanting to research, which probably means she's right, unfortunately. I get to the supermarket and I decide that while I'm there I'm going to buy something for us both to have for dinner, something nutritious and nice that we can eat together.

'Excuse me, doll?' says a lady who's somewhere between her late fifties and early two hundreds.

'What's up?' I ask.

'You're taller than me,' the lady says.

'A little,' I concede. I'm no giant but the lady is pocket-sized. 'Want me to reach something for you?'

'Can you grab me one of those, doll?' she says, pointing.

I pick up some tinned tomatoes for her, stretching to get them from the top shelf.

'Cheers, doll. Follow me.' She walks off down the aisle,

leaving me to either follow her or sneak off in the opposite direction. I go with the former.

'Can you just grab me some cumin from up there?' she asks.

'Of course.'

I hand it to her.

'You in a hurry doll?' the lady asks. 'I need some stuff from other aisles as well.'

I look around for the hidden cameras. I'm sure this must be some kind of prank. This could take a while, but I've not got anywhere to be, have I? What if this were my gran and I found out someone hadn't helped her?

'Shall we do our shopping together?' I offer. 'Then I'll be here to help whenever you need any.'

'Grand,' says the lady, before taking off at a shocking speed, with me trotting along behind her.

I help the lady reach things for the best part of half an hour. It's nice to be useful.

That's when I see her. Or, at least, I think I do. The supermarket has huge windows that look out onto the street. A lot of the window space is covered with branding and I can't see her face, but that's her hair I think. Or is it? Have I just been thinking about her and the walkout so much over the last few days that now I see her everywhere? I only saw her in real life for a minute or two; how can I possibly recognise her from the back of her head?

'I have to go, have you got everything you need?' I ask the lady.

'You've been great, doll. I'm fine now,' she says. I'm out of the supermarket and rushing down the street a few seconds later, my own shopping completely forgotten about.

I see her ahead of me. I don't really know what I'm doing.

I follow her. I just have to see if it's actually her. After that I don't really have a plan.

She turns her head around at one point to look into a shop or to flick the hair out of her face. I get a quick glimpse of her profile.

Yes. That's her. That's Catriona.

Okay, my curiosity is sated, I can stop following her now, but my feet don't want to. I want to see where she's going.

Come on Wendy, you know what this's called don't you? Stalking. You're a stalker now. What are you going to say to her? That she was part of one of the most surreal days of your admittedly kind of sheltered life and you've followed her to say something? Something vital?

To say what?

Catriona turns a corner when I'm only a couple of steps behind her and I dart behind a bus stop so as she doesn't spot me.

What am I doing?

This is daft. I pull out my phone and frown at it as though I just got a really troubling text message. That way if anyone is watching me they won't wonder why I'm suddenly turning around and heading back the way I came; they'll just think, 'Why, golly, she must have received an urgent message insisting she come home immediately.' The perfect deception.

But I've followed her this far, what's one more corner?

I rush after Catriona, strutting around the corner as quickly as I can without it being a run or, God forbid, a jog.

She's standing right there. Waiting for me.

'That's good,' Catriona says.

'What?' I say gormlessly, embarrassment working its way up my neck.

'I thought I'd lost my shadow.'

We stand there looking at each other. I wish I had the speech skills to be considered a raconteur. I'd be lucky to be considered a racoon.

'Wendy,' she says. There's a slight smile, which breaks the tension. She's taking pity on me.

'I wanted to thank you,' I blurt, and I realise that it's true, not just an excuse for following her around like a creep.

'I wanted to thank *you*,' Catriona replies.

It's not what I'd expected her to say at all. All I can manage is another gormless, uninteresting, 'what?'

'You made it really obvious which side I should be on. I dodged a bullet not working there.'

'You're thanking me for getting fired in front of you on your first day?' I ask.

'Fired? You quit,' she reminds me.

'Thank you for standing up and leading the walkout. I mean, I know it was only five of us or something and it wasn't massive or anything, but it was epic, you know? It was so cool,' I stop myself from saying that she was like a Delacroix painting of Liberty – I don't want to sound like a total loser – but I think it. She was inspiring.

'Me?' Catriona says. 'I was following you.'

And perhaps for just a fraction of a second, I allow myself to consider the possibility that maybe, just maybe, *I* was Liberty on that barricade.

This is pathetic – I sound like a kid – but I want her to be my friend. I don't make friends easily. It's words. It always has been. Words are the problem. Isn't it terrifying that every time you open your mouth and make those sounds, they affect a change in the world? If I go into a shop and ask for a loaf of bread, a tin of beans, and a pack of instant noodles then I'll be given those things and the world will have changed in a small way because of something I said. And that's fine, I'm not bothered by shopping, but I have felt the weight of that weird responsibility since I was way too young to really articulate it, which is ironic of course, because now I can articulate it, but I wouldn't.

Ever since primary school I'd worry: what if I was in a class and I said something wrong? What if saying that made people feel differently about me and that had an impact further down the line? What if I accidentally hurt someone's feelings in ways I never knew? Worst of all, what if people laughed?

The trouble is when you stay quiet all the time eventually people notice if you say anything at all – and not in a good way.

'It speaks,' they'd say.

'Wendy, don't you ever shut up?' they'd laugh.

Children can be such dicks. Eventually you learn just to keep your mouth shut all the time. I kept myself to myself. If life were a freshly made bed, I'd try my best to lie on it without creasing the sheets.

And so, while a normal person would probably have said something like, 'I'm Wendy, it's nice to properly meet you', I say: 'I write poetry.'

'Yeah,' says Catriona, 'that sounds about right.'

I feel like I've passed a test.

She gestures at the sandstone tenement we're standing next to.

'This is my flat,' she says.

'Oh God, I've followed you home like a stray.' I wave my hands around in clumsy apology. 'I'll leave you alone now. Sorry.'

'Do you want to come up for a coffee?' Catriona interjects.

It sounds like she wants to be friends with me too. I'm so relieved I almost run away.

'I'm Wendy. It's nice to properly meet you,' I say instead.

'Cat,' replies Cat.

Cat's flat is small but suits her perfectly. It's the kind of flat that a letting agent might pitch as a 'studio'. The kitchen, living room and bedroom are all one room, but at least you get privacy in the toilet. Like all tenements the ceiling is high, the floorboards have gaps and the boiler in the open-plan kitchen is ancient. Despite all of that, the flat is welcoming. Cold, granted, but welcoming. I use my powers of deduction: most people hang paintings on walls, most people don't have an easel, most people only buy paintings that are finished – she's an artist.

'Nice place,' I say. 'Really bohemian.'

'It's a shithole,' Cat says, moving over to the kitchen area. The kitchen cupboards are in the corner of the room, grouped around an uncomfortable-looking oven, as though they're all huddling together for warmth. 'Sorry about that.'

'In your defence you didn't know you were going to get stalked today,' I observe, trying to figure out if it would be impolite to sit down before being asked. Trying to figure out if it's impolite to look at the half-finished paintings, or if it's impolite not to.

'Stalked? You were stalking me?' Cat asks.

'It's what I was worried you might think,' I admit.

'I'm a daftie,' Cat sighs, closing the last of her cupboards. 'I don't have any coffee.'

'That's a relief,' I say. 'I hate coffee.'

Do you remember magic-eye puzzles? If you looked at them exactly right, you'd see the 3D shape hidden inside? Cat squints at me for a second before making a face like I'm one of those puzzles and she's just seen the 3D fairy pop out of the flat page.

'You hate coffee,' she says, 'but you hate being rude more.'

'I'd have drunk the whole mug and not complained once.'

Cat looks around for something else to offer, obviously at least slightly shackled by the idea of politeness herself; a good host should offer their guests something.

'Do you smoke?' she says at last.

'I don't really see the point in tobacco,' I say.

'Yeah,' says Cat. 'Me neither.'

I have no idea what is happening. It's as though she's slipped into speaking Spanish or something, but doesn't think it matters because she thinks I'm from Spain. Only she isn't speaking Spanish. So, what is she speaking? Oh my God. She's speaking drugs.

Drugs. I think she means drugs. I think she wants me to smoke one of those things. A doobie? What do people even call them? I don't know the lingo. I'm fairly sure that 'lingo' isn't in the lingo.

Joint. Joint? I think it's joint.

Suddenly I feel really, really uncool, so I tell her what happened to my parents. And now I'll tell you too.

5

Perfectly Matched

I'm an orphan. I live with my gran, and I'm glad to have her. I don't resent my parents for leaving: they had no choice. My grandmother has told me all the stories about them both – their crazy life, the sacrifices they made. They were heroes.

I know it sounds insane, but my parents were spies. Spies, during the Cold War.

They met at a high-stakes poker game. Dad had this trick where he made sure that no one knew who he was by immediately identifying himself by both his first and second name wherever he went, and just in case anyone was still in any doubt after that he also had a signature drink: prosecco, neither shaken nor stirred. Mum had a penchant for puns delivered in a sultry voice. They fell in love when neither of them would fold and both kept their nerve in the face of an ever-increasing pot, great rewards for the victor and a terrible loss for the loser. Neither knew when the other was bluffing, neither could identify any tells, both realised they had met their match, not just at poker, but for life. In the end it didn't matter who won, because all those winnings went towards their wedding.

Both were such accomplished spies that they successfully kept it a secret from each other that they were MI6 agents throughout an entire year of marriage. Eventually their boss decided it would probably be easier for everyone concerned if they were both told that the other was secretly a spy. For one thing it would mean they could take one car to work. Both were a little startled to find out the other had been keeping such a huge secret from them, but neither could really hold a grudge; it would have been too easy to demonstrate the hypocrisy.

They became a legend in MI6. The dream team. There wasn't any mission too impossible for them.

But secrets run deep in my family. My mum wasn't what she seemed; she was a double agent, a sleeper working for the KGB, deep undercover in MI6.

One day she got the order.

A brown envelope fell through her door to activate her. Kill orders, to dispatch an important target within MI6.

To kill Dad.

At the same exact moment, my dad got a call from MI6. They'd realised that Mum was a double agent. He was ordered to kill her.

Dad felt betrayed, obviously, so they both stealthily set out to find each other and prepared to take part in what they realised may turn out to be a protracted ten-minute fight filled with unlikely, but entertaining, action.

Everything was extremely tense. They both knew they were

in the house with a trained killer who they were going to have to use their own training to kill. Dad was trying to see round a corner using the reflection of a photo of his mother-in-law, angling it around to get a good look without breaking cover. Suddenly half the wall over his head just disintegrated. That was thanks to Mum, blasting at him with a shotgun.

Dad was too quick, he dodged, weaved, and fired back a few shots from his silenced pistol. Mum was basically a ninja, though, and she rolled down the stairs, deftly avoiding every single shot.

She tried to kill him with the shotgun again. He just walked casually out of her line of sight and she narrowly missed him. Bits of wall were flying everywhere; the architecture was less capable of dodging. Dad tried to shoot Mum again, but his legendary accuracy seemed to be failing him suddenly. The trouble was that he was only really used to fighting unimportant people with no backstory and it's extremely easy to kill them with pinpoint accuracy because they aren't essential to the plot. Managing to successfully fire a gun at someone with a name and character development was, weirdly, a lot more difficult.

Mum somehow got hold of an AK47 and she slid along the floor firing blindly. Dad grabbed a meat cleaver and tossed it at her. It took a nick out of her ear but caused no significant injury. Mum shot a gas main and there was a massive explosion that, though visually impressive, harmed neither one of them, nor did any real damage to the house beyond the superficial. What it did do was start a series of small fires on various surfaces around the house. It wasn't the kind of fire that created a great deal of smoke or dangerous chemical fumes, so there was no risk of suffocation or poisoning. It was more the sort of fire that licked and danced in the background without spreading. Remarkably harmless, but exceedingly aesthetically pleasing for a battle.

They ended up with guns to each other's faces. Just as in the poker game it had turned out that they were equally matched. They were both willing to sacrifice their own lives for their missions. Why wouldn't they be? They were highly trained agents. But as they were staring murderously into each other eyes they realised something: they could, after a year together, finally tell when the other was bluffing. When they saw that lack of conviction in the eyes they were looking into, they each also realised that they themselves were bluffing, too. They just couldn't do it; they loved each other too much.

And legend has it that's the night a certain someone was conceived.

Mum and Dad knew they were in trouble – they'd both failed their missions – they'd both be burned by their respective agencies and would have to go into hiding from the very spies they had worked and trained with for their entire careers.

But they were the dream team, and those other spies would always be second-rate. They knew they could get out of the horrible tangle they'd found themselves in if they only worked together.

There was one major obstacle: they'd need money to get away from MI6 and the KGB. Lots of it.

Mum was always resourceful. She had this big bag of drugs from her last mission. It was full of all the drugs: heroin, cocaine, amphetamine, tequila, caffeine, Calpol – the lot. If they could sell them, then they'd have enough money to disappear for good. They'd fade into the night and never be seen again.

Dad used his underground network of snitches and contacts and found a buyer, a guy called The Knife. He had a scar across his face and was super-ugly, but film-ugly, not really ugly –like he was still pretty nice to look at, but the scar let you know he was bad news. And even though Dad was a super spy and trained to notice things like scars that are obvious indicators of villainy, his powers of perception weren't at their peak – he was too busy worrying about the hordes of spies, both Russian and British, who could show up to claim his scalp any moment.

Mum and Dad arranged to meet The Knife in an old abandoned warehouse. It was a secluded-enough warehouse that no one would suspect their illicit drug deal was going on inside, but big enough and close enough to a road that everyone could just drive their cars right in and park them at jaunty angles without any apparent bother. Everyone's car was matt black.

Mum and Dad arrived alone. Mum and Dad versus the world, just the way they liked it.

But The Knife's gang arrived in three Land Rovers. He'd brought a whole entourage, or, if you were cynical, a whole firing squad.

They made the trade in the traditional way. Mum carried a huge duffle bag of drugs, The Knife carried a briefcase full of crisp unmarked bills, they walked to the centre of the warehouse where they swapped bags before starting the long walk back to their own car. That's the dangerous part – the part where all the betrayals are most likely to happen.

The Knife, his gait slightly longer than my mum's, made it back to his men fractionally faster than she did. As soon as he was safely back among his armed guards he spun, aimed his gun, and fired it at my mother.

It was a shock. But it shouldn't have been, because it was a drug deal. Drugs. Drugs make people untrustworthy.

My dad must have had reflexes of mercury, he must have seen things in bullet-time. He had to save his wife and their unborn baby, even if the cost was his own life. He jumped in front of his beloved. He took that bullet for her – for both of us. As he lay bleeding on the ground he yelled at my mum to run, to run for her life.

He knew he had to buy her time, so he drew his own silenced pistol once more. Eight bullets in the clip. As The Knife's men advanced on him, he expertly eliminated one of them for each bullet he had. The Knife's men completely failed to shoot him as he executed them, despite the fact he was a stationary target on the ground, bleeding. It was probably because they were all wearing sunglasses. The Knife's men were learning – too late – that in situations like these, looking cool should come second to having good night vision. Alas, sharpshooter though he was, all too soon my dad pulled the trigger, and rather than a muffled pop, he was greeting by a deathly click. Out of ammo. He closed his eyes and accepted his fate.

Mum made it outside but when she got out of the double doors of the massive warehouse, she found herself surrounded by police cars. It was like the whole of the Greenock police were there (this happened in Greenock).

She knew she couldn't be taken in; she was KGB. MI6 would torture her for information – and that was the best-case scenario. If the KGB got a hold of her they'd be torturing her out of sheer malice. All the police were in a big circle around her, all pointing their guns, all screaming at her to get on her knees and drop her weapon.

She only had one choice. She had to curve the bullet.

My mum, with practised grace and poetry, swung her arm around in slow motion. She used a technique she learned that defies physics and logic and is seldom useful unless the perfect contrived opportunity arises. One bullet exploded from the barrel of her gun and flew around the circle, forming an ellipse of leaden death for all in its extremely specific trajectory. There were police brains flying everywhere.

Boom. Splat. 'Oh no, not Jimmy – he had a kid.'

The bullet travelled right around the circle, cutting through the poor innocent police, who were just trying to do their jobs, as though their skulls were made of butter. Eventually it claimed its last victim with a hollow thump as it – the magic bullet – entered her head. My mum's head. Her own shot went right into her brain.

She didn't want to live without Dad – she couldn't – so she curved it into her own head. So tragic.

So you see, my parents died before I was even born, all because of drugs.

6

Happy Thoughts

None of the last chapter was true.

Obviously.

But it is what I tell Cat that day in her fifth-floor tenement flat.

I've never behaved that way around another person before. I've never spoken for so long without trailing off or starting to feel unimportant or boring, but she kept on listening, she kept on smiling at the right bits, she seemed like she cared about what I was saying. I felt comfortable.

There's a silly rambling storyteller in me that never usually gets to come out. Everything I normally say and do is just a husk surrounding a little homunculus version of me, beneath all the layers, that chats away to me all day long inside. Usually I don't let the homunculus out in case people think I'm crazy.

Crazy.

I hate that word.

Now I've shown homunculus Wendy to Cat, not because she asked, but just because I wanted to.

Cat doesn't break the little fantasy world I've created. She doesn't say 'okay, but what really happened?' or, 'that's the dumbest reason not to take drugs I've ever heard, loser.'

'If my folks had been through all that, I wouldn't touch this shit either,' she says. 'Do you mind if I roll one, but?'

'No,' and I get a strange little thrill in allowing it because what I'm about to witness is, I'm pretty sure, technically illegal.

Cat takes out cigarette papers, a lighter, tobacco and a greenish brown lump. I try not to stare at the paraphernalia or the dexterity she uses them all with. If I tried to roll a joint all that stuff would wind up all over the floor.

'You're a painter,' I say, to distract myself.

'What was your first clue?' Cat asks.

I consider actually telling her my first clue – how I pieced it together from the easel and unfinished paintings when I came in. I'm quite proud of my deduction. I realise just in time that the question is hypothetical. Instead, echoing her sentiments when she found out I wrote poetry, I say: 'That sounds right.'

Her paintings are good – really good. I'm impressed but I don't know how to tell her. To be honest, I don't really know why I even agreed to come here. I had plans today – I was going to make beans on toast.

'And you're a poet,' Cat says. It's not a question, She's not asking for proof, she's doesn't add the word 'aspiring', or ask if she might have heard anything I've written.

'I write poetry,' I say.

'Doesn't that make you a poet?' she asks.

I start to say something, but it gets lost somewhere on the way to my mouth. She's got a good point, but it feels a bit presumptuous to just crown yourself a poet. It makes it sound like I've actually accomplished something.

'I believe,' Cat says.

'In what?' I ask.

'In you,' Cat fills in. 'I believe you're a poet. Bet you're a good one, too.'

'Oh, shut up,' I retort. You might think that's a bit out of character, but listen. There's no amount of shyness that will diminish the West of Scotland impulse to respond to compliments with aggression – it would be weird not to. 'You've just met me.'

'First impressions are usually spot on, but,' Cat's rolling up the paper. It makes me think of a burrito, 'Can I hear one?'

'A poem?' I say.

'A poem,' she says.

And I shrink.

'I don't know any off by heart,' I lie.

'Pish,' she replies, with a teasing smile.

She sees right through me. I hate her.

'Another time, maybe?' she offers.

'Thanks,' I say, relaxing.

Cat is twisting the end of the joint, making it look like a little Christmas cracker.

'So, listen,' I hear myself saying, 'I don't think I should let things that happened before I was even born affect the way I live my life.'

'Oh no?' Cat replies curiously.

'So maybe it might be a good…I don't know…life experience or something if I were to…you know, try a joint?' What am I doing? There is literally no expectation from her for me to do this. I've been lulled by a complete lack of peer pressure.

'Lucky you. Because I *just* rolled one,' Cat observes, 'Here.'

She hands me her joint and starts rolling another for herself.

That's when the worry kicks in again.

'So, what's going to happen?' I'm talking a little too fast. 'Am I going to get paranoid or see things or what?'

'Don't worry,' Cat says calmingly, 'you really don't have to smoke it if you don't want to.'

'I do. It's just that…' I trail off. I can't say what I want to. It's words. It always has been. Words are the problem.

'You okay?' Cat asks.

'You'll laugh,' I say. I feel suddenly vulnerable. I want to go home.

'I will. I promise,' says Cat.

And I don't want to gormlessly say 'what' again, but she seems to bring it out in me.

'What?'

'Whatever you say, I'm going to laugh. Don't even care if it's not funny – I'm going to absolutely gut myself. I've got a laugh all charged up. I'm so ready to laugh I won't even be listening to what you're saying,' Cat says, sincerely. 'Does that help?'

'Yes.' It does, though I've no idea why.

'So, what's up?' she prompts.

I take a deep breath. I wish I could breathe in her courage as well as air. She seems courageous.

'There's parts of me I don't like.' I think of that dim shape that sat with me on the couch as recently as this morning, 'What if smoking this brings them out? What if I don't like me when I smoke it? What if you don't?'

Cat doesn't laugh.

'You're not laughing,' I observe.

'No,' Cat says,

It feels incredible to bear a little piece of your soul when you think with absolute certainty you're going to be ridiculed for doing it, and then to be taken seriously.

'Thank you,' I say, and then, 'although you did promise to laugh, so now I'm questioning your honesty.'

'Oh, bloody hell.' Cat raises her hands in playful indignation. 'We can't have that.'

She laughs rambunctiously, as though she's trying to guess what a portly old man in a tuxedo might laugh like. You can hear the top hat in her laugh. And then I laugh, and then her fake laughter becomes real laughter – and just like that I'm comfortable again.

'So, how do I avoid this being a…I don't know…a bad trip or whatever you'd call it?' I delve.

'Easy,' Cat says. 'Think happy thoughts.'

'Simple as that?' I ask.

'Simple as that,' she echoes.

'Okay, I'm in,' I say.

I pick her lighter off the table and light up the joint.

7

Immune

Writing poetry and being a poet are different; the distinction is important.

I write poetry. I really enjoy it. I think maybe I might be quite good, or at least I will be one day. I wouldn't usually ever think such nice things about myself – only with poetry.

But a poet is something other people identify you as. You can't just call yourself a poet; other people have to. For other people to call me a poet I'd have to let them read my poetry.

And that's horrifying.

Or worse, I'd have to perform my poetry. I'd have to say my words in front of a room full of people.

I can't do that.

Cat and I have been smoking for a while now. We're on to our second joints and I'm a little bit disappointed to find that I'm totally unaffected. I remember hearing somewhere that you get people who are immune to cannabis. I guess that must be me. What a let-down after all that build-up.

But I'm starting to feel freer in her disorderly flat than I do in my own tidy, comfortable house. Here I don't feel like there's expectation sitting on every end table and mantelpiece. The clutter isn't asking anything of me at all.

'So, what are you doing now? Since you quit the bank?' I ask, and then regret asking, in case she has an amazing answer and then asks me the same and I have to say I've watched almost as many hours of streaming movies as there have been hours since we quit.

'Waiting for the next adventure,' Cat says.

'I wouldn't really call working in a call centre an adventure,' I say. 'It was hardly bungee jumping.'

'No,' Cat admits. She looks like she's going to say something, stops, looks frustrated.

'Well,' I take a draw from my joint and try to sound sage. 'You obviously have more to say on that subject.'

Cat gives me a quick look as though sizing up whether to go on. 'Bungee jumping is hardly bungee jumping either, but.'

I'm still feeling absolutely nothing from the joint. The thing I read was about a guy who couldn't get high because he had out-of-control anandamide levels and the anandamide competes for the same receptors in the brain as cannabis, so he didn't have any available brain receptors for the cannabis to latch on to because they were all occupied. I guess I'm a bit of a medical marvel.

'Bungee jumping,' I say, 'isn't bungee jumping?'

Cat frowns, trying to express herself. 'Adventure shouldn't cost fifty quid and come with a safety harness.'

'Okay. Yeah. I get that. I think.' I don't, really.

'You don't,' Cat laughingly accuses.

Damn. She's a mind reader.

She starts over. 'Do you ever think you were born in the wrong era?'

'Like, you wish you were born when there were fewer health and safety regulations?' I try.

'Much fewer.' Cat's eyes twinkle. 'Medieval times. I want to be out there, slaying dragons with a sword and shit.'

'I think,' – I take another draw – 'if I were in medieval times, I'd probably be a peasant who can't afford their house. And has scurvy. I mean, statistically.'

'No,' Cat replies with good-natured exasperation. 'Don't imagine yourself as a peasant worried about bloody medieval mortgages. Be a dragon slayer.'

'Maybe I could slay dragons,' I grin.

'You could,' Cat insists. 'You slew Lindsay.'

'No, don't,' I say. 'I'm worried I hurt her feelings. Pointing out her lipstick teeth was bad form.'

I wish I hadn't used that phrase. I usually only say that in my head. I guess I let my guard down more than I thought.

'Bad form?' Cat echoes. 'Wendy. You're quirky. I like it.'

I'll pick over that later – that 'you're quirky'. I'll look in every angle and curve of it for malice or teasing. I'll never find any.

'You, though,' – I jab the roll-up at her hazardously – 'you, I can imagine slaying dragons.'

'Nah. She just pissed me off. People shouldn't talk to you like that. They think because they control your access to money, they control you,' Cat says.

Cat starts to roll a third. I realise that during our little medieval interchange I was still remembering about the guy who was immune to cannabis at the back of my head, but it's just popped right back to the surface with a warning. Maybe I am a medical marvel. He was a medical marvel, as it turned out the way he couldn't experience a high from cannabis, and his anandamide surplus, also indicated other serious neurological issues. Was it a sign of brain damage? Oh God, I think it might have been. Or was it a sign of disease? Is this how I find out I'm critically ill? How do I explain this at the hospital? 'I've just discovered I have brain damage because I've been breaking the law and smoking illegal drugs?' Should I go to hospital? I should probably go to hospital. Also, importantly, I really wish I'd bought those instant noodles. How good would instant noodles be just now?

'You okay?' Cat glances up from the task of rolling.

She really is a mind reader.

Is she really a mind reader?

Wait. Is she a mind reader?

'I'm fine,' I say.

'I'll just roll *one*,' she says, with a little smile.

I don't really have the time to ask why she would only roll one when there are clearly two of us because I've just caught one of her paintings looking at me. Actually, on further inspection, all of her half-painted canvases are looking at me. Even the ones with no eyes. That one, I swear to God, it just winked. I swear.

I really do wish I had those noodles. What do noodles taste like? I can't remember. I think they taste like being born. You know, that feeling? I am hungry. I really am. All the paint from the canvases, it's all in my brain. It's still out there on the canvases, obviously – it hasn't moved anywhere – but it's on my brain. All the colours and textures are slipping into my eyes and sitting on my brain until it's just covered in yellows and blues and reds.

When did someone last speak? Seconds ago? Days ago?

The painting that looked at me first is still looking at me. It's kind. It's not like that dark thing that stares at me at home. It's a man. He's got little crinkles by his eyes. I like them. And his eyes themselves are so real, I can't believe it's paint. He feels like he's here. He feels like he's just watching over us, benignly. It's amazing.

'You're a really talented painter,' I say.

Cat looks like she's been punched in the stomach. There might be the threat of a tear in her eye, but the room is full of smoke so I don't know for sure.

'I'm sorry,' I backpedal, 'what did I say? I'm so sorry.'

'Don't say sorry,' Cat says, 'I just wasn't ready for that.'

She looks vulnerable for the first time since I met her, which I admit was really recently.

'Thanks,' she says.

I laugh and I'm not sure why, but she does too, so it must be fine. Then she gets a weird faraway look in her eyes.

'You okay?' I ask.

'I'm happy,' Cat says.

'That's good, isn't it?'

'I'm scared that the happiness isn't real. Do you get that?' Cat gambits.

It seems a perfectly reasonable question to me at the time.

'Yeah. Like I'm a part of me, watching myself be happy,' I say, 'analysing it from the outside, saying "this is nice".'

Cat's eyes widen. She's just realised that I *do* get it.

'Sometimes I think,' she says, gesticulating her way through, forming her thoughts like playdough, 'if I ever feel real happiness, I'll get in my car and drive as fast as I can into a tree.'

That seems perfectly reasonable to me at the time as well. I can feel all the colours of her paintings still seeping into the folds of my cerebellum. I feel the room slowly getting bigger and the walls moving away from us. I nod in understanding.

I see it in my mind's eye. The metal, twisted and broken and man-made, crushed up against the tree, splintered and natural, and Cat inside, delicate and dead. It's artistic, and she's an artist; it makes sense.

Then she laughs. I don't get the joke.

'Just to mess with people,' she says. 'It'll be totally unexpected – they won't ever understand why.'

'Is that art?' I ask, with a lazy mouth. 'Messing with people?'

'Messing with people is what art is all about,' Cat confirms.

Something clicks – a little urgent nudge in the ribs. The tone of my voice shifts.

'You wouldn't really, though?' I ask.

'No. Of course not. I'm just high.' Cat closes her eyes. 'Although…'

'Although?' I prompt.

'To die would be an awfully big adventure.'

We sit quietly for a second.

'Cat,' I say, 'I'm going to make it my personal mission to make sure you never know happiness in your entire life.'

She looks at me dumbstruck. Then she laughs until she snorts. I join in. We both laugh like it's the funniest thing anyone has ever said, then we laugh because we can't remember why we're laughing. We're high. So high. We're flying. We're daedalists.

A few hours later I walk home. Everything feels a little slower than normal. My thoughts weigh something. It's a quiet night.

Where there are people there's always conflict. In Glasgow city centre on a weekend you can taste it in the air, mingled in with the yellow smell of dropped chips. All of those people trying to get something from each other, and all feeling stuff because of each other.

Looking at a road with no cars on it feels like looking at something inanimate resting. A road has a use but just now it's not being used; that feels peaceful.

I wish I could go somewhere with no people and see how the world works without us, but I can't, because I'm a person, so just by being there I'd ruin it.

But if it's quiet it feels like you can see it, just up in the distance, that perfect place of real solitude.

'You're home late, love,' my gran says.

'I'm sorry I worried you. I meant to bring us home a nice dinner. But I messed up,' I say, guiltily.

'Don't you worry about that, darling. Did you have a nice night?' Gran asks.

'I think I made a friend,' I say.

'I'm really pleased to hear that,' she says, genuinely.

I sit next to her on the couch. We watch TV together for the first time since I quit my job.

After a while she asks, 'This new friend – they aren't going to lead you astray are they, darling?'

'No,' I say. 'She's nice.'

Paranoia taps me on the shoulder.

'Gran, do I smell like…'

'I'm sure I wouldn't know anything about that, love.'

Contentedly, we watch celebrities in a jungle eating insects. Cat's given me something, though she doesn't know it –

I feel like I have some inspiration. I feel like I could maybe write some poetry. Something special. I know exactly how it will go. It's right there in my head; I just need to write it down. Tomorrow. I'll write it tomorrow.

'Would you like some crisps?' Gran asks.

'Oh my God, yes.'

8

Freya Rose

I don't know what time it is when I go to bed – all the clocks in my house are wrong but I don't fix them out of principle because if it's *my* job to tell *them* the time then what are they bringing to the relationship?

Falling asleep is easy, and I don't think it's just because of the weed. Talking to Cat has rubbed away some of the pencil scribbles in my messy mind, so everything seems a bit clearer and less worrying. In my dreams I wander back to my first few weeks of university. The morbid nostalgia of relived misery draws me back to a set of double doors outside a lecture theatre.

Oh, I don't know that I want to have this dream, will this be a good dream or a horrible one?

I go with the flow, let's find out.

My handful of high-school friends went to Glasgow University. The Hogwartian grandeur of Glasgow Uni never appealed to me, so I went to Strathclyde. I didn't have the safety net of familiar people as green and clueless as I was around me, so I had no one to make mistakes with. Making mistakes alone is a lot more daunting.

In those first few weeks I stood in front of those double doors a lot of times. Each day I made the effort to get up, get dressed, bring everything I would need for the lecture, travel to university, and walk to the lecture theatre, only to fall at that last hurdle.

I'd watch other first years stride in confidently, as though it was nothing. When the hall first opened, they'd move as one large gabbling mass pushing to get in first, like they were water and the doors were a pulled plug. Once the keen majority were through, the flood petered off into groups of more laid-back students. After the small groups would come the drip of rushing individuals hoping to conceal their lateness.

I would watch as all of them filtered into the lecture theatre, wondering how I could go in there without knowing what was inside, or where I would sit, or who with. I would watch as the last person went through the doors and they closed in front of me, then I would stare at them and tell myself to go in.

If you've ever stood at the end of a diving board trying to dive off, you'll know that you need to ride that first surge of adrenaline and take the jump. If you let your fear stop you, just at that moment when you would have leapt, you'll never do it at all. I'd stand in front of that door, stopping and starting, for as long as fifteen minutes some days. Ultimately, I would always picture myself walking into the theatre midway through a lecturer's sentence to have the entire hall look at me, and I'd realise that there was absolutely zero possibility I would put myself through that.

The doors may as well have been a wall.

I was relieved to find that lecture notes were available online. No attendance was taken at lectures either, so I wouldn't be penalised for not being there. Tutorials were a different matter. These small, classroom-like lessons for twenty or so students at a time were compulsory. Miss two and you were out.

A small classroom with nineteen of my peers was a lot less intimidating than a huge room with hundreds. When the first tutorial came around I did what I ought to have done with the lecture room doors – I rode the wave of adrenaline that my body helpfully created to get me into the room without hesitating.

I sat at one of three tables, not next to anyone, but not segregated either. The spaces on either side of me filled up as more students filed in. Most of the people at my table seemed to know each other, but none looked at me as though I was invading their group.

I was worried that the tutorial would be about a topic that had been covered in a lecture but missed out of the lecture notes. I kept having the same waking nightmare over and over that the tutor would ask me a question and I'd just stare blankly, terrified to admit my ignorance, but not able to answer.

After the register, our tutor began, 'We're going to be looking at romanticism.'

I knew this topic. I liked this topic. This might actually be fun.

'Who can tell me about the Romantic poets?' our tutor went on.

'They really liked nature,' a girl at my table that the register had identified as Freya Rose spoke up.

I wouldn't usually speak; I'd spent my entire primary-school and high-school career not speaking, but this was university. Everyone was here because they wanted to be, and this was a topic I liked. I felt safe joining in.

'Definitely,' I agreed with the girl, 'but it was even more than that; it was rebellion, it was fighting the ideas of the Enlightenment; it was reconnecting with the natural world and shunning the industrial world; it was about the "spontaneous overflow of powerful feelings". Isn't that beautiful?'

I'd got carried away. I braced to be laughed at for saying that Romanticism was beautiful. The laughter never came.

'Well done,' our tutor nodded. 'Thank you, Wendy.'

'Yeah, thanks Wendy,' Freya muttered.

'And could I have some examples of Romantic poets?' the tutor pressed on.

'Samuel Taylor Coleridge, William Wordsworth,' Freya answered promptly. Then, before I could even draw a breath, 'Any to add, Wendy?'

There were plenty to add – Shelley, Blake, Keats, Byron – but Freya's voice was a warning, not an invitation.

'No,' I declined demurely.

The tutorial went on. When we reached the end, the tutor assigned us the task of discussing the works of a list of poets in groups, and to report our findings back at the next tutorial. The groups were determined by what table we sat at, which put me in a group with Freya Rose.

'We'll go to the pub tonight to go over this stuff,' Freya ordained. 'Wendy, sorry that you won't be able to make it. We can fill you in before the next tutorial.'

I started to speak, to tell her that I could make it and would be happy to, but she interrupted.

'I've seen you skulking around outside the lecture hall

but you never come in. I assume you don't have the time for lectures, so you probably won't have time for this either. Some of us are too clever for lectures I suppose,' she challenged, glaring. 'Come on, everyone. See you next time, Wendy.'

Freya strutted out, her mute retinue following her.

We all imagine university like a college movie: groups of jocks flexing and bullying; cheerleader mean girls; emo and goth kids gathered around a speaker-amp flicking their fringes; geeks and losers wedgied to within an inch of their life. That's not what university is like in Scotland. Mercifully, we don't have such clear divisions. Despite that, it's still what we think of when we think of university. That's Americanisation for you.

Freya Rose was the closest to a mean girl cheerleader I've ever met.

I walked, warm-faced and browbeaten, to my next lecture.

'That was unfair, what she said to you,' came a voice from next to me as I walked. I jumped, caught off-guard and embarrassed.

'Wendy, right?' said the boy.

'Yes.'

It was one of Freya's group. 'Kevin, isn't it?'

'It is. The register somewhat removes the fun of introductions, doesn't it?' he smiled. 'I'm sorry Freya won't let you come to the pub with us. She doesn't like to be contradicted.'

'It's okay,' I said, but it wasn't.

'I'll talk to them tonight. I'll convince them that they got the wrong impression. Leave it with me,' Kevin offered.

'Thanks,' I smiled.

We reached the double doors of the lecture theatre.

Kevin walked through, then stopped abruptly, realising I was no longer with him.

'What's the matter?' he asked.

'Nothing,' I said, too quickly.

'Come on, I need someone to sit next to,' Kevin insisted. We walked through the doors together.

9

Opportunity doesn't text

I wake up the next morning to the doorbell ringing. Seventy-five per cent of my body firmly holds me down in bed, insisting it's not for me.

I'm sprawled everywhere; my feet are overhanging two different sides of the bed, one of my arms is flopped over a third, and my other arm is under my face and embarrassingly slimy with drool.

The other twenty-five per cent of my body reminds me that my gran is getting on a bit, and if I don't answer the door she will, and she's not as good at the stairs as she once was.

I gather my shambles of limbs like a new-born deer.

I've been drunk before – I've never been a big drinker, or anything, but you don't go to university without sometimes getting just unreasonably drunk – and, because I've been drunk before, I've been hungover before. Oh God, have I been hungover. I do a quick body scan: I have an unpleasant taste in my mouth, my tongue seems to be sticky, my teeth have a lot more texture than they usually do, and when I get a whiff of my hair it's got a heavy musk to it, but other than that I feel pretty good. I don't have a headache, I don't feel sick, I don't have a strange sense of terror about what I may have done the night before. This is a revelation.

I start to hurry into yesterday's clothes, which are lying helpfully on the floor right in front of me. As soon as I pull a top over my head I can smell the same musk that's in my hair. I can't live with it. I grab something fresh from the cupboard. Hygiene prevails. I hurry out of my room.

It feels as though it's taken me a little while too long to get to the door. After all, I've gone from fully unconscious in my bed to semi-presentable, semi-awake, rushing down the stairs in a semi-detached. I'm not sure if the phantom ringer will have waited, but as I approach the door I can see the distorted shape of a person through the small frosted-glass window.

When I open the door, I find Kevin. It's really nice to see him, but I'm also a little disappointed. Who did I want it to be?

'This is so weird, I was just dreaming about you,' I almost say, then realise that would make me sound like a massive creep.

'Hello Wendy,' Kevin says. 'You look tired.'

I haven't looked in a mirror today. I conjure up a mental image of myself with gigantic cartoonish bloodshot eyes like a parody of a stoner. I look at the floor to try to hide the evidence of my delinquency.

'No, I'm great. Been awake for ages,' I say.

After that day when we first sat together at a lecture, I got to know Kevin really well. Freya made life extremely hard, but Kevin always stood by me; he's a good guy. Although, this is definitely against social rules.

'Why are you at my door?' I ask.

'I wanted to touch base. Check in with you. I've something to give you,' he replies.

'Texting first is, like, the law,' I point out.

'I did,' Kevin protests.

He probably did. I don't have my phone; it must be somewhere upstairs.

'You're meant to wait for a reply. Clearly,' I counter.

'Sorry,' he says. 'Shall I walk down the road a bit until you can answer me, then I'll come back?'

'Just come in.' I give him a withering look.

Kevin sort of insisted on becoming my friend despite my best efforts to distance myself from everyone in university. I would always keep a two-metre perimeter between me and groups of happily chatting freshers. After seeing Freya's zombified followers I started to treat popularity like a virus and I wanted to avoid any risk of catching it. I didn't think it was the kind of thing I would survive.

I shouldn't have worried too much I suppose. I may not be immune to cannabis, but empirical tests have shown I'm basically the vaccine to popularity.

We have a bit of history that goes beyond friendship. We spent a few nights together in uni, but always when we were drunk. Each time we decided not to define ourselves as a couple or start a romantic relationship because our friendship was too important to risk. I think really we both secretly wanted to take that risk; it's just that neither of us were brave enough to admit it sober.

In my gran's living room Kevin pulls an envelope out of his bag and puts it on the table.

'I heard about your mishap at the call centre,' he says.

'Mishap,' I grin. 'I didn't stub my toe or spill a coffee.'

'As I understood it, you were fired?' he ventures.

'I quit,' I correct.

'Whatever, the point is…' he begins.

'No, not whatever,' I interrupt, 'I quit. That's the point.'

He recoils a little.

'Wendy, are you okay?' he asks.

Did I just lose my temper a bit there? Yeah, I think I did. Bad form. Actually, I think I've maybe been a little snarky from the moment I saw it was him at the door. It's weird, I'm glad he's here, I don't feel like I've seen many people recently, so why the attitude?

'Sorry,' I say, 'I'm tired. What were you saying?'

'The point is,' he recovers seamlessly, 'the timing is perfect. A position just opened at my work.'

'No? Seriously?' That really is quite exciting.

'It's not been advertised yet, so I'd appreciate if you don't tell anyone I told you,' he goes on. 'You can get in ahead of anyone else. They need a graduate with an IT degree.'

That might not be the degree you'd expect me to have, but I do. Kevin is a cyber-security software developer. His job, and jobs at his company, have a salary. Those are measured by what you get paid in a year, not in a week. That's major. And in terms of job security his office is top notch: the pay is utterly insane, even for an entry level graduate, and the hours, by comparison, are utterly sane. No late nights or split shifts or zero-hour contracts. Nine to five – what a way to make a living.

The only downside is that it's about as far from poetry as you can get. With words you can do whatever you like, but code isn't like that. It needs to be right or it just won't work.

Still. A lot of people would give their big toe for this sort of job. They'd be delighted to be able to finally afford things – a mortgage, a car, a life. All that stuff sounds great, right?

Intimidatingly great.

'We'd see each other far more frequently,' Kevin says, 'We'd be colleagues.'

He smiles, he's got little crinkles by his eyes. I like them.

What? Shut up. Forget I wrote that.

Maybe seeing Kevin every day wouldn't be so bad. That could be, maybe, quite nice.

After a few years at the company, I could become a consultant. I know that's what Kevin's aim is. We could become consultants together. We could be making well over a hundred grand a year each– can you even imagine?

I hug him and say, 'Thank you.'

'What does your hair smell of?' he asks unexpectedly.

I let him go. I try to think of an excuse but my brain splutters and stalls. I just say, 'I'll fill in the application form.'

'Excellent,' Kevin says with smooth corporate hyperbole. I'd say he's picked that habit up since he started his job, but really he's always talked with the same vocabulary as an office memo. 'Good luck.'

We stand in the living room for a second, saying nothing.

'Anyway,' he begins.

'Yeah, of course,' I agree, without knowing what he's about to say.

'I should get going,' turns out to be the rest of the sentence.

'Me too,' I reply, even though I have nowhere to go.

We pass nonsensical platitudes to each other until eventually he's out of the door and gone.

'He's a nice boy,' my gran observes wryly from the kitchen, where I had no idea she was lurking.

'Yeah.' I aim for airy and dismissive, but it comes out a bit too high-pitched. I wander, with the application form in my hand, back upstairs, a study in forced casualness.

The poem.

I was going to write a poem. I can still feel the residue of it in my thoughts. Maybe if I act fast I can tease it onto paper before it wisps away with last night's dreams.

I power up my laptop and I jump onto my bed with it perched on my knees. I open my word processor. I have the aplomb to crack my fingers like a concert pianist.

On a white page a little black cursor blinks at me expectantly.

Obviously, the formatting is all wrong here. I need to make sure the line spacing is right, and the page size and the header and footer, and the font. All of these things are crucially important when you're submitting poems to people, and if I ever decide I'm going to do that I don't want to look like a rookie who doesn't know her iamb from her anapaest. I spend a half hour or so sorting out the layout.

When I'm finished that little black cursor blinks at me again. I don't like its attitude.

What was the poem? I had it. It was right there, fully formed, and all it needed was committing to type. It was going to be the great poem of our generation, It was going to make that show-off Robert Burns look like absolute shit.

This is Kevin's fault – he showed up and distracted me, vanished it like the person from Porlock vanished the Pleasure Dome of Xanadu. Stupid Kevin.

The person from Pollok.

I remember I took a note. I scribbled it on a receipt in my pocket before falling asleep last night. It might be a clue, a beacon towards my masterpiece.

I go through the pockets of yesterday's clothes, still huddled in their smelly floor pile.

Eureka, I have it – the receipt that will be my guide. I've written on it. I can see the pen indentation through the folded paper. All is not lost.

I unfold the receipt to reveal my note: 'Buy instant noodles.'

I throw the receipt in the bin, but I wish I was throwing it into a roaring fireplace to burn it to oblivion.

That's okay. This just means I'm back to square one. Last night's poem has gone to the place where unwritten poems go – a magical realm full of the greatest poems ever conceived but never inscribed. I'll just have to think of a new one.

The black cursor keeps blinking, as though to say, 'I'm waiting.'

I'd been thinking about Felicia Malcolm recently, hadn't I? About how magical that summer had been when Cavalier had protected me from her. Imagine if that summer had been a person, if that nostalgic warmth had been physicalised.

'Shall I compare thee to a summer's day?' pipes up the ghost of William Shakespeare from beyond the grave, 'thou art more lovely and more temperate.'

Pre-emptively plagiarised by the bard himself. You win this round, Willy.

Okay, scratch that. I remember the colours in Cat's paintings had a profound impact on me. I need to write about something colourful.

Isn't it amazing that colours are naturally occurring? We can just look out the window and be bombarded by colour.

It's unbelievable that flowers can be something as vibrant as yellow. If we wore yellow clothes we'd be making a statement. People would really take notice, for better or worse. Yet we could be walking around in the hills one day and just be taken by surprise by, say, a daffodil.

'I wandered lonely as a cloud,' another William bubbles into my consciousness, 'that floats on high o'er vales and hills.'

Damn it.

'When all at once I saw a crowd,' he continues.

'A host, of golden daffodils,' I finish out loud.

Wordsworth, you son of a bitch.

How can anyone ever write anything when all these old dead guys have already written everything?

I heard somewhere that there are only seven stories in the world. Seven. And all the stories you've ever read or heard are really one of those seven stories in a glitzy disguise. That means that seven people got there first, and now the rest of us have nothing new to say. They selfishly snatched them all up before we got a chance.

Cat's right: I wish were born in a different era. I wish I were around in ancient Greece to be the first person ever to write a tragedy. That would blow people's minds.

I have an idea. Has anyone ever written a poem about war?

This is hopeless.

I hear my phone vibrating in the pocket of my coat – my coat, which is hung on my curtain rail in an act of ingenuity I don't remember being a part of. I also don't remember swapping phone numbers with Cat last night, but I must have because when I look at my phone it's a text from her.

It just says, 'I believe.'

I start to write. It's not a work of art or a masterpiece or anything, but I'm writing and it feels good.

Eventually I hit a block and I decide I can't concentrate because it's too cold. I go downstairs and turn on the central heating.

Heat brings inspiration. I distinctly remember a Sherlock Holmes mystery where Holmes, thwarted by Moriarty, insists that Watson snuggle him until his muse arrives.

All right, that may have been some dodgy fanfiction.

Twenty minutes later I realise that the radiator hasn't warmed up so I wander back downstairs to investigate.

The heating has been turned off again.

I shiver. Not just because the house is cold.

10

Fugitive

Sometimes I worry my mind isn't on my side. I feel like it's lying to me.

Actually, forget it. Forget I said anything.

Sorry, I was telling you about the heating but that's going to have to wait.

Turns out it actually was a really bad idea to hide in my own home, seems like that's not the last place they'd check after all. Seems it's pretty high up the list of places to check.

They came. They found me.

I made it through the whole night without anything happening. While writing this confession to you I rummaged around my gran's attic to see if there was anything useful there, and it turned out to be a treasure trove. I found a tattered baseball cap and an old pair of sunglasses with big brown marble-effect frames. I've no idea whose the sunglasses were – Elton John's, based on the look of them. I've never seen anyone wear them in my lifetime, so I guess whoever wore them predates me. The cap smelled of dust and was about the right shades and combination of blue and pink triangles to have been a bit of a showstopper headpiece in the eighties.

I also found a trench coat. An honest-to-God brown fabric trench. It was stylish in an old-school kind of way, even though it was a little too big for me.

I was looking out of the small, mostly grimed over window of the attic when they arrived. That's the only reason I had time to escape. I saw the yellow and blue of the police car pulling up outside my house – distinct colours even through a dirty window. They didn't have their lights or sirens on. Of course not. They wouldn't want me to notice them and run. Smart.

I grabbed the masterpiece and my cobbled-together disguise. I rushed down the attic ladder and the stairs to the ground floor as stealthily as I could – wincing at every creak and praying I didn't accidentally damage the stolen art.

My gran was my saviour. Not deliberately – I'm sure if she knew the trouble I was in she would have willingly been my accomplice, but she did this by accident. Both hearing and sight become a little less reliable at her age and, since I hadn't said hello when I came in, she had no idea I was home. I'd sent her a text from the attic late yesterday evening to tell her I wouldn't be back until the next day. I didn't want her to worry. She was telling the two uniformed police officers exactly that at the front door as I snuck out the back.

'Wendy isn't here, I'm afraid. Is something the matter?'

I hope she wasn't too upset when she found out what I did.

I'm glad it's uniformed officers at the door. I'd have hated to have heard the voice of Detective Davies. He'd been so kind to me. Who's Detective Davies? I'll get to him, soon. I'm getting ahead of myself again.

I'm going to be honest – I thought that would be it for me. I didn't think that the police would be so sloppy as to have two officers come to the front door without positioning another at the back to catch me if I tried to sneak out, but when I emerged from my back-garden gate, muscles tensed and ready to be huckled, there was no one there.

My legs were still complaining from last night, the last time I had to run. I thought they weren't going to do what I told them. They signed a petition recommending we simply walk away from the house, but as there were only two signatures, I ignored it. I ran as fast as I could.

The coat flapped around and I pictured myself in my mind's eye like one of those cool action movie heroes, the ones who are always in exactly the right weather conditions so that their clothes billow dramatically but their hair remains perfectly styled. Then I remembered my outrageous combination of headwear. That's okay. I'm already an art thief – I don't need to look cool doing it.

I ran to a bus stop. I still had a collection of spare change from a taxi I had to get yesterday. I got on a bus. Three different people nearly put their elbows or hands onto or through the painting. Can you imagine if the *Mona Lisa* had never been seen because someone on a bus burst their elbow through it before it made it to the Louvre? Or if the *Girl with a Pearl Earring* was just the 'Girl with a Smudged Ear' because someone couldn't keep his hands in his own personal space? You want to deprive the world of its next cultural touchstone just because you don't like being considerate on crowded public transport – how entitled and selfish do you get? I kept my composure. I didn't want to draw attention.

Now I'm in a café. I'm sitting in a booth at the back.

A café is an even worse place to hide than my grandmother's attic; I'm right out in public.

But here's the problem. First of all, the police are the lesser of two evils. If I get caught by the police then they will arrest me, but the other guy? The guy this painting technically belongs to? He's another story. I don't think he knows much about people or compassion or – based on the coat *he* was wearing – fashion, but what I bet he does know is value. He knew this painting's worth; he'll want it back. He seemed like the kind of man who had *friends* – friends who wouldn't have a conversation with me before taking back what was his. I don't want to get caught at all, but if I do, I hope it's by the police and not by him.

Hiding is hard. It's something that I was totally unprepared for.

I bought the coffee I'm nursing with the last of the loose change I had rattling around inside my purse. I bought it so I had a reason to be sitting in the café and wouldn't get kicked out. I don't know why I bought coffee to nurse – you know I hate coffee. I panicked.

I can't use my debit card; they'd be able to track that. It wasn't so important last night – at that point everyone knew where I was – but now I can't buy anything else. Using my card would be the same as turning myself in. Effectively, I have no money.

I don't have a car, but if I did, I wouldn't be able to drive it. That's the whole point of registration plates.

Being found at my gran's clearly shows that they are looking in any place I could sensibly go, so I can't go to anyone I know and ask them to hide me. I'm also not sure anyone would take me in – not after all that's happened. Even if they did, I couldn't trust them. Sure, there are people who might protect me just now, but what if, down the line, the police offer a reward? Or lie about what I did to make me sound worse than I am? Can I really rely on people not to turn me in if they're being offered a life-changing amount of money? I'd rather not find out.

Plus, the other guy – the guy in the red velvet coat – he might have other ways of making people speak.

I don't have my phone any more. I'd forgotten what a liability phones are. I had it in my pocket right up until the last second before I left the attic. They can track your phone, you know? Even if you have location services off. I abandoned it. Otherwise the little traitor would have led them right to me.

Then there's the CCTV cameras. They're everywhere and I think those things have facial recognition. My wacky disguise should confuse them, but I feel like it's drawing attention to me in the real world. I don't really blend in among the customers here. It's making people look at me, but I'm afraid to take it off. For all I know, the police have my face on news bulletins on every channel, and the cut on my lip is damning, and I can only hide it behind this coffee cup for so long.

That said, I am carrying around a framed painting protected by nothing but a dustsheet. I'm a bit distinctive, disguise or no disguise.

I don't really know how I get out of this. I wish I'd somehow thought to withdraw all my cash last night, or to have withdrawn it in phases and leave it somewhere secure to pick up. I didn't really have the chance though. Plus, it probably wouldn't have occurred to me even if I did. When Cat and I were planning the heist we never got this far. I'm out of my depth. The whole heist thing was her idea in the first place.

If Kevin is reading this he's probably thinking, 'Where's Cat now, when you need her? I told you so.'

I'm getting this all in the wrong order. I'm talking about things I haven't told you about yet. Sorry – I'm just having a tough time organising my thoughts because this environment is, well, it's weird.

This café is decorated in shades of rich chocolatey brown and I'm sitting underneath a massive wall, stencilled with a reassuring message about ethically sourced Arabica beans.

People are eating toasties, booths made for four are being used by people on their own who are sheepishly scrolling through their phones. The staff are uniformed and friendly, their conversation with customers is soothingly banal, the names on the takeaway cups are hilariously misspelled. What's weird about all of that? It's all so normal. My life has changed irreparably, and this place is all so normal. Can't they all see that I'm not a part of their world just now? Can't they see I'm just hiding in it? I keep thinking that all these people might be actors and soon a false wall will fall, revealing a swat team behind it.

I don't think we call them swat teams here; I think they are called Armed Response or Tactical Support teams or something. I know a different country's police forces better than my own – that's Americanisation for you.

Wendy.

Be rational.

In reality, no one here seems to be watching me. I don't think anyone knows who I am or what I've done. Everything is okay. For now, at least, everything is okay.

I've still got a lot to explain to you so I'm going to keep telling you my story.

Okay. Deep breath. Here's what happened next.

11

Make a Scene

Cat and I text back and forth but don't see each other for a while. It's the strange thing about adult friendship, you can't just pop around someone's house and ask if they can come out to play. You always assume that everyone is busy, and you don't want to bother them. Everyone assumes you're busy, too. Maybe Kevin has it right, with his unannounced visits?

No. He doesn't. I hate them.

I don't tell Cat that all I've been busy with this week is lying in bed, pretending to sleep in the hope that I can trick myself into actually sleeping. The thing that watches me out of the corner of my eye is sitting cross-legged on my bed behind my back, I can feel myself being pulled into the furrow its weight makes in the mattress, I know without looking at it that it's got a sharp pointy smile below those inquisitive eyes now. Time passes.

Tick-tock. Tick-tock.

But even though I can't sleep, I can't stay awake either. I'm too tired. I float about doing neither and waiting for something to change. Actively waiting – like change is a house guest who should have been here ten minutes ago. I check my mailbox – and even my actual physical letter box – countless times an hour, as though I think that change is going to drop into my life at any instant, with an offer that's only valid for the next twenty seconds. I don't want to miss that.

I get a text from Cat: 'You about right now?'

And I head out of the house so fast I almost forget to reply, but I don't forget to grab the thing on my desk. It's something I've decided I'd like her to see.

I find Cat between her flat and my house on Kilmarnock road, near the River Cart. We'd both headed towards each other so we could meet in the middle. Cat is practically vibrating with anger, not directed towards me I don't think, but definitely potent. It's building up and I can see she's in danger of exploding. She needs a lightning rod.

'Wow,' I say involuntarily, taken aback by her wild energy, then, 'Okay, tell me. What happened?'

Cat blows out air, gestures meaninglessly around with her arms, doesn't know where to begin.

'I just…' she false starts.

'It's just…' she tries again, then tries to explain everything in one sound of frustration. It's expressive but doesn't help with the specifics.

'Start at the start,' I try to help.

'I was just talking to someone,' Cat manages.

'Who?' I probe softly.

'Just, someone. Just a person,' Cat seems momentarily

evasive, 'but they said…'

Her cheeks turn red. Embarrassment, anger, or both.

'What did they say?' I prod.

'It's stupid,' Cat retreats.

'Promise I'll laugh at you,' I try.

It works. She blows a little laugh through her nose and visibly releases a bit of tension with it. Not a lot, but a little. People walk around us giving us a wider berth than is really needed.

'Art isn't a real job,' she says, with a shrug both remorseful and irritable, as though she's apologetic to be so wound up over something so minor, but annoyed at herself for being apologetic at the same time.

I've heard the same plenty of times but with 'poetry' in place of 'art'.

'Hey, it's okay,' I rationalise, 'some people are idiots.'

'They are,' Cat agrees, 'but it's not that. It's that…who chooses?'

'Chooses what's a real job you mean?' I try to keep up.

'Chooses what has value,' Cat replies. 'These people look down on the guy pushing trollies back to the supermarket in a car park, but do you know what happens when he isn't there? You wind up with a car park full of bloody trollies. But they love their hedge-fund managers, don't they? Those arseholes get rich from other people's misery, but they all bloody love them. Our values are a total state. It doesn't matter how many chandeliers you have in your house if there aren't any bloody foundations.'

I feel like I ought to step in and calm Cat down. But to be honest she hasn't said a single thing I disagree with. Interrupting her flow would imply that she's being unreasonable. I don't think she is.

'If someone tells me that "art isn't a real job" they better never have looked at a billboard, or hung pictures on their walls,' Cat continues.

'Or even picked a particular breakfast cereal because they liked the box,' I add.

'Right?' Cat says, spurred on. 'Every book in their bookcase, record in their record collection, and box in their cupboard better be covered in plain white paper.'

'If "art isn't a real job" they better have never even read a book,' I say.

'Yes, Or watched the TV,' Cat says. We're egging each other on, getting louder.

'Gone to the cinema.'

'Seen a play.'

'They ought to be dressed in brown sacks.'

'They better not want to tell me about their favourite bloody song.'

'Or movie.'

'Elitist, bastard, hypocrites.'

Cat yells the last word, then stands eerily still, breathing as though she's just been for a run.

I want to cheer. I want to grab a banner and march across the country to the parliament.

Then I look around and burst out laughing.

Cat seems utterly bemused.

'Are you laughing because you promised you would laugh at me, or because I'm crazy?' she asks.

Ugh. I hate that word.

'No,' I reply. 'Look around.'

Cat looks. Everyone passing us has walked to the other side

of the road. Not a single person in sight shares our pavement. Everyone is hurrying past and staring at the ground or, if they're brave, stealing glances at us.

'Oh Christ,' Cat breathes, 'they must think we're having a blazing row.'

'Whereas actually,' I point out, 'we're just having a spirited conversation about the arts.'

Cat laughs along with me and now we probably seem even more crazy than before. No one crosses back to our side of the road.

It occurs to me, academically, that, generally, if I thought a whole street of people were looking at me and judging me, I'd die of humiliation, but I feel absolutely fine. Cat needed this and what other people think doesn't really matter to me right now.

'Maybe I shouldn't be screaming my head off in the middle of Shawlands,' Cat says, looking embarrassed.

I take a deep breath. I throw my head back. I scream at the top of my lungs. Cat takes a second to catch on, then she joins me. We scream as loud as we can until our throats start to hurt. We scream until the seagulls and crows that fish scraps from the communal bins behind the tenement blocks get annoyed and start screaming back at us. We scream until we don't feel like screaming any more.

'Feel better?' I ask.

Cat nods, 'Better.'

'Good. Lets get out of here in case anyone called the police.'

We hurry at first, just in case, then slow to a walk which ambles aimlessly through the labyrinth of streets that branch off from Kilmarnock road, turning whenever the mood takes us.

'You can support the arts right now,' I say, with trepidation.

'Can I? How?' Cat asks.

I pull the thing from my desk out of my pocket. It's a little red notebook. It's battered, and creased, and falling apart a bit.

'You can read these.' I don't make eye contact. 'I mean, if you want to.'

'Are these your poems?' Cat's eyes light up. I love how she pronounces 'poems'. She says 'poyums'.

'Some of my poems. Some old ones. You don't have to,' I flounder.

'I'd love to,' Cat replies with enthusiasm.

'You're sure?' we both say at once.

Then I give her the book. It must have been heavier than it seemed – I suddenly feel a lot lighter.

12

Trolley Boy's Tale

Cat suggests we go to a coffee shop, but I convince her that it would be a better idea to grab sandwiches and sit on a bench in Queen's Park.

'So,' I say, trying to figure out the misnomer that is an easy open sandwich, 'did you just ask me to meet you because you were having a revelation about how artists are undervalued?'

'Would that be wrong?' Cat replies, opening her own sandwich with annoying ease.

'No, not at all.'

The box says that I should peel off the perforated strip, but nothing looks like it's perforated.

'I just thought you'd probably get it, I guess.' Cat takes a bite of her sandwich. It looks good – wish I could bite a sandwich right now.

'Hey, if you need someone to stand in the street and scream with you, then I am, it turns out, your girl.' I don't know if maybe I'm supposed to fold something to get into it?

'You okay there?' she says while chewing.

'Yup.' I just rip the damn thing.

We're sitting near the duck pond. Sometimes it freezes over in the winter. People start to skate on it or just run about on it. It always seems like a really bad idea – it gets cold here, but not so cold that you can trust a pond to be frozen solid. Every year I expect to hear about someone falling through the ice. It's not frozen today. Today the weather is pretty nice.

'You know what's wrong with the world?' Cat asks, with a self-deprecating smile.

'What?' I ask.

'Capitalism,' she says.

I don't know how to respond. I just look at her, trying not to make any expression at all, whatsoever.

She sniffs a little laugh.

'Your face,' she says.

'Sorry,' I laugh.

'I know what I sound like,' she admits. 'I sound like those guys hanging about on freshers week, yelling slogans into a loudspeaker, stoatin' about in second-hand Russian greatcoats from the army surplus places in town.'

'Oh God,' I say. 'The guy who says he's a communist, but actually he means he just wants everyone else to pay for stuff for him?'

'Because he doesn't believe in money. Aye. Him.'

'Why do those guys always smell so…strange?' I ask.

'So strange,' Cat agrees.

'Ooooh, Capitalism,' I say, waving my fingers around like I'm delivering the gruesome conclusion to a ghost story.

'Capitalism,' Cat joins in. 'Oogie boogie boogie.'

'Oogie, boogie?' I laugh.

'That's my scary ghost noise,' Cat explains.

There's a guy throwing a whole loaf of bread out, slice by slice, on the other side of the pond. He's gathered quite an avian audience. A little sparrow is trying to join the feast but keeps getting bullied out by bigger birds. It flies over to us, lands, and hops around at our feet hopefully. Cat starts breaking off pieces of her crust and dropping them for the little bird. She does it with the guarded attitude of anyone who's ever walked across George Square trying to eat their lunch. You can't let a single pigeon see you have food, you see, because Glasgow pigeons are a different breed from other pigeons. They've got a hive mind like bees and they descend like locusts.

'But, see, if you think about it,' Cat says, 'it's a pretty good trick. Imagine having a system that unquestionable, that anyone who criticises it just gets written off as…'

'Crazy?' I offer.

Cat nods.

A little boy cycles past on a bike with no stabilisers. He swerves across the whole path with each pedal but stays upright.

'So who told you art wasn't a real job?' I ask.

'Just…' she hesitates, 'some guy. He saw me carrying my portfolio back to the flat.'

I feel like there's something there she isn't being totally honest about, but it's not important. What is important is that I, without asking, know what an artist's portfolio is. A big painting-sized briefcase sort of thing that's used for taking the work that you think showcases you the best as an artist from one place to another.

'Where were you getting your portfolio from?' I ask.

'I apply to tons of stuff. Try to get my art out there,' she says. '"Thanks but no thanks" is usually the best I can hope for. Most of the time I just get dinghied, but I've been going back and forth for a while, talking about my paintings with Lily Caplan.'

'Lily Caplan,' I say with wide-eyed wonder. 'Who's that?'

Honestly I could tell by her cadence that it was a big deal and I got excited, but I don't want to pretend I know who she's talking about because that seems like the kind of little lie that could spiral into all manner of unlikely comedies.

'Don't worry,' Cat reassures. 'You're not meant to know who she is. She's not a celebrity; she's a gallery owner. Scottish art scene big shot.'

'Okay, so she had your portfolio?' I'm on tenterhooks.

'Yeah, she wanted to see all my best work. Today we had a meeting,' Cat teases.

'So? What happened?' I urge.

'Nothing really,' Cat admits. 'Just a talk. She likes my stuff though. She said she'd be in touch in a few weeks.'

'That's amazing.' I'm really thrilled for her. Her art is so good, and I feel exceptionally lucky to have met her just before what I'm sure is going to be her big break.

'Don't get carried away,' Cat cautions, 'you'll carry me off with you.'

'Oh, pardon me.' I raise my hands in playful indignation. 'We don't want that.'

'I've heard it, you know?' Cat says. 'When someone says they'll contact you in a few weeks it might mean they'll be in touch tomorrow, or in a few weeks, or in a few months, or – probably – never. They'll just ghost you and stop answering emails. I've gotten to this bit enough times to know not to let myself care too much.'

'Okay,' I say. 'That's reasonable.'

'Thanks,' Cat replies.

'Cat?' I say.

'Yes?' Cat smiles at the corner of her mouth.

'I believe,' I say.

She nods happily and we sit for a minute in comfortable silence. Then I realise that I was so caught up in Cat's news that I forgot all about the sandwich I worked so hard to free. Eating this sandwich is proving to be a real emotional rollercoaster. I finally take a bite.

'I've figured out why the trolley boy is so happy working at the supermarket car park, by the way,' I say with my mouth full.

'Oh, you have?' It's really reassuring how quickly and seamlessly Cat catches on to my flights of whimsy.

'It's simple really. Have you heard of Sleeping Beauty?' I ask.

'The fairy tale?' Cat checks.

'Yeah,' I confirm, then, 'Wait, yes, *of course* the fairy tale. What else could I have meant?'

'That's what I secretly call the security guard,' Cat admits.

I think of the security guard at the supermarket nearest to us, the one Cat probably does her shopping at, the one I saw her through the window of after being recruited as a shelf reaching assistant. His head is always on his desk and his snores louder than he probably realises. Sleeping Beauty. It's a reasonable moniker.

'You think trolley boy is there because of the security guard?' I delve.

'I thought I better check,' Cat shrugs.

'The fairy tale,' I reconfirm. 'We all know that the princess was put into an endless sleep, we all know she could only be awoken by true love's kiss, and then what happened?'

'The prince kisses her; she wakes up,' Cat fills in. 'It's non-consensual, a bit creepy, and people try not to think about it too much.'

'That's what they tell us happened,' I say. 'You'll be pleased to learn there was no creepy, non-consensual kiss at all.'

'I am,' Cat confirms.

'Allow me to elucidate,' I offer. 'You see, when that evil queen cast her curse on poor Sleeping Beauty, she didn't realise just how terrible it was. The princess could only be woken up by the kiss of her one true love. More than that, Sleeping Beauty would live forever, suspended in time, because of the spell that was on her. It's not reasonable to think that Sleeping Beauty's one true love happened to be a prince whom she had never met who was just wandering around during her natural life span and in her kingdom. One true love suggests something grander. It suggests there is a soulmate out there somewhere in the wide, vast, world that you will meet at some point during your life, and now Sleeping Beauty's life was infinite. How many billions of people will exist in an infinite time and on a planet as large as ours?'

'How many?' Cat says, enraptured.

'I don't know; I'm not good at maths,' I say, 'but what I do know is that people forgot all about that castle where the princess slept. Over time it fell to disrepair and collapsed around the princess. Sleeping Beauty was protected by the spell that shielded and doomed her all at once. She was preserved inside her glass coffin.'

Cat raises an eyebrow.

'No, the glass coffin wasn't just Snow White,' I intercept

her question. 'It was Sleeping Beauty too; trust me. Anyway, time went by, centuries passed, layers of dust and silt and dirt buried the princess. Eventually a developer came along. The developer had no idea there was a princess asleep beneath his feet. It was a lot like the princess and the pea, in a way, only the princess was underneath the mattress this time and the mattress was hundreds of years of accumulated subsoil. He concreted over the whole area. Now it would be a centre of commerce instead of the empty field it had been for as long as anyone living, or any written record, could remember. So it was for decades, as businesses rose and fell above Sleeping Beauty's head, then, at last, her true love was born.'

'Trolley boy,' Cat breathes.

'Spoilers,' I smile. 'His parents would think he was a strange child. He'd cry constantly except when they took him to the supermarket. He'd sit happily in his child seat, in their car, in that car park. He'd scream if they tried to lift him out of it. They spent many a frustrating night driving the boy down to sit in the empty car park, so he'd finally sleep. They slept in the car most nights.

'He never really focused in school. He never got good exam results. He was always a bit distracted by the allure of that car park. He was always waiting for when he could next go and sit on the grass verge beside the tarmac. His teachers would tell him that unless he knuckled down and studied, he'd never be able to go to university. He took their advice, since he didn't want to go to university, he knew all he had to do was *not* knuckle down and *never* study, then he wouldn't have to go anywhere; he could just stay near the car park.

'He still went through the typical stages of teenage rebellion, still drank underage and hung around with the wrong crowd, but he did it all in the car park of the supermarket. What better place to shoplift bottles of vodka?

'But eventually his fellow delinquents grew up and stopped wanting to hang around in the cold – what would be the point now that they could go into pubs? And he grew up too. He grew out of delinquency, but he didn't grow out of the car park. As they all scattered to the corners of Scotland, getting salaries and husbands and wives and cars with impressive letters at the start of the registration plate, he stayed put. One day the supermarket advertised for a trolley boy. He applied immediately. It was the first thing he'd ever wanted in his entire life beyond that vague constant longing he'd felt since before he could even talk.

'Imagine his delight when he was told he could work where he was always most content. Imagine the joy he felt when he was given that job, that lots of people would recoil in horror at the suggestion of having to do for a year of two, let alone forever. Imagine how fulfilled he was when he found out he could be in the car park every day for the rest of his life.

'And that's where you can see him. The trolley boy. He spends all day in that carpark, and they pay him for it. They don't know he'd do it for free. He doesn't know what it is about the place – he just knows it's the only place he feels complete, and safe, and happy. There are lots of jobs people say are romantic: pilot, sailor, and – dare I say – poet, but really there are none more romantic that the trolley boy's. Sometimes people mock him and look down on him. Sometimes they treat him without any respect at all, but he doesn't care. He pushes trollies back to the front door with a face filled with resting happiness, he waves at people as they slow their vehicles to let him roll his metal mesh trains past them. He always feels complete because he loves that car park. He loves it with all his heart.'

'Wendy,' Cat says, blinking, 'we need to go dig Sleeping Beauty up from under that car park.'

'Maybe, tomorrow,' I laugh.

Cat finishes the last bite of her sandwich.

'Why a bench instead of a coffee shop by the way?' Cat shivers, 'A nice, warm, coffee shop.'

'This whole being unemployed thing,' I sigh. 'It's starting to have a bit of an impact on my coffee-shop-going capabilities.'

Cat acknowledges that with a pained empathetic expression.

'Well if you won't let me go dig up a car park,' she says, 'we could at least go rob a bank or something.'

'Rob a bank, yeah?' I doublecheck.

'Or something,' She completes, 'Mon, let's pull a bank heist.'

'Okay,' I say, 'I'm in.'

We sit and watch the world pass by for a minute or two as I catch up with what remains of my sandwich.

'I've always liked that word,' I say, '"Heist."'

13

Tomorrow

Kevin comes around again. This time he texts first.

Full disclosure: he did text first the last time too, but this time he waits for a reply to show I'm actually conscious.

We're in my gran's kitchen and my gran is, conspicuously, nowhere to be seen. Kevin has explained to me at the door that he's just checking in again to make sure I'm all right. Just checking in. Just touching base.

'Just going to stick the kettle on,' Kevin suggests.

'No,' I reply in horror, 'I'll do it; you're a guest.'

'I'm hardly a guest, now, am I?' Kevin points out, 'I've been here enough times that I really ought to be pulling my weight. No special treatment for me.'

'Well,' I hide the truth in plain sight by disguising it as a light-hearted joke. 'Now it would be rude of me not to let you.'

'Excellent,' Kevin notes. 'So, you'd like a coffee?'

'No, honestly, you're fine.' I once got a coffee with Kevin in first year rather than just tell him I don't drink it. It didn't seem like the kind of little lie that could spiral into all manner of unlikely comedies, and yet, here we are, five years later and I'm considering switching to decaf.

'It's no trouble,' he reassures, 'I'm happy to. I can't just make myself one and not you. That would make me a terrible guest.'

'You literally just said you're not a guest. You can't just change your mind whenever it's convenient for you, buddy,' I say.

No.

Sorry.

I don't say that.

I'm lying again. I'm sorry. I'm really trying. I don't say that because that would be a bit confrontational. Bad form.

'Oh, go on then,' I say instead, as though I was only refusing it in the first place because I'm on a coffee fast, but I just don't have the willpower to stick it out.

Kevin puts my kettle on, helpfully.

I decide that I'm at least going to pass him the sugar – then I won't feel completely useless. I open the kitchen cupboard and notice, abstractly, that there is very little food in there. Just a few boxes of pasta. I make a mental note to ask Gran if she needs me to go to the shop. I must have made the mental note in disappearing spy ink though, because I don't recall ever mentally seeing it again.

'Did you fill in the application?' Kevin asks.

'Get off my case,' I say, picturing the application still lying untouched on my desk upstairs.

I don't say that really.

Sorry.

Bad form.

'Yeah,' I lie. 'I sent it in the day after you gave me it.'

I can't even remember how long ago that was.

I heard once that if two blocks of lead – or any two blocks of any element, as long as they're the same – were to meet in the vacuum of space, they would merge into one object without the need for any sort of melting. They'd merge on contact. That's because there's no elements in between them, because space is a void, so there's nothing to let the two blocks of lead know they aren't already one block of lead. There would be no helpful air molecules squished in between them to let them know where one ended and the next began. They'd just become one solid unit, seamlessly. Literally. Without any seams. Well, that's days of the week for me just now.

'Brilliant.' Kevin has his back to me, spooning coffee and sugar into mugs. 'They shouldn't take too long to get back to you, they're very efficient.'

'Thanks,' I say. 'At this point I'd take pretty much anything. I've seen advertisements for delivery drivers, but I don't have a car. Or a licence.'

It should be true that I've been desperately seeking work, but really I've given looking for a job about as much attention in general as I have Kevin's application form.

'Well, of course,' Kevin says compromisingly. 'But you didn't go through four years of university to have to do just *anything*.'

I bite my tongue.

'No,' I agree convivially, but I don't like the implication. Who chooses what has value?

In first year at Strathclyde uni you get to do a lot of subjects.

I took English, IT, philosophy: a bunch of things. When I went I'd meant to do English as my degree from second year onwards, but after first year Kevin and I were talking about how IT was where the money was. An English degree might be interesting but with an IT degree you were securing a lifestyle. If you played it right you could be set for life before you were thirty. Kevin had worked it all out at high school. We agreed IT was the smart move, so we took IT. So did Freya, unfortunately. Whatever. She's not important just now.

Kevin takes a lot of pride in remembering how I like my coffee; how much sugar and milk. I wonder if I'll ever tell him that the reason I only take a small amount of milk is because putting it in coffee is a waste of milk.

'Although…' I begin.

'What's up?' Kevin asks, looking up from the alchemy of coffee making. It's as though as soon as I agreed with him he erased the conversation from his head entirely.

'There's nothing wrong with being a delivery driver,' I say. 'I was talking to Cat yesterday, and…'

'Oh, Cat from uni?' Kevin interrupts.

'No, not Cat from uni. I didn't even speak to her when I saw her every day, why would I now? Get over university; it's finished. Move on.'

Sorry.

There's something about this conversation that makes me want to lie to you. I didn't say that. I said this. 'No, from work. My old work. The call centre.'

'Understood,' Kevin says, handing me my coffee carefully. It's in my favourite mug. I'm being too hard on him. I'm tired. That's all. At least I'm not letting it show.

'Was she telling you how much they were struggling

without you, and that they regret ever firing you?' He takes a sip from his own mug.

'No. She quit too' – and I put a bit of emphasis on the word 'quit' as opposed to 'fired' – 'at the same time as me, actually.'

'How did that work?' Kevin asks.

'I really haven't told you about what happened at all, have I?' I realise, a little surprised. I guess as a friend I've been a bit negligent.

'That's not an issue,' he shrugs. 'It's not an enjoyable thing to happen. I doubt you want to relive it.'

'It was enjoyable, in a weird way,' I tell him.

'It was?' he leans forward, conspiratorially, interested and ready to listen. It's been a while since we've really spoken.

'Yeah,' I laugh, 'it really was, and I met this girl because of it – Cat – she's pretty cool.'

'Tell me more.' Kevin still has the same look of interest in his face, but it seems to have frozen a little. Maybe I'm imagining it.

'Okay,' I say. 'This is crazy. You know that smell in my hair when I last saw you?'

Kevin nods. I look around over both shoulders, paranoid I'll be overheard by a passing police officer even though I'm in my own kitchen. When I speak, I whisper, painfully aware my gran has a knack for lurking soundlessly. I lean towards him, so that I can't be overheard by any bugs that might have been planted in the house by MI5 without my knowledge, and say, 'That was weed.'

He tilts his head, like he's trying to fit my words in his ear and they've got stuck.

'You don't smoke,' he says eventually.

'I just tried it,' I say.

'Isn't it addictive?' he chides.

This from him? He'd happily be the guy who goes up for a round and comes back with a side order of shots without asking. He bought me *plenty* of shots. He wasn't worried about them being addictive.

I feel chastised. It feels as though his reaction is unfair. Being annoyed about unfairness makes me feel like a stroppy toddler, which I hate even more.

'Yeah,' I say, shaking it off. 'It was stupid, really.'

He considers me, creasing his forehead.

'No,' he says at last, 'I'm being a prude. I'm just jealous that I've never done it.'

My shoulders unknot.

'Was it fun?' he asks.

'I think so,' I reply. 'It was really weird.'

'Wait, let's do this correctly,' he insists. 'Start at the start. How did you both quit at once?'

'It was a walkout,' I'm delighted to share, particularly because he finally said 'quit'.

'No way?' Kevin prompts me to go on.

We have a proper conversation for the first time in a while. We drink coffee until I get the jitters and feel sick. It's nice.

When he leaves my gran appears again behind my back, as though she has the power to travel wherever she wants in our house by teleporting through shadows.

'You two should go somewhere nice together, darling. Don't always just sit in here,' she suggests.

I see her dreams for my future. Kevin and I in a relationship, a home of our own, maybe children, a stable job. I see it all so clearly.

My stomach lurches.

I don't have space in my head for any of this. It's full up. I can't go somewhere nice with him. I've not had a job for, literally, I don't know how long, I can't afford somewhere nice.

'Yeah,' I aim for airy and dismissive, but it comes out bitter and irascible for some reason. I head back upstairs. A study in suppressed torment.

Sleep won't come again that night. No sheep to count, no sandman to bewitch my eyes.

'Make something of yourself. You've no excuse any more, Wendy,' I think. 'No school, no college, no university, not even a part-time job you can say you're doing until the right 'forever job' comes along. You're a graduate now. You can't hide behind education any more, you need to have some sort of use. If you're going to become something, then you better do it.'

'I'll do it tomorrow,' I promise myself.

Just like I did yesterday.

14

Pixie Cove 🧚

A few days later Cat and I go somewhere nice.

Cat asks me to meet her at a little restaurant in the Merchant City for lunch. It's called Pixie Cove, which is an incredibly whimsical name for a café, even by my standards. I get there and find her sitting at a table near the door, with a mischievous look in her eye.

'What do you think?' she asks as I sit down.

'Of here?' I ask.

'You like it?' Cat raises an eyebrow.

'It's nice,' I say, non-committal.

Cat scoffs, 'What do you really think?'

I look around. The décor is bland, the servers bored, the menu innocuous. Everything has a sort of false boutique sheen to it. It has the veneer of a small business run by someone with a passion and a dream, only the soul is cynical. Under the façade of this plucky small business, I suspect, lurks a commercial puppet master. Pay no attention to the man behind the curtain.

'Is it a chain?' I conclude.

'How did you get that?' Cat looks impressed.

'I'm somewhat of a detective,' I confess.

Cat gives me a small quiet round of applause, 'It's a chain. A secret chain restaurant. Do you still think it's nice?'

It's a little unusual that I came out for lunch and instead I'm getting a quiz, but I'm enjoying the intrigue. I want to know where all this is going.

It's hard to see the niceness of the place now I know that it's all a lie. It's difficult to look past the deceit and say for sure if I'd find this place charming if I hadn't realised the charm was market-researched, but there's something to it, putting aside the duplicity.

'Yeah. Sort of,' I say indecisively.

'Would you be gutted, but, if we never ever came here again?' Cat tilts her head.

'Ever?' I ask.

'Ever,' Cat pointedly over-enunciates.

'I suppose not?' it's more of a question than a statement. I don't really know what's going on. I look at the menu. 'It's expensive.'

I feel a little hand of tension grip my lower vertebrae. I can't really afford 'expensive'. To be honest I can't really afford 'cheap' at this point.

Cat shrugs. 'Overpriced, I'd say.'

'You're not going to try to say it's on you, are you?' The little hand tightens its grip. I can't let her pay for me – that would be horribly bad form. I'd be humiliated. Cat must realise that?

'No way,' Cat's eyes glint with mischief. 'I quit too,

remember? I'm a burden on society just like you.'

Now I'm confused. 'So, if neither of us can afford to be here, then why are both of us here?'

'Have you ever…' Cat looks around, an echo of my own behaviour when I told Kevin about my illicit smoking session, '…done a dine and dash?'

'You mean run away without paying?' I ask.

Cat shushes me, worried I'll be overheard. She looks around again. She nods.

'We can't,' I contest, but the hand of worry has released my spine and I feel something else instead. It's stomach-churning, but even though it's not exactly a nice feeling I suspect it may, possibly, be excitement. 'What if…'

'I've checked,' Cat replies.

'You've checked?' I ask.

'I knew you wouldn't do if you thought it might hurt someone, so I checked. The staff don't get charged for theft; it comes out of the company's pocket, and, by the way, while I was checking I found out the company's really shit. There are loads of ex-employees online saying that working here is awful and the company keeps all their tips.'

'But two wrongs don't make a right,' I say, without much conviction.

Cat doesn't say anything. She knows she doesn't have to argue her case any more than she has.

'Why would you tell me this now?' I try to hide my face like a criminal. 'Now I have to act natural throughout the whole lunch.'

'I wanted you to know you could order whatever you like,' Cat explains, as though it's perfectly reasonable. 'Plus, the anticipation is the best part.'

I realise another implication. 'How can I possibly talk to a waiter or waitress without them knowing?'

Cat adopts a dramatic caricature. She does a *voice*, like a 1920s American gangster. 'Let me do the talking.'

I can tell it's not the sort of thing she'd usually do – she cringes a little at her own bad attempt – but she knows it's the sort of silliness I like. It works. I snigger despite my nervousness. I deliberate internally. I'm good at deliberating internally. I have a whole internal process that has an appeals system and everything. Deliberating something internally can take months or even years. Big choices shouldn't be made on mere caprice.

Caprese salad. That's what I'll have.

'Okay,' I feel a rush of exhilaration, 'I'm in.'

Cat grins. Before I can change my mind, she calls over a waiter. I try to cover my entire face with a menu without looking suspicious.

'Hello, good sir,' Cat says, in a posh approximation of the accent of stereotypical landed gentry, the waiter's expression suggests he is elsewhere in mind if not body, 'we should like to order a spot of lunch.'

The waiter takes out a notepad. His sigh isn't vocalised, but it exists in his posture at all times.

'I should enjoy a coffee to drink,' Cat goes on, not put off by our stern server, 'and my associate will have something other than coffee, as she secretly detests it.'

She remembered. There's really no reason why she wouldn't. I still like that she did.

I turn my menu around and point to a soft drink. If our waiter isn't speaking, I don't feel as though it's rude of me not to either, I don't want him to be able to recognise my voice in a line-up.

Our waiter scribbles what may be the drinks order or may be a handwritten resignation; we have to assume it's the former.

'We shall be eating today as well, my good man, I hope that's no trouble.' She's still doing the accent, and I can see her starting to regret it. The waiter's withering indifference is starting to shake her.

'I'll have a plate of your finest macaroni and cheese, if it comes on a plate. A bowl or paper tray or chopping board is fine if that is your way. I don't care about the...uh,' she flounders for a word, looks at me for help, then before I can offer any, goes with, 'receptacle.'

I snort a laugh. The waiter glances at me distastefully. He offers no clarification on the means of mac and cheese delivery.

I point to my chosen salad. I stay silent.

'Cheapest thing on the menu,' Cat observes.

Our waiter jots, then he wanders away wordlessly.

'Yes,' Cat calls after, though not loud enough that he can actually hear, 'sally forth and return with nourishment, forthwith.'

'Cat,' I reprimand her. 'You're making us look suspicious.'

'Thought he'd never leave,' Cat laughs.

'Why were you a gangster one second then posh the next?' I ask.

'I don't know. I just opened my mouth and Downton Abbey came out so I was stuck with it.' Then she adds, reverting to her artificially plummy character, 'Besides, I think what really made us look eccentric was you, my silent cohortian.'

Cohortian. Good word.

'Oh, by the way, while we're here, stealing lunch and that,' she begins.

'Oh God,' I tease. 'Is there more to this? We're not going to murder someone are we?'

'*I* might,' Cat taunts playfully. It's the nicest death threat I've ever received. 'No. I read your poems.'

'What?' I wonder if she knows that she may as well have just told me she's looked into my soul. 'I only gave you the notebook a few days ago.'

'I read it all for the first time that night. I wasn't about to just fling it in a corner and leave it, was I?'

'The first time?' I'm astonished. She's read it twice?

'There was no chance I was getting every little nuance by just reading each poem the once,' Cat explains. 'I've read some of them five or six times.'

'Which ones?' I ask. She still hasn't said she liked them. Why hasn't she said she liked them?

'My favourite is Daedalus,' Cat says. 'I don't know anything at all about poetry, so I have no idea if it's breaking any technical rules or whatever, but I do know that when I read it, I felt like it was saying something that I've been trying to say for a while but couldn't.'

'It's about flying.' I'm surprised when my voice comes out raspy. I was going to say more but my throat betrayed me.

'It's more than that,' Cat says. She doesn't seem to think it's silly or embarrassing that I obviously want to cry. 'But, Wendy, that's just my favourite. I love them all.'

I love putting words in order on a page and making something that I think is bigger than the sum of its parts. I love having time to arrange them and play with them. I wish I weren't so afraid of words in the real world, I wish they didn't turn into glue in my mouth so often. Life is an unlimited cascade of parallel possibilities and every single word alters the path. That's petrifying; it's fossilising. How can people handle that responsibility?

It's words. It always has been. Words are the problem.

My gran has read some of my poems. She's always supportive. She says they're good, but I don't believe her. I don't believe she really likes poetry – she likes *me*; that's all. I believe Cat. There's a miniature sun made of gratitude right in the centre of my rib cage and its beams are tearing out of me, but, because we're in the real world where words can't be retrieved once they leave your mouth, I don't know how to tell her how much it means to me.

'You believe?' I say at last, lamely.

'I believe,' Cat replies.

Our lunch arrives and the moment breaks.

'That was suspiciously quick,' Cat points out to me as the waiter walks away again.

'Right? I know mine is just a salad, but how do you make macaroni and cheese at that pace? Looks like it's microwaved.'

'How shit is that?' Cat says.

'I'm glad we're robbing them,' I say.

A surprised laugh escapes Cat. Then she says, 'You know what's wrong with this place?'

'Capitalism, oogie, boogie, boogie,' we say in unison.

'So, is this instead of the bank heist?' I ask, taking in the full forbidden grandeur of my lunch. Just now it's both stolen and not stolen. Schrödinger's salad.

'This is the warm-up heist,' Cat explains. 'To see how well we work as a team.'

'Obviously,' I say. 'How silly of me.'

'We should hit a gallery though, not a bank,' Cat expands. 'I know the layout of a lot of them like the back of my hand and

I have the contacts to sell a painting, too.'

'That's smart thinking,' I play along. 'Although I think it's about time I told you what *really* happened to my parents.'

'Now is definitely the time,' Cat invites me to continue.

So, I tell her. And now I'll tell you, too.

15

The Mermaids

It's hard for me to admit this, but my parents were confidence tricksters. Conmen is the common parlance, though, in this case, it's con-people. This was long before the time when a con was just an ad on the internet that promises a quality product but delivers a cheap knock-off. This was back when conning people was a thing you had to do face to face, when to con someone, you needed style and pizzazz. They travelled far and wide, running elaborate scams. They were the top of the most wanted list from Thurso to Dumfries.

They were honourable people. Their marks wouldn't be the old or the vulnerable; that would defy their code. They hit those whose bank balance was large but whose morals were bankrupt. They preyed on greedy credulity, the desire of wealthy people to believe they could gain even more than they already had.

They were pros at all the top grifts, the short count, jam

auctions, pigeon drops, rainmaking – the whole shebang. They could talk someone into a knot and then they'd charge to untie it. They were confident in their tricks of confidence; perhaps a little too confident.

My parents' circumstances had changed, and that's what led to them doing something that might have been risky. That change was me, the baby they had on the way. Their swindles were making them enough cash that they could survive in the manner to which they were accustomed when it was just the two of them, but a third member of their infamous troupe would try their means. Sure, they had enough that we could all have lived comfortably pretty much indefinitely, but who wants to live comfortably when you can live fabulously?

They needed to do one more big con, one more job so they could hit the mother lode and then never have to scam ever again. This job would need a team.

They were going to hit three casinos at once. For a caper like that you need a team of crack specialists, all exceptionally talented in their own chosen field, and with varying yet complementary characters. Some of them have to rub each other up the wrong way – that's a requirement for any criminal escapade – but all of them must ultimately operate to a similar moral code and be the kind of ne'er do wells you can really root for.

My mum was the mastermind; Dad was the grifter. They were joined by the hacker, the gadget guy, the safe cracker, the driver, the muscle, the fixer, the inside man, the thief and the new kid. Eleven in total; it just seemed right. They all told each other that whatever happened they'd never do this again. They also all agreed that if they were to ever do it again, they'd probably do it with a crew of twelve. It also just seemed right.

The plan went off with only the right amount of hiccups to create dramatic tension. My parents and their team of rapscallions knocked over all three casinos and made off with enough moolah that they could all live like royalty.

But you're probably getting a sense that this all went just a little too smoothly, and you'd be right. Months went by and my parents became increasingly complacent. They started to decorate their nursery and prepare for their life as well-off parents to a wonderful baby girl. It was on the day that they brought their new baby-crib back to their lavish mansion-crib that they learned that they hadn't got away with their crime at all.

In their living room they found five men waiting for them. All were in suits. Four, my parents could tell, due to their exceptional skills of observation, were wearing concealed firearms. The fifth was the last person they wanted to see sitting on their new premium-quality couch.

All three casinos were owned by one man – a man whose name was Mr Huge; huge amounts of money, huge amounts of power, huge capacity for anger. Mr Huge was in my parents' living room.

But how? The new kid had sold them out. Their misgivings about letting a young unknown upstart onto their crack team had been right all along.

He demanded his money back; they told him they'd already spent it. He demanded to know who their accomplices were; they refused to tell him. He demanded to know how they did it; they kept schtum. He saw no reason, given how unhelpful they were being, not to just kill them.

But, as we know, my parents preyed on greedy credulity – the desire of greedy people to believe they could gain even more than they already had. My dad reasoned with Mr Huge. He insisted that a man like Mr Huge must have use for a man and woman of their particular talents.

Mr Huge took the bait. He told my dad he liked the cut of his jib.

Mr Huge had a huge foe, a crime kingpin with a wealth that rivalled even his. They called him Hoarder because of his habit of acquiring anything of value he could to add to his impressive collection. Hoarder had a painting, a lost and hitherto unknown work of art by Edgar Degas. It was called *The Mermaids*. Huge said he'd seen this painting only once before Hoarder had snatched it up and hidden it from the world. He said he felt as though it were singing to him. Singing, to him and only him, promising him such power and happiness. Mr Huge said it was the only beautiful thing he'd ever seen in his life besides his huge vault of money. He told my parents they must free *The Mermaids*. Only then would he let them live.

They had to reassemble their team – all except the new kid, of course – but this time the team were much more reluctant. They'd all agreed that the last job would be just that: the last job. They were spread across the globe by this point, each living in their own personal paradise. Why would they come back to rainy Scotland to steal a painting when the risks were so high? It says a lot about what incredible people my parents were that when the time came every single member of the team returned. They couldn't leave my mum and dad to die, even if coming back might mean they'd die as well. With everyone gathered, there was only one thing left to do: arbitrarily inflate the number of people in the crew to twelve. They got a different, completely unrelated, new kid and brought in an explosives expert just to make up the numbers.

Everything was going smoothly. Each team member had found one specific moment during which their precise talents were essential. The explosives expert had even managed to find an excuse to use an exceedingly small explosive and do so in such a way that it seemed crucial, despite the fact the job logically had no need of an explosives expert. Intricate meshes of lasers had been contorted around, trip wires had been stepped over, security guards had been effortlessly knocked out in a way that presumably caused no lasting brain damage. When the crew finally saw *The Mermaids*, they all had to agree, it was beautiful. They felt it pulling them in. They could hear the surreal representations of the mermaids singing to them, luring them. They grabbed the painting and made their escape.

Then someone sneezed.

New kid. They knew they shouldn't have replaced new kid with a new equally unreliable new kid. Why would they never learn?

New kid had sneezed directly onto the painting. They'd removed it from its frame to make it easier to smuggle, and so it was completely unprotected from the snot. It wasn't just the new kid who was too green for this job; his phlegm was as well. Before anyone could stop him, the new kid tried to wipe the offending matter off the painting.

The paint, dampened by his sneeze and the resulting moist lump it had left on the canvas, came away too. *The Mermaids*, through no fault of my parents', was irreparably defaced.

What a comedy romp.

But not for my parents. Now they had no choice but to go back to Mr Huge and own up. They would have to tell him they'd destroyed the only thing he ever considered beautiful and face the dire consequences.

Mr Huge took the news poorly. He flew into a rage. My parents were confused as to why he didn't kill them on the spot. Relieved; granted – but confused. Huge explained to them that if he couldn't enjoy art any more, then he'd make sure no one could. He told my parents the blood that would be spilled in the next hour was on their hands. Then, with a villainous flourish, he exited their story.

It was my mum who cracked his code. He was so bitter at having lost the only work of art he cared about that he intended to blow up the National Art Gallery and eliminate the works of art inside, but there wasn't just art in there; there were people.

They only had an hour to stop catastrophe. My parents got in their car and sped to the National Art Gallery as fast as they could, swerving between other drivers and skidding around corners. My mum went through a speed camera without even slowing down and as it flashed, my dad realised something: if she didn't care about the speeding ticket, then she knew this would probably be a one-way trip.

Their crew was down to two now, but they were used to that. With slick professionalism they assigned tasks. Dad was to get to the bomb. Mum would get all the people out.

Evacuating the building wouldn't be easy. Mr Huge had sent his bruisers down to the gallery to make sure that no one could foil his evil plan. As Mum made her way towards the fire alarm, which she intended to pull to clear out the gallery, she suddenly found herself the eye of the storm in a hurricane of bullets. She took cover, amazed that Mr Huge's henchmen were such terrible shots. The good news was that the gunfire had served the same purpose as tripping the fire alarm would have – people were exiting the gallery at a reassuring pace, screaming notwithstanding. The bad news was the shock had caused my Mum's water to break. She went into labour there and then. She knew she couldn't let Mr Huge's men harm her baby, so she grabbed a Fabergé egg and beat them to death.

My dad found the bomb. Once he did, he realised he had no idea what he was doing. This would have been the perfect time to have an explosives expert on hand, but there's never any around when you need them. There was every chance, at that point, that if he had turned and run he could have escaped the gallery in time, but how would he be able to live with himself if innocent people died because he hadn't even tried to stop the explosion? He had no way of knowing whether the gallery had been successfully evacuated or not. For a nerve-racking three minutes he did his best to deactivate the deadly device.

My mum had heard that labour took a good few hours at least, but knew she didn't have time for that. She efficiently gave birth to me, cut the umbilical cord with a nearby priceless ceremonial knife, and passed me to a fleeing escapee, telling her to take diligent care of me. She said my name was Wendy.

She could have escaped too, of course, but not without my dad. Instead she went deeper into the gallery to find him. They were together in the end, my mum and dad, and that ticking LED bomb timer. As the seconds ran down, they knew they'd been lucky in life to have each other. They were blessed because they had found true love, and even though their lives would soon end at least they would still be together. They also knew their legacy would live on.

It does: it lives on in me.

So you see, my parents died right after I was born, all because of an art heist.

16

Dine and Dash

None of the last chapter was true.

But it is what I tell Cat as we eat our lunch.

'So,' Cat asks, 'no heist?'

'Let's not be hasty,' I insist. 'I just think we have to learn from the mistakes my parents made. Otherwise their deaths will have been in vain.'

'So,' Cat corrects, 'no new kid.'

'Exactly.' I eat my last tomato slice. 'We've got to keep our team close-knit.'

It's stupid that literally fifteen to twenty minutes or so ago I couldn't think of the most appropriate way to accept a compliment and now I've just spent the whole time we were eating our lunch on a flight of fantasy. It's nice to talk though, even if what I was saying was complete nonsense. It's nice to just mindlessly chat and be heard without worrying, and Cat had very much been an active participant. The phlegmy sneeze, for example – that bit was hers.

I do wish she'd taken more time on her mac and cheese. And I wish I'd taken more on my salad. Don't get me wrong, I don't mean I'm judging either of us for eating quickly or for eating everything. I don't get people who order food just to pick at it and leave it. Food's brilliant – why wouldn't you eat it? What I mean is now we're both finished.

We realise, seemingly at the same moment, that if we're both finished then the time has come. It's now or never.

'Are we really doing this?' I ask, my heart racing.

'It'll be an adventure,' Cat says with suppressed anticipation in her voice.

'No dragon to slay,' I point out.

'No,' Cat agrees. 'No safety harness, but.'

'No safety harness,' I nod, resolutely. 'So what do we do?'

'Just walk out,' Cat coaches, adopting an exaggerated cowboy drawl, 'real casual like.'

'So, do you just, like, do a random accent when you're nervous?' I ask.

'I feel seen,' Cat replies, 'and I don't like it.'

We stand, acting natural, and begin nonchalantly walking towards the door which, thanks to Cat's expert table-picking, is only a few feet away.

There's an employee near the back of the restaurant who, unlike his colleagues, is wearing a pinstripe shirt rather than a plain one, and doesn't seem to have to wear an apron. It's the universal code for manager. He's the one who spots us.

He calls to our waiter. 'Michael, have they paid?'

We pick up the pace. I'm trying not to break into a jog. The door feels like it's getting further away.

'Michael, stop them,' shouts the pinstriped manager.

Our waiter, whose name is Michael, as it turns out, gives Pinstripe a sardonic look that makes his thoughts on that suggestion very clear.

I knew I liked him, deep down. He's our hero, Captain Apathy, to the rescue.

'Oh, for God's sake,' Pinstripe realises if he wants anything done right, he'll have to do it himself. He starts pushing past tables to get to us.

'Run,' Cat shouts, breaking cover. A bell over the door jingles politely as we career out of Pixie Cove.

We run full pelt. We hold nothing back. You know the old axiom, 'prepare for a marathon not a sprint?' Wise words. Doesn't always apply though. We dodge past confused pedestrians.

I almost literally run into a guy. I look at his face, hoping that a second of eye contact will let us get our wires straight and figure out who's going around who.

'Wendy?' Kevin says.

'Kevin?' I reply, bewildered.

What are the odds?

Then Cat's voice at my shoulder reminds me, 'Wendy, no safety harness.'

Pinstripe is gaining on us. Shouting things like 'get them' and 'stop her' to a street full of people who, thankfully, are as interested in what Pinstripe wants as Michael was.

I'd love if I'd said something suave to Kevin. What I actually do is scream directly in his face, offer no explanation at all, then keep on running.

Cat and I get into a rhythm, running side by side. People start getting out of our way, rather than us having to dodge them. My legs start to burn but I ignore them. I'm not necessarily dressed to run, but I ignore that too. My shoes are doing fine. I can feel my heartbeat, which was uncontrollable as we were sneaking out, start to regulate. My lungs do the same, pushing my breath in and out rationally rather than in the unproductive gulps they were moments ago. I'm aware that my eyes are behaving differently, it's as though my field of vision has narrowed but sharpened. I feel like I'm processing information faster, preparing for the possible pitfalls up ahead by disregarding my peripheral vision entirely. I didn't know I could do that.

Neither of us are picking what turns we make. We're like a very exclusive flock of birds, understanding each other's intentions subliminally and following each other so smoothly and thoughtlessly that we don't know which of us is the leader. I'm dimly aware of crossing George Square, passing a few of the buildings where I used to have classes, barrelling through the bus station. After that it's all a blur.

Pinstripe doesn't look like he'd be that fast, but you never know. We don't look back. We just keep on running, together. I pick up the pace, Cat follows suit. I do it again, she matches once more. She gives me a look that says, 'Oh it's a race you want?' and widens her stride, pulling out in front of me by a few inches. I catch her up. We both try to go faster and can't. This is top speed for both of us.

I can't maintain this pace for long, but I wish I could just get that tiny bit faster. I feel as though my feet are barely touching the ground and there's a wisp of a hope in my mind that if I could just get a little tiny bit faster then maybe they wouldn't touch it at all. Maybe we'd both just lift off the pavement. We could outrun gravity like a plane on a runway.

Okay, so my understanding of aeronautics might not be

great.

Then my heart, lungs and legs all seem to fall out of synch. The bliss of everything working in beautiful tandem is replaced by the sudden awareness of how searing cold the air going into my lungs, and pushing through the gaps between my teeth, is. My hands, unprotected from the chilly atmosphere, are pink and stiff. My back, however, is much too warm, and I can feel exactly where sweat is running down it with horrible accuracy. My brain, foreman of the discord, issues a recommendation that I stop before all the other parts of my body decide to go on strike. I drop to a walk, take a few quick steps in a circle to let the excess energy flow away, then stop entirely, panting heavily.

'Oh, thank God,' Cat says, stopping next to me. 'I thought you were going to go that fast forever.'

I laugh, which turns into a cough, which turns into a coughing fit, which turns into pretending none of the coughing happened.

'Did we lose him?' I pant.

'The restaurant guy?' Cat asks. 'Yeah, like a mile away. Not even exaggerating.'

'What? No,' I say, 'we didn't run a mile.'

Cat gives me an earnest, though amused, look.

'Wow,' Is all I can manage.

We *are* quite far from Pixie Cove. It didn't feel like we'd been going for long. I thought he was still right behind us, but I can feel time decompressing now. It's as though it was compacted by all the other sensations of running and I forgot to notice it, but now it's returning.

'How long were we running for?' I ask.

'I don't know,' Cat says. 'More than five minutes, less than ten?'

'Yeah?' I gasp.

'Think so,' Cat says. Then she looks at me and beams, red-faced and happy.

We're on Buchanan Street. It's wide and pedestrianised. I guess whatever part of our brains we left in charge of the route we took led us to somewhere that it would be easier to navigate around passers-by. Cat looks further along the street. She notices something.

'Come on.' She runs away.

'Oh, God,' I say, hoping I can manage even the laziest of jogs. I huff after her.

She's heading towards a balloon stall outside the shop that, to me, will always be Borders Books despite the fact it stopped being that when I was, like, ten years old. A man, half street vendor and half party clown, is making balloon animals. I see examples hooked to the side of his cart. They're the usual fare: cartoon character favourites, rendered in balloon, bulbous and bloated but somehow still adorable. It's not those she's after though. She hands the man a crumpled bank note as I jog towards them and he hands her two helium balloons in return. I arrive just as the transaction draws to a close. Cat pushes a balloon string into my hand.

'Ready?' She looks into my eyes expectantly.

'For what?' I ask.

And Cat charges away full-speed again, helium balloon trailing behind her.

I gurgle in exasperation. I wish I could say I sighed but it seems the exertion of the chase has transmuted all my sighs to more watery substitutes. I run off after her.

Cat is running up Buchanan street, glancing impishly

behind her to make sure I'm still there. She leads me across a few intersecting roads and around jaded shoppers who've seen far stranger things in the city centre. She drops back a little so I can fall in by her side again just as we reach the steps of the concert hall.

'Okay, one last sprint. You ready?' she asks.

'No?' I suggest.

'Come on.' She explodes into a run, and I do too.

We bound up the long stairs of the concert hall, feeling like a couple of Rocky Balboas. There it is again, that sensation of weightlessness. It's not as strong, thanks to the tiredness in my muscles and the fact we're going up a staircase, but it's there – like we could take off.

'Think happy thoughts,' Cat shouts as we reach the top, 'then let go.'

We both do. I expect the balloons to fly forward past us when we let them go, but actually they go backwards. Science.

They spin and teeter in the air gracelessly, finding their feet like I did when we left the restaurant, then they right themselves. We watch as they silently ascend. You don't often see a freed helium balloon without the soundtrack of a heartbroken child. These ones seem so peaceful. So full of poise.

'For Daedalus,' Cat explains, with wonder.

'For Daedalus,' I echo, delighted.

We watch them get further and smaller. Everything seems quiet. The sounds of the street are far off and inconsequential.

'That's actually kind of littering,' I point out.

'Add it to the rap sheet,' Cat jokes.

I imagine myself up there with the balloons. Or rather, I imagine I am one of them. My one, whichever that is. I envy it.

I imagine myself drifting idly through the freezing air, sinking upwards through the clouds, observing how everyone down below is diminished by distance into insignificance. I imagine coming out of the other side of the damp cloud barrier to see a world that looks like the morning on a snowy day, before a single footprint has spoiled it. I imagine having nothing above me but stars beckoning weakly through the blue glow of the ozone layer, and nothing below me but whiteness. I imagine the quiet and the lack of any other life, being free of expectations or responsibilities. I imagine I can – serene, unobserved and unreachable – just float away.

*

17

Proud and Insolent Youth

A few feet in front of us John Malkovich is walking away from an exploding plane.

Cat, sitting next to me on her couch, gives her review.

'This is the dumbest shit I ever saw.'

Cat doesn't have a TV, not because she doesn't like TV, but because with all the easels and canvases around there really isn't space for one, and even if there were it would probably get paint all over it. We've propped her laptop up to create our own tiny makeshift cinema. The bottom of our tower of entertainment is a weird little stool. Cat assures me it came with the flat, and that she suspects it may be in some way cursed. On top of the stool we've stacked a bunch of ragged law textbooks for the laptop to perch on top of. I don't know if they came with the flat or not.

Nicolas Cage jumps through a tiny window while fire licks his boots, his long hair swishes as the displaced air from the explosion rushes past him.

'It is,' I say fondly. 'Do you want me to switch it off?'

'Absolutely not,' Cat replies.

'You sure?' I say, reaching out to close the laptop.

'Make a move and the bunny gets it,' Cat exclaims, holding a finger gun to a couch cushion.

'Woah, okay.' I sit back with my hands up. 'Lets not be hasty.'

'So, action films?' Cat asks.

'Yeah. I love them. It's really hard to worry about life when there's a movie in front of you just throwing bright colours and loud noises and terrible one liners at you. It's distracting. Like waving keys in front of a baby, you know?'

'But instead of keys it's a guy with a machine gun,' Cat notes.

'And a white vest,' I add. 'Always a white vest.'

'Always?' Cat asks. 'How many of these have you watched?'

'Umm,' I make a show of counting on my fingers. 'Approximately, all of them.'

On the screen someone is throwing shotguns to people like party bags.

'Hey, Cat?'

'Yeah?'

'I want to go back and pay for the lunch we stole,' I say, awkwardly.

'What?' Cat replies. 'But Wendy, we totally smashed capitalism today; we live in a socialist society now. You want to undo all of that?'

I'm relieved at her light-hearted hyperbole.

'Yeah,' I admit.

'Even though you're skint?'

'It's the right thing to do,' I shrug.

Cat rolls her eyes.

'Oh God. Is that the look you give people you've just lost all respect for?' I ask.

'This look is for when I've just found out I admire someone,' Cat admits, then adds, 'begrudgingly.'

A witty one-liner from John Malkovich brings us back to the movie. We make an unspoken agreement to go make reparations after the movie ends. We watch the plot unfold for a while.

I draw in breath to say something, think better of it, and say nothing.

'What's up?' Cat asks.

'Oh, you noticed that?' I say. Cat gives a nod and I decide to be brave and just say it. 'Usually when I'm watching movies like this, it's because I should be doing something else, but even if I really want to do the thing, I just can't; it feels like my feet and legs have been wrapped in concrete.'

Cat doesn't make a big deal. She keeps her eyes on the laptop. Guns are firing, cars are exploding. 'I'm going to say a couple of kind of intimidating words, is that okay?'

'Yes,' I scoff.

'Yeah. Look who I'm talking to. Of course it's okay,' Cat smiles. 'Have you ever heard of executive dysfunction?'

'No,' I reply.

'You should google it,' Cat suggests.

My mind races. There *is* a word for it. The way I've been feeling has a term, and if it has a term then it can't be that uncommon. I want to know more about it, but before I can say anything else we hear a scratching sound coming from the door.

'Is that keys?' I ask.

The whole mood changes instantly.

Cat jumps to her feet. She rushes, not to the door, but to the corner of the room, her muscles are taut, her eyes are wide. I stay on the couch, paralysed by confusion. The front door swings open, a woman in her forties walks in, without a trace of hesitation.

'You can't just show up here.' Cat's voice is tight. She doesn't shout but it's clear she wants to.

'What else am I meant to do?' asks the woman. She's like a hurricane tearing through the peace of our afternoon. 'You won't answer the phone, you won't answer texts.'

I expect Cat to have a blistering comeback. She doesn't. She looks at the floor, scolded.

'You lost your job, Trini?' says the woman, throwing a package on the kitchen counter.

'How do you know?' Cat's face is beginning to flush.

'They called me, Trini, probably because you wouldn't answer your phone. I'm your emergency contact.'

I can see Cat's arms start to shake, like they did in Chay Turley when I thought she was about to hit Lindsay.

'What have you got to say for yourself?' the woman demands.

Cat's chin creases. She glances at me, and when I catch her eyes they're filled to the brim with embarrassment.

The woman is marching around the flat looking at things with distaste. Next to the parcel she threw on the counter she spots Cat's ashtray. The next moment she is advancing on Cat brandishing the stub of a joint.

'Do you expect me to keep on paying for you if this is what you're going to do?'

'Paying for you?' I think. 'What a horrible thing to say.'

Cat must think so too. Her head springs up. 'I don't expect anything from you.'

'Good,' the woman spreads her arms wide. 'Great. At last. I'll take this with me then?'

She throws the joint back into the ashtray and picks up the parcel, pointing it at Cat like a gun.

Cat's jaw tightens. She looks determined.

Then, suddenly, her resolve breaks. She looks down again.

'No,' she says.

'No,' says the woman, throwing the parcel back on the counter.

I hope that that will be the end of this, whatever this is. I just want the woman to leave. I want to check Cat's okay, but the woman has spotted something new. Furious incredulity twists her mouth. She's looking at the canvas Cat has on her easel.

'I've not seen that one before, Trini,' she accuses.

'It's new,' Cat says quietly.

'New?' The woman hold her arms out again, a self-proclaimed martyr. 'New canvas, new paints, it's a brand-new painting.'

'Yes,' Cat mutters, wincing.

'Then it's mine.' The woman strides over to the unfinished painting and grabs it indelicately in one hand.

Cat finally moves from the corner. She shouts, 'No, Mum, please.'

Mum. It's her mum. Of course it is.

Cat's mum stops Cat with a belligerently pointed finger. 'I paid for the paint, I paid for the canvas, so this is my painting.'

'Mum,' Cat begs.

'Thank you, Trini. It's lovely,' her mum cuts her off viciously.

Things fall into place. The person who had upset Cat so terribly the day we'd screamed beside the River Cart wasn't just a random person on the street. The reason it had hurt so much was that it was her mother.

'Sort out your life, Trini,' her mum continues. 'You can't go on like this.'

Cat's cheeks are burning red. She's not just embarrassed, she's utterly humiliated.

And who helped *me* when I was humiliated? Who stood by my side?

I finally get to my feet. As evenly as I can I say, 'Hey.'

There would have been more, but Cat's mum turns the full force of her anger on me. She must have been expecting this from the moment she saw me in the flat.

'And who's this, Trini, one of your layabout friends? What do you do, love? No, let me guess: unemployed? Just a burden on society?'

She can tell she's right by my stunned face.

'Take my advice, stay away from my daughter, She'll drag you right down with her,' says Cat's mum. Then she leaves. Gone as suddenly as she arrived.

I want to comfort Cat, I want to say something that'll help, but I don't know what.

Cat excuses herself. She walks with forced composure to the bathroom. Once the door is closed I hear her trying not to cry. Trying, and failing.

'You're still here,' Cat says, relieved.

'Of course I'm still here,' I reassure.

'About lunch,' Cat says, 'I've decided my mum is paying for it. She owes you, after what she said.'

'I'm sorry I didn't stand up to her better than I did.'

'You did fine,' she says, then adds with a grateful laugh, 'Did you see her face when you spoke to her? She was raging.'

I laugh back, but Cat still seems awkward and uncomfortable.

'Anyway,' she says, 'this package is just a great bloody brick of money. She won't do a bank transfer because then I "won't appreciate how much I'm being given". So I can go pay for lunch, or I can just give you the cash, or whatever. I get if you want to leave. It's fine. I get it.'

Cat holds the package in one hand. With the other she plays with her own sleeve, watching her fingers and not me.

'We could go back to Pixie Cove and pay tomorrow,' I suggest.

'Why not today?' she says.

'Well,' I say, 'have you ever heard of *The Bourne Trilogy*? Pretty sure I know where to stream all three.'

'You don't want to leave?' Cat asks, swallowing a hopeful sob.

'Not one bit.'

Cat sniffs, 'Thank you.'

We settle back onto the couch. The laptop screen, still paused at the moment when Cat's mum entered the flat, reminds us of happier times. That's okay. We'll recapture them.

'By the way,' I point out, '"Trini" doesn't suit you *at all*.'

Cat laughs, 'Tell me about it.'

18

Revenge

In second year at Strathclyde uni a girl called Chloe punched me in the face. Not a slap, not a tap – a full-on, closed fist, right hook punch.

She didn't hit me so hard that I was knocked unconscious or that I toppled backwards and hit the deck like I would have in an action movie, but it was hard enough that I had to half-squat, holding my face, as I tried to get my ears to stop ringing and figure out what was happening. The punch had come out of nowhere. She'd just walked up and hit me. Before that moment I didn't even know Chloe.

'For your information,' Chloe screamed at me, 'I've only slept with three people in my entire life.'

We were on the pedestrianised part of Rottenrow, a road that becomes a path that joins a few of the university buildings. Between classes it was always heaving with students rushing from one lecture to another.

'But even if it were a hundred,' Chloe went on, 'a woman can sleep with as many people as she wants and it doesn't make her a slut, alright?'

'What? Yeah,' I said hazily, still trying to piece together what was going on. 'I agree.'

'Don't give me that, acting all innocent. Do you know the shit I've put up with because of you? They could have kicked me out. He could lose his job,' Chloe said, trying to shake the pain out of her hand.

Yeah, Chloe, If you think your hand hurts imagine how my face feels.

'Who are you?' I asked, trying to stand up straight.

Chloe went for me again, but got held back by another two girls who were with her. As they pulled her away she shouted back, 'Keep your mouth shut about me, or, I swear to God, I'll shut it for you, alright?'

I picked up my bag, trying not to look at all the students I knew were watching, like my life was one of my gran's reality TV shows.

'You okay, Wendy?' someone asked, disingenuously. It was Freya and a gaggle of her fans – the last thing I needed.

'I suppose that was bound to happen, really,' Freya went on without waiting for me to reply. 'Spreading rumours about someone being a whore is one thing, but you can't just make up that someone slept with a lecturer, Wendy. That's really cruel.'

'I didn't,' I protested.

'Oh didn't you?' Freya purrs, 'My mistake. I thought you were the one who had started all of those nasty rumours. I guess I was wrong.'

'You told her I said that stuff about her?'

'She had a right to know, Wendy,' Freya said. 'Still, no hard feelings? It was an honest mistake.'

Then Freya and her friends walked away. They only managed to hold in their laughter until they got a few metres further along Rottenrow.

In first year Freya had been unfriendly and sometimes a little malicious. Something had changed when we moved into second year. She'd gone from passively attacking me when we were together to actively devoting her time to torturing me. I avoided social media; all of the Strathclyde student group pages were filled with rumours or crudely Photoshopped memes about me, my mentions were full of 'banter' at my expense, my direct messages were a wasteland littered with abuse from fake accounts.

'She's obsessed,' I told Kevin in his sparse room. Kevin stayed in student accommodation rather than travel into Glasgow city centre every day. He said it was so he wouldn't miss out on any of the 'vital social aspect of student life.' I didn't have that option; students halls are expensive, but then I also wasn't really a massive believer in the 'vital social aspect of student life.'

'Do you genuinely believe Freya orchestrated it all so that Chloe would attack you?' Kevin asked, lounging on his bed.

'She totally did. You should have seen her.'

'She's crazy,' Kevin said, and I cringed a little inwardly. I hated that word even then. 'Some of the guys are a bit sick of her too.'

'They are?' I asked, trying not to seem too keen to hear bad things about her.

'She's terrible on a night out,' Kevin confides. 'Never gets a round, but expects everyone to include her in theirs.'

'Seems pretty rude,' I say.

'As I understand it she's the first person in her family ever to get into university. She must not know the etiquette.'

'Yeah, Kevin, I don't think knowing that you're meant to go in on a round is a university thing, and even if it was I don't think knowing how to act at uni is inherited,' I teased him.

'Fair enough,' Kevin said, 'then, yes, she's just being rude.'

'Exactly,' I said. 'Bad form.'

Kevin made a face. 'What?'

'Bad form? It's from one of my favourite books when I was a kid.'

'Right,' Kevin said. 'That's cute. Probably prudent not to say things like that around other people though. You don't want to give them more ammunition to bully you with.'

'What's wrong with "bad form?"'

'Nothing,' Kevin said, 'but you know what people are like.'

The number 38 bus from the Southside of Glasgow into the city centre wasn't awful. The bus itself was modern and roomy and you'd only really get trouble on it at night after the pubs or clubs closed. On days when I decided not to stare listlessly at my phone for the whole journey, and instead stare listlessly out of the window, I would see Freya sometimes, walking through Pollokshields with earphones in. I'd try to hide behind my hair, scared she'd notice me noticing her. I thought it was strange that she didn't stay in student halls though, given how important the 'vital social aspect of student life' obviously was to her.

On a Thursday night Kevin and I found ourselves in a pub on Hope Street famous for karaoke and bad choices. We were there with a few people from our class and some other people Kevin knew.

'I'm just in first year, but don't hold that against me, like. Kevin and I have been mates since we were weans,' a guy called Gary told me, shouting way too close to my ear. Our table was crowded with empty glasses and a good number of them were Gary's. He kept trying to focus his eyes by gently swaying backwards and forwards.

'Gary,' Kevin said, coming back from the bar with drinks and a surprise round of shots, 'don't you have an essay due tomorrow. Maybe you should consider calling it a night?'

Kevin gave Gary an encouraging slap on the back to emphasise his point, then started handing out the shots to the others. Masked from Kevin by someone's rendition of 'Hold Back The River', Gary replied, 'Chill mate, Freya's doing it.'

I got the same feeling you get when you misjudge how many stairs there are in the dark.

'What did you say?' I asked.

'Nothing. Don't worry about it, it's just there's this girl that'll write essays for you if you've got the dough. She only does it for first years though, so she's no good to you.'

'And she's called?'

'Freya,' Gary said. 'You must know Freya. Kevin's pal.'

Yeah. I knew Freya.

I set up a new email account. I was paranoid enough that I paid for a VPN so nothing could be tracked back to my IP address. I spent a day mentally preparing for what I was about to do.

It was such a risk. What if she found out it was me?

My jaw still hurt from Chloe punching me. There was a gif going around because someone had helpfully captured the moment on their phone.

I hoped she *did* find out it was me, when the time was right.

I wrote Freya an email asking if she was the one who writes essays for first years, spinning a sob story about how I've messed up and can't possibly finish mine in time, and begging for her help. I said I'll pay anything. With grim satisfaction I typed that I wanted her to write me an essay about Romanticism and Romantic poets.

She wrote back within minutes asking who told me to email her. That didn't confirm anything – I'd have to keep the charade going a bit longer. I typed that Gary said I should get in touch, and hit send.

A few minutes later another email from Freya lit up in my catfish inbox. It said that Gary was an idiot and that she didn't like to be emailed by people she didn't know.

She was being careful. I could feel my chance slipping away. I hit reply and typed, 'please, I'm desperate, I'll pay in advance.'

I sent it and sat in silence broken only by the soft whirr of my laptop's fan. The gap before her reply came through made me lose hope – I was sure I'd spooked her. Then it arrived.

'A Romanticism essay will cost you £200 and I can't get it to you until Wednesday. Send the payment to these details. I'm doing nothing until it's in my account.'

A digital smoking gun.

'You didn't know she was doing this, did you?' I asked Kevin in his room in halls. If I was going to bring down Freya, I didn't want to accidentally make Kevin collateral damage.

'Of course not,' Kevin said. 'I wouldn't want Freya writing an essay for me. I'd get a better mark writing my own.'

'I can't believe her,' I said.

'No, nor can I,' Kevin replied. 'Though…'

'What?' I pressed.

'Look, this will sound a bit utilitarian, but in the end it's only first years she's helping, isn't it? It's not as though she's passing people's degrees for them.'

'You don't speak like you're from Pollok,' I said, momentarily derailed by the realisation.

'That's because when you speak with a certain accent people stop listening to what you say and only hear how you say it.'

'Isn't that their problem?' I asked.

'Not if they're the ones in charge. Then it's your problem. In a way that's the point I'm making with Freya.'

'You're not on her side, are you?' I asked.

'No,' Kevin assured. 'Here's how I see it. We've got a certain amount of time to achieve all the things we want to achieve. Any head start we get now means it's more likely we'll actually hit the milestones we want to hit. If these first years have found a way to get a head start, then so be it, and if Freya has found a way to monetise what she wrote last year, then is there really any harm?'

'It's cheating,' I pointed out.

'It is, you're right, I agree,' Kevin said emphatically, 'but when you're buying a massive house in Newton Mearns or the likes, five or six years from now, no one will know if you cheated in uni. They'll just know you can afford it.'

I couldn't see myself buying a house six years from then. I couldn't even see myself buying one ten or fifteen years from then. To me, the milestones that Kevin was talking about looked more like teeth, eating away at my future before I'd even had a chance to live it, fast-forwarding me to my sixties or seventies, when I'd be a Wendy haggard from working her entire life but still without any real pension, any retirement plan, anyone to support me, or any idea how I'd survive. Maybe Kevin was right. Time was already running out.

Tick-tock, tick-tock.

'She can't just get away with it,' I told Kevin.

'She might not,' Kevin said, 'but you don't need to get your hands dirty, do you?'

The next week, out of the bus window, I saw Freya walking towards town with her earphones in. I had an axe over her head and she didn't even know it, I just wasn't sure whether to swing it.

Later I was grabbing lunch at a takeaway café near where my next lecture was. Freya and a group of students from my year came in while I waited for my sandwich. Just my luck. There was no one else there but the staff and first years, and Freya's disciples saw this as a chance to try to score some points with her, with the added bonus of showing off to the newbies.

'How's your jaw, Wendy?' one boy jeered.

'I could watch her getting battered all day,' said another.

'I have been, on a loop,' said a third.

The lady behind the counter handed me my lunch with a sympathetic smile.

'Enough,' Freya said sternly. She wasn't talking to me, she was reprimanding her friends. I was as shocked as they clearly were. Was this where Freya drew the line? Maybe she did have a shred of decency?

'Leave her alone,' Freya smirked. 'Just like her parents did.'

I put my head down and stormed out of the café. Time to get my hands dirty.

All I had to do was send one anonymous email and Freya Rose would be gone. What she'd written to me might not have been conclusive proof that she was definitely helping people cheat – she could maybe have talked her way out of it – but I knew the name of one of the people she'd written an essay for. I was sure they'd be able to compare Gary's usual work to the essay Freya wrote and tell that they were different. After they'd confirmed she'd done it once, they'd be able to look through other essays handed in by first years to find things written in her style. One email, and I'd never have to worry about Freya again.

I sat with my laptop on my knee, composing my exposé, and dreaming of what the rest of my life at university would be like without her in it.

An image of Freya walking through Pollokshields flashed into my head. I waved it off.

I knew that getting Freya kicked off the course might mean some of the people who she wrote essays for would be kicked out too. I felt bad for them, but not bad enough that I was willing to come into class every day fearing what Freya might do, or go home every night dreading what people were saying about me online.

Without meaning to I thought about Kevin telling me that she never buys drinks, and that she was the first in her family to go to university. I thought about Freya's caution when I contacted her out of the blue being overridden by the promise of being paid in advance.

No. Never mind those things. Freya was a monster. I couldn't cope with another two years with her.

I realised something: she didn't stay in student halls, even though popularity was so important to her, because she couldn't afford to.

If I got her kicked out, my life would be so much better, but her life would be destroyed.

Moving my mouse felt like pushing a car. Every inch of screen resisted the movement, but, inevitably, my cursor eventually landed on the button. I clicked. Not send. Delete.

I deleted the email Freya sent me. Then I made sure it was gone from the recently deleted folder too.

I swore at myself so loud that I'm amazed my gran didn't come up to check on me. I wanted to change my mind, call the email back from the ether, and annihilate Freya Rose forever. Turned out the moral high ground was paved with regret.

Whatever. It was the right thing to do.

19

Learn Solemn Things

For days after the encounter with Cat's mum, I feel like something has pulled me down into muddy water.

I lie in bed each morning feeling like the bedsheets are made of lead. The many actions it would take to get up feel like an over-filled to-do list.

Get out from under the bed covers.

Put my feet on the floor.

Stand.

Dress.

Figure out why I even bothered.

I should shower, only showering would be decisive, and would suggest I have something to do. As everyone else gets into their cars or buses to go to work I am preparing for a day of nothingness. I think of the application form still sitting on my desk. Maybe I'll do that today, I think each day.

I should do that today.

Once I'm in the shower, on the days when I get that far, I can't think of any reason to leave. The world is still outside the door, waiting. It's nice in here. It's warm. I can feel fat drops of water hit my scalp, I've not given them enough distance from the showerhead to stretch into less podgy orbs, they're closer to a tiny water balloon than a rain drop. The sound of the water hitting the shower floor and how it changes if I move a limb is hypnotic. I don't know why I'd leave, not when it took so much effort to get here. After a while I tell myself it wouldn't be normal to stay in a shower for longer than forty minutes. Or longer than an hour.

I'm tired. It makes things seem drab and bleaches the colour from them. My eyes want to close, but sleeping during the day would make my gran worry. I stay awake and tell myself I can sleep at night, when normal people do.

'Are you still watching?' my streaming app asks. I select 'yes'.

I visit the fridge from time to time, just to see if anyone has moved in that I haven't said hello to. I'm not hungry, though, and the fridge is pretty empty.

'Executive dysfunction', Cat had said. I should look it up, but I don't ever seem to get around to it.

The thought of leaving the house is the most terrible of all. If I make plans, I get a burning impulse to cancel them. Cancelling plans is always a relief. Walking out of the front door would be the most worrying transition imaginable.

I scroll through my own Instagram page as though it can help me figure out who I am. I look at old selfies and the captions below them.

'Who wrote this?' I think. 'Who are you? Why are you smiling?'

If I'm honest, though, the only reason I look so fulfilled is because everyone has learned how to lie online. Everyone is conducting their own independent customer research without realising it. We all change what we put online based on what gets the engagement, and what gets ignored. As the amount of people who like our posts grow, the amount of ourselves we are revealing narrows, our self-image becomes purified and sanitised. It stops being who we are, and it becomes who people want us to be. We learn from the little endorphins realised from the notifications we receive – like rats in a lab.

I stay up late. It feels wrong to go to bed when you haven't achieved anything since you got out of it.

Time passes by. Sometimes too quickly, sometimes too slowly, but mostly unobtrusively. Time pretends it's benign.

Until three in the morning.

Exactly three in the morning.

At three in the morning time becomes sinister. I stop hearing the grumble of the engines of cars, or seeing the overspill of their headlights scanning my bedroom wall. There's silence and darkness. Everyone is asleep. Everyone but me. What's wrong with me?

For all I know everyone has died and I'm the only living human on the planet. All I want is someone to talk to, but I have nothing to say.

I start to feel guilty that I'm not doing my bit around the house and begin cleaning every room top to bottom. During my sudden fit of productivity I find something.

The books at one end of a shelf on the bookcase in the living room aren't in line with the books at the other end. All the books on the far left of the shelf are a few centimetres taller than the ones on the far right. They're all the same kind of book, and I'm sure they had previously all lined up. It's jarring.

I investigate. I pick up a handful of three books to see what's underneath.

Papers. They're all folded once, neatly, and laid flat underneath the books. There are just enough of them to lift the books they're under a noticeable amount, otherwise they would have been perfectly hidden. Not a single white corner protruding.

Hidden, I realise, is the right word. These have been put here deliberately. Given I didn't do it, and there are only two of us living here, it doesn't take my skills as a master detective to figure out who by.

I know I shouldn't. It's a terrible idea, but I'm not able to stop myself. I unfold the top sheet of paper. It's a bill. There's a lot of red. It's overdue. I unfold a few more. They're all overdue bills.

That dark intangible watcher who haunts me looks through the bills with me. I see him there in the corner of my eye – his favourite spot. He grins his oversized grin. He reaches out and places one hand over my heart. He pushes down, firmly.

I don't know why people think dread is similar to fear. It's not. It's far more insidious, far more familiar. Fear comes on fast; dread creeps in slowly. Fear makes you act, for better or worse, but dread assimilates you; you become nothing but it.

Tick-tock, tick-tock.

It all comes together – the heating mysteriously being turned off, the cupboards empty except for no-frills essentials. Some master detective I am.

Did I really think that two people could survive on a pension for one? I don't even know how long ago it was I walked out of my job. I have no idea how many weeks I've been nothing but a burden. I didn't realise any of this was happening.

Because I didn't want to.

I still don't want to leave the house but it's an open airlock. All the oxygen has been drained out of every room. I heard it leave, like the flush of an airplane toilet. I can't breathe here. I put on a jacket like armour, zip it up more than the weather requires, and rush out of the house without saying goodbye

20

Application

Outside has people. That's the terrible thing about outside. Fresh air, birdsong, and distant dog barks are all nice. The only issue is that other people like them too.

I read about this thing called a kinesphere. It's sort of like a metaphorical bubble that surrounds us at all times. If you stand on one spot and move your arms and legs around as far as you can in every direction, the orb you can trace is your kinesphere. Your own bubble.

If that all sounds a bit like new age nonsense, then it might help if you call your kinesphere your personal space. I think everyone gets the concept of personal space. We all know when someone is way too close.

The most interesting thing about kinespheres is that we can control them. If you're in a spacious room with a handful of people, then you'll probably feel uncomfortable if someone you don't know well comes and stands in your kinesphere.

But on a crowded bus that same person could come and stand much closer and it wouldn't be uncomfortable at all, you'd just shrink your kinesphere down so that your personal space was defined as being a bit closer than usual. But say you're in a huge field and there's only one other person in that field and you don't particularly trust them. Then you'd want to extend your kinesphere five or six metres from you.

Here's my theory. My kinesphere is stuck on field mode. I get that feeling that you get when someone is standing way too close to you, but I get it on crowded streets even if no one's really that close. When people feel like someone is in their personal space it's natural for them to take a little step back. I want to do that, I want to take that little innocuous step back from everyone on a whole street, or block, or city, all at once. I hunch my shoulders, and march into town.

I start going from shop to shop. I'm trying to gather application forms. I need a job. I need money. My gran needs money. I think this is getting pretty serious.

I know I have an application form at home, but when I think about that one, I get a premonition of the Wendy of the future, overladen with responsibility and deadlines, thinking 'remember when I wanted to be a poet?'

One of the first things we ask people when we're making small talk is 'What do you do?' Like we're opening up a tool box instead of meeting another human being. We define people by their jobs. Why do we do that?

Oh my god.

It's...

It's capitalism isn't it?

Oogie boogie boogie.

I go from shop to shop. I do it in a sort of angry, antisocial haze, without even making eye contact with the person behind the counter as I talk to them. I'm doing an abysmal job of making first impressions.

I don't quite have the brass neck to ask for an application form from Pixie Cove, even though we slipped an envelope through their door the very next morning with an apology note, the money we owed, and even a pretty nice tip.

After a while I have a ragtag collection of applications. I say collection – it's a duo. Lots of places tell me they only take applications online, far more places tell me they don't have any openings. I buy a pen in a shop that isn't hiring and sit on the steps of the Galleries of Modern Art, with the statue of The Duke of Wellington (wearing his historically accurate orange traffic-cone hat) just in front of me. I use my knees as a desk. I'm going to fill in these two forms right *now*, before I lose momentum. If I tell myself I'll do it later then really I'll be admitting to myself I won't do it at all.

Sometimes, in action movies or sci-fi, the plot will revolve around a society run by robots. They'll show how inhuman and inhumane the robots are by making sure they only refer to each other using clean, sterile, serial codes rather than tolerate the inefficient individuality of names. They might even take humans' names from them and assign them numbers too, and the people subjected to that torment are seen to have lost something of themselves by losing their name. That's how we know the robots are evil.

The forms ask me for my national insurance number, phone number, house number, previous house numbers, numerical date of leaving and entering each house, numerical date of birth, passport and driving licence numbers, and sort code and account numbers.

At least in a robot society we'd only have to remember one serial code. I mark down all the requisite digits.

The forms ask me to give examples of times I've been helpful, or times I've gone over and above to make a customer's experience great. I hate it. Who helps an old lady across the road and thinks 'I must remember this for my next job application'? I make up some pleasing lies.

Then comes the personal statement. I write them an airbrushed version of me.

They ask why I'm right for the job. I feel as though they're asking the wrong person. I scribble down some paradoxes: I thrive in a team, but I work well alone. I always take the initiative, but I follow my bosses' instructions to the letter.

They ask for a reference from my previous employer. Lindsay surfaces in my mind, like a great white shark bursting from the sea.

'The life and energy that I used to see on your first week here has quickly turned into dour-faced stupidity.'

That might be a problem. I skip it.

Qualifications. The only part that makes me look good. I fill in the boxes.

A final box bears the legend, 'Sign'.

I resist writing, 'Sagittarius'.

I look at the two application forms – my entire life boiled down to four sides of A4 paper. The worst part is it's not even autobiographical; it's at least fifty per cent fiction.

My life: based on a true story.

All my personality and character has been baked out of me as I wrote. I feel like a crisp, now. An unsalted, sad, crisp.

I return the forms, back again the same day but covered in black ink in block capitals, like vandalised homing pigeons. I start to walk home, a little calmer than when I left.

On the way I see a bar I've never seen before. It's one of those basement bars, the kind with the intimidating staircase as soon as you enter and a penchant for painting all the walls black. It's called The Little Panther. None of that is what draws my attention. I wouldn't usually really care about discovering a new bar.

What I care about is the sign outside their door, handwritten in chunky marker pen.

'Poetry open mic night.'

There's an email address to request a slot.

My head spins and my heart skips.

I apply for that too.

21

Follow The Leader

Two days later, Cat and I are in her car.

In Scotland you're never more than an hour from the countryside, usually less. There are places in the world where the same can't be true. If you were in the centre of, say, London or New York, then driving for an hour would only result in you being slightly less in the centre of London or New York.

I've never been to the countryside. I've never left Greater Glasgow before. It sounds ridiculous, but I don't drive, and it would have been bizarre to just hop on a bus up to the Highlands for no reason, or to ask a taxi to whisk me away to Loch Lomond and damn the expense. I'm dimly aware that I've spent my entire life never travelling further than about thirty miles from my home. The whole time I've existed I've stayed within a territory smaller than most big cats have.

But today that's changing. I'm in the passenger seat of Cat's car, there's an endless soundtrack of early noughties tunes streaming through the radio, and the windows are wide open. Soon we'll be heading towards the hills and away from concrete and streetlamps. Everything feels just like a movie.

'Where are we going?' I ask.

'Nowhere,' Cat says, but not dismissively. She says it as though it's exciting.

'Nowhere beats anywhere,' I reply. I like the sound of a place where there aren't queues. 'I'm pretty sure I was told not to get into cars with strange people, though.'

'Lucky you're such a wee rebel, then,' Cat responds.

'So why are we going nowhere?' I ask.

'Did you ever see a movie where a knight slays a dragon in a cul-de-sac in the southside?' Cat queries.

'Don't think I saw that one,' I admit.

'Exactly. Adventures don't happen in cities – there's too much pollution. It gives them bronchitis,' Cat says.

'Totally understand,' I say. 'So what kind of adventure are we going on?'

'You know,' Cat says. 'A quest, an escapade, a voyage of discovery.'

She glances around to catch my unconvinced expression.

'I've no idea,' she confesses. 'I just thought it might be nice to get away from everything for a day.'

I let out a huge breath that I feel like I've been holding for weeks. 'I think that sounds absolutely incredible.'

We pass through the centre of the city and out the other side. The buildings get smaller the further from Glasgow we get. We go from tall commercial buildings and tower blocks, to smaller multi-storey flats, to little two-storey houses, to bungalows and then, abruptly, to nothing at all. One moment we're in suburbia, the next there's not a single home in front of us as far as the eye can see.

I've seen mountains in the distance before, I've been in parks, walked on grassy hills, and there are plenty of trees where I live, but there's something about just being suddenly freed from the bonds of the city boundaries that feels like diving into the sea. I've no idea how far the next big city is, I'm not even sure if there is another big city on this road. I don't know what's out here. There's no safety harness.

The mountains we can see are still in the distance, but they seem so much closer now without the interference of a jagged city skyline between us and them.

I hang my hand out of the window as we travel, letting it surf on the wind and feeling the difference in the air depending on what angle I tilt it to. We're going relatively fast, and it seems even faster when I look out of the side window rather than the front. The ground close to the car is going past so quickly that my useless human eyes can't understand the movement; it's just colour and blurred nonsense.

I have a sudden sense of awe. The road we're driving on has all been laid down by someone. Every metre of it is real, took time to put there, has a texture, and its own story. It's got dents, and bumps, and maybe even the odd pothole. There are stones in there to aid the grip of the tyres and they're interspersed with absolute randomness; every inch of the road is the same, yet completely different. There are miles of that. Hundreds of them. Thousands.

But what's really mind-numbing is the grass. Every blade of grass is real. There are insects and birds and maybe the odd hedgehog hidden in there, and those blades of grass weren't put there by anyone. They got there through a process of seeding, and pollinating, and photosynthesis, and rhizomes, and lots of other plant words I don't fully know the meaning of. If every inch of tarmac is different, then every inch of grass is unfathomably diverse. How many blades of grass would we pass today, and every one of them living and growing and individually full of fascination?

That's just the stuff directly next to the car – I haven't even begun to try to think about the magnitude of everything in front of us. I'm almost afraid to look up.

I can't express any of that in words. I just can't figure out how to say it, so instead I just say,

'There's so *much*.'

Cat nods and smiles in understanding.

I see some sheep. I try to be mature enough to resist saying 'sheep'. I am overjoyed when Cat has no such self-control.

'Sheep,' she enthuses.

'Sheep,' I agree, with similar glee.

So now we know there are sheep.

We perform similar rituals when we first see horses, cows and an exciting unexpected Shetland pony.

We snake around the narrow roads of Loch Lomond, fearing for our life whenever a bus or truck flies around the corner towards us. We drive down A roads, then B roads. We navigate C roads and passing places. We eventually find ourselves driving down roads that probably don't even deserve a letter but do deserve a little bit of maintenance. When we're sure we've given society the slip we pull into an odd elbow shape on a single-track road that we guess passes for a layby this far away from road markings. This seems as good a place for an adventure as any.

'Look,' Cat points out of her window. 'There's a footpath.'

Then she opens her door and jumps out of the car without

any further overture. I'm uncertain enough about myself that I don't get out to follow her straight away. I wait a second in case she doesn't want me to.

'You think she drove you all the way here so you can wait in the car?' I ask myself.

I get out. Cat has taken a few steps along the path. She turns around and shouts back to me, 'I packed us both lunches. Like a pure loser.'

I go with Cat into the unknown.

We follow the path and we learn as we go that signs that say 'footpath' are often actually gravestones memorialising the ghost of a footpath. We also learn that our footwear is woefully inadequate. One thing that Scotland seems to boast, alongside an enviable level of access to the great outdoors, is a truly unenviable level of mud. At first, we try to pick our way around the bogs. Not long after that we make the decision that our shoes are damp and muddy anyway, so we might as well embrace the havoc and just wade through them. We both live in fear of accidentally venturing into a bog both deeper and with more suction than the others. I'm afraid that all that training I did as a kid, escaping quicksand in my living room, won't translate to the real world. The other thing we learn is that, even in the absence of any livestock, there would still appear to be shit everywhere. It's a strange, smelly enigma.

As we trek across the fields towards our uncertain destination we keep ourselves motivated by eating Cat's packed lunches.

'How far are we going?' I ask.

'We'll do half on the way there and half on the way back,' Cat assures.

'Can't argue with that,' I say. 'How long will we keep going for?'

'We'll either try to get back to the car before it gets dark,' Cat suggests, 'or we can build a wee house out of mud in a field and have a sleepover.'

'It's good that you have a really well thought-out plan.'

'Oh.' Cat's eyes widen.

'Don't.' I know what's coming.

'It would be our...' Cat pauses for effect, '...Wendy house.'

'Great.' I exaggerate my eyeroll. 'Now I have to hate you forever.'

'I'm honoured,' Cat says humbly.

I think it takes a lot of affection to tell someone you hate them without the fear of them thinking you might, you know, hate them.

'There,' Cat shouts.

'What?' I'm suddenly sure we're about to get gored by a bull I've somehow missed.

Cat points emphatically.

'A tree?' I ask, because that's what it is. I'm not so much of a city girl I don't know a tree when I see one. I'm only confused because there are plenty of trees around. This one is standing all on its own, granted, and looks maybe a little more remarkable than the others in a gnarled, character-filled sort of way, but it is, irrefutably, a tree.

'Come on,' Cat says. 'You can't be telling me you don't know a good climbing tree when you see one.'

She starts jogging towards the tree, jumping over patches of dark mud as she goes.

'Really?' I shout after her. 'We're going to climb it?'

'Kid on you're a squirrel,' Cat suggests.

'I hope you know what you're doing,' I say, jogging after her. 'I don't want to have to call the fire brigade and tell them...'

'Don't.' Cat shouts back.

'Tell them my Cat is stuck up a tree,' I finish.

Cat sighs.

'Now *I* have to hate *you* forever.'

She reaches the tree, turns her back to it, and puts out her clasped hands in front of her, the universal sign for giving someone a boost. She raises her eyebrow in question.

'Okay,' I say, 'I'm in.'

22

The Lost Girls

I'm playing a new game. It's called 'try to pretend you're not terrified of being in this tree'. The rules are in the name.

We've both managed to scramble up to a high branch wide enough for us to sit on side by side. It took some graceless swinging of limbs and I discovered that I have an astonishing lack of upper body strength, but we got there. We also both have shallow scratches all over our arms. Trees are friendly as a rule. Even an Ent has to be talked into fighting. This specific tree, though, is a pointy trunked arsehole. Its bark is its bite. We both keep having to wipe away small beads of blood from our arms.

Despite all of that, It's amazing being up here. I hear a distant distressed-sounding cry that at first I think is a lady shouting for her lost dog but over time I realise is probably a pheasant. There's the rattle of a woodpecker, and the dinosaur trill of a grouse.

Not a single seagull. Which makes the whole trip worthwhile even if I get nothing else out of it.

Then I hear a new sound from high above us. It's like a cat mewing, but amplified. It has an echoey quality that makes it hard to pinpoint. It sounds sad. Mournful.

'What's that?' I ask, quietly.

'Buzzard. Look,' Cat points to a specific spot in the cloudy sky.

I see it. It's too far to pick out much detail but there's something mythical about it: a real bird of prey, rare and beautiful, here with us now.

'I've never seen one before,' I confide.

It circles in a wide radius. It looks like it's travelling so gently and slowly, but given the area it's covering it must be going much faster than it seems. I never see it beat its wings; it just glides – glides and cries that melancholy cry.

'It must be so incredible,' I whisper.

'Flying?' Cat says, 'Like in your poem?'

'Yeah,' I say, and then, 'sorry.'

I'm not sure where the need to apologise comes from, but it's overwhelming. It's like she saw a part of me I didn't mean to show her.

'Don't be daft, you've nothing to be sorry about. You're totally right, it must be incredible. I'd love to fly too. Who wouldn't?'

'Yeah,' I say, relaxing.

'Funny, though,' Cat nudges me gently. 'The lassie that wants to fly is freaked out being up a tree.'

'Yeah,' I reply. 'That's because I *can't* fly. It's not heights I'm worried about. It's the ground.'

Cat smiles puckishly. She begins to swing her legs and

holds her arms out like she's the first across the finish line in a marathon. She's not holding on at all, she's just trusting the branch to keep her up.

I want to grab her to stop her falling, but I'm afraid if I do something wrong, I'll push her myself.

'Try it,' she says.

I gingerly let go of the branch, releasing the death grip my hands had on either side of me. I lift them slowly into the air like I'm concerned a murderous sparrow is going to knock me down any second. I kick my feet, just enough that I don't risk losing my balance.

'How's it feel?' Cat asks.

It feels like I'm floating. It feels like nothing is keeping me up, just like the buzzard.

'Amazing,' I say.

Cat smiles.

'I've thought a few times about what it must be like to have been a fighter pilot,' I say, before realising that it's a little bit out of the blue. My train of thought ran off without me and I didn't bother attaching it to the carriages it left behind when I caught it up.

'A fighter pilot specifically? Or just any pilot?' Cat puts her hands back on the branch and turns to listen.

'A fighter pilot,' I assert. 'I have these dreams about what it must have been like to get into one of those cockpits during World War Two. One of those planes with the cool names, like Boomerang.'

'Spitfire,' Cat supplies.

'Mohawk,' I laugh, miming the famous punk hairstyle with my hands before lowering them back to the branch as Cat did. 'I dream about getting into one of those and knowing that

I'm about to take off and fly into the sky, where people don't belong. I dream I'm looking at the old dials inside, feeling the leather of the bucket seat, worrying because the green metal all around me looks sort of cheap, then I'm taking off, and it's petrifying because I know there are other people up there who really want to shoot me. I usually wake up once I get over the clouds. That's the bit I like. The emptiness and the blueness and the lurch in my stomach as the plane evens out.

'But when I wake up, I think about the fighter pilots – the real ones, that is. The ones who knew, when their wheels left the ground, that there was a chance they might never touch it again. The ones who knew that when they went up, they might never come down. They'd just stay in the sky forever.'

I look up wistfully. I try to relocate the buzzard, but it's flown away.

'Only that's not what happens really,' I go on. 'They always came down. Some came down victorious, some came down sombre, some came down broken – either their bodies or their minds. Some came down way too fast. They probably wished they could stay in the sky forever; it was landing that killed them.

'Then there were the ones that, for whatever reason, exploded before they even got the chance to crash – those ones were nothing but flaming pieces; just debris spread over miles and miles. But they land. What goes up…

'That last one: that's what happened to my gran's dad,' I finish.

'Shit,' Cat sympathises. 'Wendy, I'm sorry.'

'It's okay,' I say, lightening the tone as much as I can, guiltily aware that I've brought it down, 'I didn't actually know him. He died before I was born.'

'Is that why you call him your gran's dad and not your great grandad?' Cat asks.

'Yeah,' I say. 'It feels wrong to just give him a title without him knowing me. He never agreed to that.'

'*Most* people didn't know their great grandparents,' Cat points out.

'That's true,' I confirm, with a touch of uncertainty. I consider saying more, but instead I say, 'I think my gran is, maybe, having some sort of financial crisis.'

'Really?' she sounds concerned.

'I need to get a job,' I sigh.

'Me too,' Cat says, looking equally crestfallen. 'I have to do something to get free from my mum.'

We enjoy our pity party for a few seconds.

'Listen, she only gives me what I need for rent, bills, and the car, and some money I'm meant to spend on food, but usually spend on art stuff, but every so often I get commissioned to draw things for people – just wee framed pencil-and-ink sketch things. I could give you some of the money from the next few I sell, if it helps.'

'No,' I say, though I'm grateful for the offer. 'It's okay. That's not fair. I'll find something.'

'If you change your mind...' Cat begins.

'How much do people pay for your sketches?' I ask, curiously.

'Like eighty quid,' Cat says.

'No way.' I'm scandalised.

'Too much?'

'Way too little,' I reply. 'Does that even cover the materials?'

'Folk don't think about that stuff,' Cat says.

We both look out over the fields and hills, as though there will be an answer to our problems out there somewhere.

'One thing for it,' I say. 'We need to get the heist going.'

'Good news on that front,' Cat straightens up, energised by the change of topic. 'Guess who's working at Lily Caplan's gallery?'

'Who?' I prompt.

'Sleeping Beauty,' Cat bounces the branch in her excitement.

'From the supermarket security desk?' I ask.

'From the supermarket security desk,' Cat confirms. 'I guess the company he works for rotates their staff around a load of different places.'

'That could really work to our advantage,' I say, enthusiastically.

'We wait for him to fall asleep and just wander off with a painting,' Cat completes my thought.

'Problems solved.' I wipe my hands against each other to indicate a job well done.

A breeze shakes the leaves of our tree. It makes a sound like the whispers of conspirators.

'Cat,' my tone hardens. 'At this point I'd consider actually doing it.'

'So would I,' Cat says, seriously.

We stare resolutely into each other's eyes.

We both crack and burst out laughing at the same time.

'Hang on a minute,' Cat says. 'See, after we actually do this heist, how do I know you won't just want to return everything?'

'Easy,' I reply. 'Because I'll be doing it for you, so you don't have to worry about your mum.'

'Gotcha,' Cat says, 'and I'll be doing it for you.'

'If we're doing it for each other, then returning whatever we steal would be really selfish, if you think about it.'

This place really is like nothing I've seen in the city before.

When I thought of the countryside, I imagined green, but the ground here is carpeted in moss so dark it looks almost black. The further north we drove, the more the landscape turned from dirt to rock. Now the soil on each hill looks like the peeled-back flesh on a terrible injury, with broken bones of rock poking from the wound. The landscape is so wild that you really can imagine there being kelpies in every dark river, fairies in every copse, and dragons hibernating in hidden caves. The hue of rank after rank of mountains pales as they get farther from us and become more and more obscured by the thickness of the air. Cat has brought me to a magical fantasy land.

Wait, am I experiencing a tranquil restoration due to the calming power of nature?

Wordsworth, you son of a bitch.

'About time we got moving,' Cat points out, and I notice the sun is getting lower in the sky, rather than higher.

'Good idea,' I agree, though I'm a little concerned. 'Might be hard to climb down the way we came up.'

'That's why we're going to jump,' Cat smiles roguishly.

'Umm, no?' I protest, 'We've got to be ten feet off the ground.'

'That's not that high,' Cat shrugs.

'It feels it,' I argue.

'Just make sure you roll when you hit the ground, or your legs will both break,' Cat advises.

'Really?' I squeal.

'No,' Cat laughs, then after a moment of thought adds, 'probably not.'

'This is a horrible idea,' I say, but I've got a little bubble of anticipation inflating in me.

'One,' Cat says.

'No, don't count,' I protest.

'Two,' she goes on.

'Wait, are we going on three or after three,' I try to stall.

'Three.'

We both jump.

We're flying.

We're daedalists.

23

Heartless and Innocent

'…But that's because it always has to be for money.'

We survived the fall, now we're back in Cat's car. We've chatted about thousands of subjects today, I don't think I've spoken with any one person for this long before in my life. Just now Cat is getting really animated about art. It's like a veneer of inhibition falls off her. I like it.

'Imagine if artists could just make the art they want to, and not always have to be thinking about whether it'll make money. Just now you can't just make something that one person will love, but some folk might hate. It's better to make something that one hundred people will just like and no one will really care about enough to hate,' Cat goes on.

'Because then you'll sell it to more people,' I say.

'Exactly. We're missing out, though. I'd rather make something that'll change one person's life than something that'll change one hundred people's afternoon.'

It's a good motto.

'I just want to check,' I say. 'You are my friend, right? You're not just trying to recruit me to your secret socialist army?'

'Is it working?' Cat laughs.

'I mean…kind of, actually,' I concede.

'Answer me this then,' Cat says.

'Shoot.'

She tries out another over-the-top accent. She becomes a caricature of a pretentious philosopher. 'Can people even really *own* things?'

'Shut up,' I laugh, hitting her arm.

'Don't hit the driver.'

I hit her again.

She shakes her head in mock disappointment. 'Bold yin, aye?'

'Aye,' I smile.

We're still a long way from home, but it feels too close.

'I signed up to perform my poetry in front of people,' I say. I wasn't sure until right now if I was going to tell anyone.

'What?' Cat's eyes widen. 'Right. I'm there. Where? When?'

'Okay, calm down,' I say. 'Don't get carried away. You'll carry me off with you.'

'Sorry.' Cat bows her head in humble apology, or bows as low as possible while keeping her eyes on the road.

'I *would* like you to come with me, though,' I say.

'Like you had a choice,' Cat replies. 'Either you'd let me come or I'd come in disguise with a wee fake moustache. What poem are you going to do, "Daedalus"?'

'No,' I say. 'I think I want it to be something new.'

'When is it?' Cat asks.

'Thursday.'

'How's...' Cat interrupts herself, looking in her rear view mirror. 'This guy is fair travelling.'

I crane my neck to look out of the back window. There's a car bombing towards us on the winding country road. It's got a spoiler, even though it doesn't look like the kind of car that would come with one. Whoever is driving it probably had a spoiler on their tricycle when they were little.

'They're going fast,' I say, concerned.

'Like eighty, ninety.' Cat sounds worried too.

They gain on us. At some point they'll have to slow down or hit us. They aren't slowing down.

'Cat, they're not stopping,' I scream, my heart rate jumping.

At the last second the car swerves out onto the other side of the road. It overtakes us. We hear the shouting through our open windows. The boy in the passenger seat is giving us the finger, his face red as he spills sexist bile. His mate is bellowing laughter as he drives. They swerve in again, too close to the front of Cat's car, then accelerate off.

Cat frowns. Her hand goes instinctively to the gear stick, but then she pulls it away.

'Cat.'

She looks at me.

'Do it,' I say.

She smiles. She drops into third gear. She puts her foot down.

The jolt of speed pushes us back into our seats, and my whole body floods with endorphins immediately. Every little adjustment of the steering wheel feels like it'll send us spinning off the road. The engine screams in agony. 'Wrong gear.' it cries. 'Too fast.'

They're still going as fast as they can, but Cat is gaining on them. I see their brake lights flash as they round corners, but Cat seems to take them without slowing.

'Can we get past them?' I ask.

'There's a straight around the next corner. If it's clear...' Cat says.

It is. Cat pulls out. As we pass the other car we hit a tiny bump. My stomach drops and I let out a little involuntary laugh. The boys in the car look stunned as we pass. I whoop victoriously.

We pull in in front of them again. I look out of the back window and the one in the passenger seat is yelling and gesticulating at the driver, his red face turning purple.

'What now?' I say, breathlessly.

'Now we leave them in the dust,' Cat winks.

We speed away, but we can't lose them. They're always right behind us.

'Christ, what are they doing?' Cat exclaims.

We'd overtaken them on a straight; they do it on a corner.

'Idiots,' Cat shouts.

In my mind's eye I picture an unseen truck coming around the corner. I see the devastation of something that big smashing into their daft little car, the flying wreckage wiping us out as well, the news reporting that five people have died in a road traffic accident. I know we should stop now; it's getting dangerous.

But as they pass I catch a glimpse of the driver's face, contorted with his contempt for us. He has the look of someone who's used to doing whatever they want without anyone challenging them. I want to punch him.

'Wendy?' Cat checks in, her jaw tight.

I nod, giving Cat the all clear to wipe that look off his face.

Cat stays on their tail, harassing them until we can reach another straight stretch of road. As soon as we find one she accelerates to pass. The driver of the other car drops a gear and accelerates too, trying to trap us on the wrong side of the road. Scenarios flash through my mind. What if we hit something and the car ignites? We can't survive explosions; we're not Nicolas Cage. The driver is spitting with rage, but his friend's skin tone has gone from purple to pallid; his eyes are too wide.

There's a red car coming towards us. Cat touches the brake slightly but at these speeds the deceleration still comes with a jolt. We pull in behind the boys. The red car passes harmlessly – but it was close.

It was really close.

'We'll get them on the next straight,' I say.

Cat shakes her head, 'We need to stop.'

'What?' I can't believe what I'm hearing.

I can see her face; she's furious. She doesn't want to stop. She wants to teach them a lesson as much as I do.

'Are you scared?' I say. It's not fair; I'm trying to goad her. The adrenaline has drowned my reason.

'Yes,' Cat replies, 'I'm scared that if I do something wrong I could hurt *you*. Then what would I do?'

'Oh,' I say, and I'm utterly ashamed of myself.

But I want to beat them. They shouldn't be able to treat people like that.

Cat still hasn't slowed out of the race, despite what she said. I can tell by how her hand hovers over the gear stick that she's still fighting an internal battle about whether she should try for another overtake.

'We should stop,' she says again.

'Wait.' I notice something. 'What's that?'

'What?'

I point to a field up ahead on the road. There's a sheep slumped over the top of a fence, her hind legs still on the ground but her front feet dangling in the air. We're going so fast that we're driving past her seconds later. As their car and ours pass the sheep it struggles. Once we're past her she stops, still slumped.

'She's stuck,' I say.

Cat takes her eyes off the road for a moment to look at me. She catches me still looking over my shoulder at the trapped animal.

'Sheep or race?' she says.

'Okay,' I say. 'Stop.'

The sheep starts kicking and panicking again when she sees us walking towards her.

'Do you know anything about sheep?' I ask Cat.

'This is the first sheep I've met up close,' Cat confesses.

'Me too.'

The sheep either decides we aren't an immediate threat or, more likely, she's just exhausted. She slumps again, her torso leaning on the thin wire that tops the fence. It looks painful.

'Should we get someone?' I ask.

Cat looks around, taking in miles of fields. 'Who?'

We move slowly closer, trying not to scare the animal any more than she already is. She keeps her glassy eye locked on us, its alien-looking rectangular iris unmoving. Her heavy breaths flare her nostrils.

'Looks like she was trying to jump out,' Cat says.

'Poor thing.'

Cat reaches out a hand slowly. The sheep struggles once, then settles down again and accepts Cat's touch. She places her hand on the sheep's head. She makes soothing noises. 'Shh, you're okay. You're okay.'

'She's lucky this wire isn't barbed,' I say, grateful there aren't sheep guts hanging from where it's pressing on her flesh.

'Can you see how she's stuck?' Cat asks.

While Cat distracts the animal with calming noises, I start trying to figure out why it can't get off the fence. The sheep's wool is damp and oily. Her long face is quite intimidating up close.

I notice that one of her front legs is folded under her more than the other. I push her wool up a little and see the top wire of the fence has looped around it. It's digging into her leg, tracing a narrow line of blood along its edge.

'I see it,' I say. My voice must be too loud though, because the sheep bucks, kicking her free front leg into my arm. It leaves a shallow cut, covered in mud and, if I'm honest with myself, a fair amount of sheep shit. I suck air through my gritted teeth.

'You okay?' Cat asks.

'Yeah,' It hurts like a stubbed toe. I want to swear the pain away, but I know that'll scare the animal more. 'It's the wire; it's wrapped around her leg.'

It shouldn't be possible for the wire to wrap around an animal's leg, because it should be taut. This one has come free of a few old fenceposts and it's got just enough slack. Trying to avoid the sheep's intermittently kicking legs and bucking head, Cat and I devise a plan to free her.

I grab the wire on either side of the sheep's leg, gun-shy from the ragged hoof, and push it together. The loop around her leg loosens slightly. Cat gives the sheep, essentially, a great big hug and, with all of her strength, pushes it backwards. The sheep panics entirely, her eyes loll, her legs flick, one unfortunate jerk of her head connects with the side of Cat's head with a dull thump. 'Bastard,' Cat shouts, but she doesn't let go. We manage to push the sheep free from the wire, she lands gracelessly on the ground inside the fence, then she lies there, puffing hard through her nose.

We watch in suspense, I have no idea what we do if her leg is broken.

Then she stands, shakes, and wanders off into the field as though she's already forgotten the whole embarrassing incident.

'Wow,' I pant.

'We just saved a sheep,' Cat says, her shoulders covered in mud and strands of fleece.

'We just saved a sheep,' I grin.

'Heroes,' Cat announces, then offers me a smooth low five.

'Is your head okay?' I ask, 'That sounded nasty. You barely flinched.'

'I got in a lot of fights at school,' Cat says.

'I'm shocked.'

'Are you, aye?'

'Probably too late to catch up to those guys,' I point out.

'Ugh,' Cat says. 'Fannies.'

At the far end of the field the sheep joins her flock. There's no sign of a limp.

'I feel a bit guilty that she wanted to be free and we just stuck her right back in her wee pen,' Cat remarks. 'Eventually some hungry farmer will slaughter her.'

'Downer,' I accuse.

'Sorry.'

The sheep bows its head and starts nibbling a patch of grass. She probably hasn't eaten for a while.

'She needs to be in the pen, though,' I say. 'She can't survive outside it.'

As we drive south the sun is starting to redden. Beams of sunlight radiate from the clouds in that enchanted way they do when the conditions are exactly right. Every cloud has a gold lining, which is better than silver by anyone's reckoning.

The car smells like mud, blood, sweat and damp wool. It's not a bad smell; we've earned it.

The radio is still pumping out the hits, but we're both content and tired now. On the way out we had extended periods of car karaoke; on the way back we're happy to let the familiar tunes wash over us. I think the collective term for a group of pop songs from the noughties is a 'nostalgia'.

It's good that Cat's driving, because if it were me, I'd turn the car north and keep on going until we ran out of petrol or out of road.

24

grow Up

My gran meets me at the door after I hop out of Cat's car.

'Did you have a nice day?' she asks.

'I did,' I smile.

'Where did you go?' she asks.

'Nowhere,' I say. 'It was beautiful.'

'As long as you had fun, darling,' my gran says, unconcerned by my whimsy.

I head upstairs and grab a pen. I don't want my creativity scared away by that expectant blinking cursor again, so the old-school approach feels right. I know that using a computer is less wasteful and more environmentally friendly, but all of the poems I'm most proud of have been written on paper, in my battered red notebook, and since I can't write in that just now – Cat still has it – I use the pad where I keep my captured words. It's been a long day, but I'm not making the mistake I did last time. I'm going to get my feelings onto the page before they evaporate. No waiting until tomorrow, no worrying about formatting, no going back over what I've done until after I'm finished. And it'll probably help that this time I'm not high.

Under the glow of a dim desk lamp I scribble into the night.

The next day, the house feels less like a prison than it has in a long time. I've got a bundle of paper covered in my – frankly, horrible – handwriting. It may not look pretty, but a lot of the poems I've written feel right. They don't feel as though I'm *trying* to write poetry; they feel like I *am*. I know there's something in there that I can perform at Little Panther.

Yes, the idea of performing my poetry to anyone, let alone a group of strangers, does still make me want to dig a hole in my bedroom wall and live in there, emerging only to forage, but I feel less afraid now than I did before. I feel like it might work out.

The doorbell rings. I'm beginning to detest the doorbell. It's so demanding. It doesn't matter what you're doing you have to drop everything. We're all trained, like Pavlov's dogs.

When I answer, Kevin is standing there.

'Okay,' I laugh. 'This time you definitely didn't text.'

'Sorry to bother you. May I come in?' His politeness is like a poorly attached mask with the string taut and ready to snap.

'Yeah,' I say, suddenly concerned. 'Yeah, of course.'

I lead him to the living room, glad that my gran is upstairs and, in theory, out of earshot, though in practice, of course, I don't think she's ever out of earshot. Her ears have a Benjamin Button-like quality: the older she gets, the better they become.

'What's the matter?' I ask, gesturing to a seat, preparing to offer coffee.

'Something has come to my attention.' Kevin doesn't sit; he seems agitated. 'Today we got a list of people interviewing for the job opening – and you weren't on it.'

I feel a little bite from my conscience.

'Oh no,' I perform. 'That's gutting. I guess I wasn't qualified? Thanks for letting me know in person. You didn't have to do that.'

'You are qualified,' Kevin accuses. 'I questioned them as to why you weren't selected, and they informed me they didn't get any application from you.'

'They must have lost it,' I say. 'Would you like a coffee?'

I don't want to lie to him, but it seems the route of least friction. If I admit to him I never submitted it then we'll have to argue about it, or at the very least talk about it. What am I supposed to do? Tell him the truth? That I was afraid of rejection? That I was even more afraid of success?

'No, thank you,' Kevin replies. 'Wendy, I doubt they lost it.'

I'm hurt, because he doesn't trust me, because he's right not to.

'What do you mean?' I ask. 'I told you I handed it in ages ago.'

'I realise that.' Kevin paces back and forth. 'Are you certain you didn't forget?'

I think of the application form, still lying unmarked on my desk upstairs. I worry that it'll beckon to him somehow, like a tell-tale heart.

'I'm not a liar,' I say quietly, my face turning red.

But I am.

'It's such a great position.' Kevin is a dam of sticks trying to hold back a tsunami of aggravation. 'I can't fathom in the slightest why you wouldn't just make the effort.'

'I said – I handed it in.' I'm so annoyed that he doesn't believe me, despite the fact I know I'm not telling the truth.

'You didn't though,' Kevin says, finally getting past his need to skirt around the issue. At least now it feels less like he's handling me; less like I'm a difficult client. 'Did you?'

There's nothing to say. There's no way to avoid this being confrontational. Now it is, and there's no way out.

'Is it because of her?' Kevin pries. 'That girl?'

That seems a strange cognitive leap. I feel a needle of anger stab into the back of my neck.

'That girl?' I mimic. 'What girl?'

'This Cat girl,' he comes back immediately.

'What are you talking about?' I try not to let my voice rise. 'Who calls people "that girl"? You sound like someone's dad.'

'This is a serious matter.' Kevin's exasperation comes out as a tense fidgeting of his fingers. 'You meet her and suddenly you're quitting jobs? You're doing drugs? And, correct me if I'm wrong, but didn't I see you both running out on a bill at a restaurant a few weeks ago?'

My thoughts get caught on the phrase 'a few weeks ago' like a woollen jumper on a nail. I pull them free.

'What are you saying?' I'm hiding my ire behind sullenness and sarcasm. I don't want to full-on lose my temper. That would be extremely bad form. 'She's a bad influence?'

'Yes,' Kevin says. 'I don't care if you think that sounds ludicrous, or if you think I sound like someone's dad. She is a bad influence. I know people like her, Wendy. One day she's going to convince you to do something you don't want to do. She's going to talk you into something that's dangerous, and that will put you at genuine risk. She'll make you feel it was your idea all along, and if things go wrong, you'll abruptly find

188

that she isn't there to take the blame. She'll have orchestrated the whole thing so that all fault lands squarely on your shoulders.'

'No,' I shake my head. 'That's not her.'

'Whose idea was the walk-out?' Kevin responds, 'Who quit and brought all those other people with her?'

'Me,' I insist. He won't take that from me.

'Really?' Kevin asks. 'Because it certainly didn't sound that way when you told me about it.'

Why does he have to be here? Why does he have to do this right now? I was having a good day. They're so rare, and I just wanted to enjoy it. He's demolishing that and, worse, he's trying to tarnish the person who made it good in the first place. He won't. I won't let him. How dare he?

'Will you stop?' I shout.

And now that I've shouted there's no way to undo it. I can't go back to disinterest, I can't go back to denial. I can't pacify myself, and Kevin certainly can't.

'I'm not some stupid little girl, okay?' I say. 'I don't need you to look after me. You think I'm so naïve? You think I'm that vulnerable?'

'Alright.' Kevin has the nerve to act as though this is unprovoked, as though it's some hysterical explosion. 'Calm down. I'm trying to help you.'

'Well stop,' I yell in return. 'I don't want your help.'

'Come on,' Kevin appeals, acting as though I'm being unreasonable. 'Who remained by your side all through uni, through thick and thin, regardless what was going on?'

'So now I owe you?' I challenge.

'I didn't say that,' Kevin sighs. 'You didn't use to be like this. This isn't how you used to behave. I preferred the old Wendy.'

Now I'm more than just angry. Now I'm furious. I have to hold on to the fury because if it cools even slightly, I'll start to cry. It's a frustrating response my body has to anger, and I don't want it to happen because it'll make me look weak. I grasp the fury with both hands.

'The old Wendy?' I taunt. 'The pliable, quiet, Wendy? The one who was just eager to please everyone and didn't want to get in anyone's way? Her? That Wendy? I bet you liked her. What's not to like? She's totally agreeable. That was never me. You just thought it was because you were one of the people I was hiding the real me from.'

'This is the real you, then, is it?' It's infuriating that the angrier I get the more he seems to calm down. The more I shout the more he seems in control.

'Yes,' I scream. 'You finally got to meet me. You should be honoured.'

'The fact is,' Kevin says authoritatively, 'you can pretend that a life of running around with Cat, getting high and stealing and whatever else you've been doing, is sustainable, but in reality you can't survive without a job. You need money to live, Wendy, that's just how it is.'

'I'll get a job, without your help.'

'When?' Kevin demands. 'It's been four months.'

'What?' I'm stopped in my tracks.

'Four months,' Kevin repeats. 'That's how long ago you left your job.'

'No,' I reply, but without conviction. I don't know if he's right or not. I don't even know if he's close.

'You don't need me to prove it, do you?' Kevin asks. 'Because I have a calendar on my phone; we can count together.'

'Don't patronise me,' I growl.

'I'm sorry,' Kevin says curtly. 'I'm just concerned for you. How long do you think you can keep this going?'

I know that I've spent whole days in bed, but can it really have been four months since I left Chay Turley? A third of a year? It can't have been.

A voice in me whispers, 'it has'.

'Look,' Kevin seems to soften, seeing the fire in me dowsed by the revelation. 'I'm sure whatever you've been doing has been fun, but there comes a time when you, and Cat, will have to grow up.'

'Get out,' I mutter.

'Pardon?'

I don't repeat myself. I walk from the living room to the front door and open it.

'Fine,' Kevin sighs. 'I'll be here when you need me. Just call me when you calm down.'

He wants the last word. I can't stand it. I close the door enough that he can't leave.

I know I said I would try not to lie, and I've been trying, but I've been lying about Kevin. I made it sound like we made the choice not to 'define our relationship' together. We didn't. He suggested it and I went along. I made it sound like we made the choice to do IT together. We didn't. He talked me into it, and I went along. I thought maybe, one day, Kevin and I would get together. I lied to you about it all because now I feel so stupid, I didn't want to admit to you that I changed the course of my whole life, and studied a subject I don't even care about, just because he asked. I thought you'd think less of me.

'Did you sleep with Freya?' I ask him.

I've taken him by surprise, but he recovers quickly.

'Oh honestly, what's that got to do with anything?' Kevin

rubs his temples.

'Did you?'

'Yes. Alright? Is that what you want to hear?'

No. Of course not.

'More than once?' I ask.

'Why are you doing this?' he retorts.

'Kevin,' I demand.

'Yes. Happy?'

I'm not. My mind is full of all the ways Freya tortured me. The exclusion, the rumours, the weaponisation of social media. I remember being punched in the face by Chloe, a girl I'd never even met before, because she thought I'd been spreading lies about her, and how I went to university every day never knowing if one of the thousands of other students might attack me, because of Freya's machinations.

'At the same time as you were sleeping with me?' I ask.

I know from the moment of hesitation that the answer is yes. He starts to trot out an explanation that's he's probably had rehearsed and ready to go for years.

'We're done, Kevin,' I interrupt. 'I don't want to see you again.'

'What?' Kevin's voice is close to shouting. I get a twisted satisfaction from that. 'Because I had sex with someone? It's not like we were a couple, Wendy.'

All that time I thought we were friends and might one day be more, but really Kevin only wanted me around so he could keep his options open. I open the door fully again, giving him space to leave.

'Bye,' I say, but hope it's clear that what I'm actually saying is that I hope he dies and that I'm the one to kill him.

'Do you know what, Wendy? Fine. Fine, I'll leave,' Kevin

spits, without actually making any move to go. 'I don't need this shit. You're insane, do you know that? Look at you. You're crazy.'

Crazy.

'Piss *off*, Kevin,' I shout.

He doesn't. He looks me up and down. He takes his time. Then he give me a sardonic eyebrow raise that seems to say 'or what?' He wants me to realise that if he doesn't want to leave, then I'm probably not strong enough to make him. He disappointedly shakes his head.

'Bitch,' he says.

'No.'

It's my gran. She's on the stairs behind me, just like the last few times Kevin visited. I hadn't seen her, nor had he. She's clearly heard quite enough.

'Leave,' she says simply.

I see Kevin consider refusing. His face is visited by a sneer, then he walks out of the door.

25

Little Panther

Every collection of people, no matter how big or small –
whether it's cities, towns, villages, offices, or classroom – has
tribes. Finding people who you can form a tribe with is a
natural human thing to do. We make tribes out of anything
we can. We name our generations and create groupings
based solely on the year we were born, as though every single
human that came into existence in a thirty-year window has
something in common with all the others, and we bond with
people around the world who we have never met and never
will meet through that feeling of generational comradery.

We do the same with religions, beliefs, political views,
nation, sports, books, interests, hair colour – everything. How
many people have bonded because they both happen to like
the same TV show? Or both like dogs? We grasp at anything
to feel belonging and banish loneliness.

Having a tribe makes us feel safe and secure. We need a tribe so that when we grow old there will be people to help when we can't help ourselves, so that when things are hard we aren't alone, and so that we can fill in for each other's weaknesses. We're tribal animals.

The only problem with our innate need to find common ground with others is that it encourages us to make a stand. Do you support a football team? Well, the good news is now you have a tribe of other supporters backing you up, the bad news is now you have rivals – people who support a different team, who aren't part of your tribe. Our vast generational tribes criticise and generalise all the others, whole swathes of the population wage battle over avocados. Our religious tribes have had wars throughout history. Our national tribes thrive on stereotypes and xenophobia, as though someone born in one hemisphere is made of totally different stuff from someone born in the other. Our tribes bring us together and separate us. Our greatest strength is also the source of all the conflict the world has ever seen.

The tribe of Little Panther's poetry open mic nights are a special kind. Poets aren't exactly the first to be invited to sit at the table with the cool kids. The Little Panther tribe are a crew of misfits and outcasts, the kind we root for so much in fiction but dread being bundled in with so much in life. That kind of adversity leads to a tightknit tribe. They may not have been beacons of popularity throughout their lives, but here they are.

And I'm an outsider.

I look around the basement bar with an expression I hope is approachable and friendly. I weigh up the pros and cons of taking a seat at a table all by myself. I don't want to draw focus to the fact I'm alone – what if everyone avoids me? Worse, what if they don't?

Walking down the stairs to the bar was a struggle. There was something about the black glossed walls and metal staircase that had a very 'leave this place' vibe. I'm not sure how that works as a business model. It smelled like spilled drinks, mingled aftershaves and perfumes, and the wayward tobacco clouds that over the years had drifted in from the smokers outside.

A man at a makeshift box office consisting of a folding table, chair, and a little money lockbox was waiting for me at the bottom. He was a lot more welcoming than the stairs that led to him. A sticker in cheery blocky text on his chest read 'Hi, my name is Roger'.

Roger didn't see me immediately – he was too busy calculating the amount of change the person in front of me was due – but even when his expression was flat, the lines on it were an origami template for a smile. When he saw me, his face folded along those lines to reveal the kind of expression you'd expect from Santa Claus, not a balding middle-aged man in an oversized band t-shirt.

'Hello, traveller,' he'd said. It was an incredibly silly thing to say, but he said it with such charm and mystique that I couldn't help but like him. 'Ticket for one, is it?'

'I'm actually…' I made some hesitant noises, restraining my urge to bail out, 'I'm actually reading tonight. That is, my poems. I'm reading them out. On stage.'

'Well,' Roger said amiably. 'That would make you one of our guests of honour. Carry on through, traveller, and enjoy your evening.'

There are people in the world who can leave you feeling their warmth for a long time, even if you meet them only briefly. We should always remember that we can all do that, if we want to, but now I'm here, and Roger is still on the other side of the door I came through. I'm out of my comfort zone and my depth.

An efficient-looking man with a clipboard starts striding over, giving me a little wave as he approaches. I wave back, my grin solidified and sore.

'You must be Wendy?' he asks when he reaches me. I don't know if he knows by my lost expression that I'm new to the club, or if it's just because he knows every other person there already.

This fellow has a clipboard, and knows who I am. That means he must be one of the organisers of the event. Despite that, he doesn't seem to have a sticker like Roger's. I'd assumed Roger's name badge had been standard issue. Realising that he must have brought it from home makes me like him even more.

'Yes,' I confirm. 'Wendy. That's right.'

'Great,' he says, ticking my name off his list. 'It's great to meet you.'

'Thank you,' I beam, hopelessly.

'Grab a seat somewhere. Take in some of the other performers; they're all great. I'll give you a little call when it's your turn. If you just keep your ears open for your name that would be great.'

He hasn't introduced himself. I've named him Mr Great in my head. I'm thinking of christening him Great Scott for the delicious pun-value of it, but I don't know if his name is Scott and I feel like it would be too serendipitous if it were.

'Now, listen,' he says. 'We know it's your first time performing, but we're a very welcoming bunch, so don't worry about your reading. The important thing is getting the first one done and under your belt. No one expects you to be great.'

Oh. Perhaps, Not-So-Great Scott.

I'm sure he was trying to help, even though he's just told me not to worry too much because everyone already expects me to be shit. His pep-talk would have come across a little better if he'd waited for me to actually say I needed it. My nervousness must be written all over me in neon.

'Thank you,' I say again, with the same frozen grin.

'Great.' He shakes my hand and moves on to his next task.

I don't sit down. I look around, like I'm going to find an anchor to grab onto in some corner somewhere. People are sitting at round wooden tables that are covered with carved graffiti. Most of the audience are wearing black, the walls are black, I imagine even their coffee is black. No one looks aloof or unapproachable, but no one looks like they're in need of a new friend either. Everyone here seems to have someone, or a group of people, to talk to. I stand awkwardly, like the last kid to be picked in PE.

A poet takes the small stage at the far end of the room and there is a polite round of applause. I'm confused by how he talks. He's taking odd gaps and using some really weird inflections. He really seems to know what he's doing, and the audience don't seem to find his strange lilting delivery unusual. I've never heard anyone talk like this before. When he leaves the stage, I applaud with the rest of the room, but I can't recall a single word he said, only the way he said it.

Another poet takes the stage. People seem excited to hear her so she must be well thought of. When she starts to speak, she has the same inflection as the one before her, the same unnatural speech patterns.

I realise, with horror, that this must be how poetry is meant to be spoken. I was so stupid to come here. I've only ever seen poetry written down, I didn't know there was a way it was meant to be said. I'm going to sound like a fraud. Should I try to mimic it?

Then something happens to me.

I get a rush, like I've stood up too quickly. The room feels off kilter, as though the floor is at a very slight angle that's getting infinitesimally steeper each second. I steady myself and wait for it to pass. It doesn't. Icicles push their way out of every one of my pores. They spring from my arms, my legs, my face – everywhere. Around the icicles, television static is dancing on my skin. Some of it creeps into my peripheral vision, giving my sight a white corona. I can hear it buzzing. What's happening? I need it to go away. I can't focus with all these people around. They have to give me some space. They have to move away. They have to stop speaking. I remember the lights in here being dim and now they seem far too bright. I can't stay here. I need to get out. I need to be away from all of them and all of this. The static in my eyes is spreading and I can't see properly. I can't find the exit.

I have to get out of here.

I have to.

I have to leave.

I can't find the exit.

I have to leave.

I feel hands on my shoulders, firm but assuring.

'I'm here,' says Cat.

26

Spit

'Look at me.' Cat's voice is resolute but kind, like her hands on my shoulders. I glance at her face, but then my eyes start to dart around.

'Nobody's looking,' Cat says. 'Promise. We're at the back of the room and they're too busy listening to the lassie on stage.'

I stop looking around. I look at Cat, who's standing directly in front of me.

'Think about breathing, okay?' Cat coaches. 'In and out.'

She regulates my breathing with me, prompting every in-breath and out-breath. As she does, I feel her kinesphere, her bubble of personal space, grow and encapsulate me. If I keep looking at her, I can imagine the walls of her kinesphere are opaque, we can't see anyone outside the orb, and they can't see us.

'Let's count your breaths, yeah?' Cat suggests, like it'll be a fun game. 'We'll count ten of them.'

I count with Cat. Every time we breathe out we add one to the tally. I can feel the icicles start to melt and the static starts to decode.

'What's this place like,' Cat asks. 'Tell me what you can see.'

The walls of her bubble turn translucent, I look around like I'm observing the room from behind safety glass.

'There are stupid red lamps on every table,' I say.

'Stupid?' Cat asks.

'So stupid,' I confirm.

'And?' she prompts.

'Wooden tables. Old coasters. Mismatched chairs,' I hesitantly play freestyle I-Spy. 'Everyone is wearing so much black. The walls are all black too.'

'That'll be why they call it Little Panther. Most panthers are black,' Cat says gently, still looking into my eyes.

'Panther is actually a colour, not a species. Panther just means a black big cat. There's no such thing as a panther, just black jaguars and leopards,' I say.

Cat looks at me in amazement, like she can't believe I would pull a fact like that out of the air, given the current circumstances. To be honest, I don't really know what the current circumstances *are*; I just know that things aren't normal.

'Is that true?' Cat asks.

'Yeah,' I say, as the static withdraws from my vision and hearing, and all the corners and edges of the world come back into focus.

'Everything's okay,' Cat tells me.

'Yeah,' I say again.

'There's no danger here,' she says.

'No,' I agree.

'And we're here together,' she reminds me.

'Yeah,' I say one more time.

I shake my head, like I'm trying to clear water from my ears. Cat gives one last reassuring squeeze then lets go of my shoulders.

'You ever had one of those before?' Cat asks.

'No.' I feel confused and tired. I want to lie down and sleep. I distantly hear the audience applaud the poem's end and wonder how long I was gone and where I went.

'You did well. Let's get a drink and grab a table,' Cat says. 'Hi, by the way.'

I throw my arms around Cat's neck and hug her tightly. We've never hugged before. I guess we both like our own kinesphere to stay intact most of the time. But just now I have to – I'm so glad she was here, I'm so happy to see her.

'Hi,' I say.

I feel better immediately. Now we're just two people sitting at a table, indistinguishable from all the other people sitting at tables. I'm not a misfit standing at the side of the room any more. I don't feel like anyone is looking at me. I've gone for a soft drink rather than alcohol, at least until I've performed. Cat and I watch poet after poet deliver their lines. Some are excellent. Some are less good. I'm reassured by how many there are. Provided I don't entirely mess up I'm unlikely to stand out from the crowd, which is comforting. I guess that's what Great Scott was trying to tell me.

'It's weird how a lot of them talk, isn't it?' I whisper to Cat. 'Is it just me?'

'It's not just you,' Cat replies.

'Do you think that's how you're meant to perform poetry?'

I ask.

'I've no idea,' Cat admits. 'They seem to think so.'

'Do you think I should try to speak like them?' I ask.

'I think you should try to speak like you,' Cat replies confidently.

We settle in. We start to really enjoy ourselves. We get caught up in the narratives of some of the best pieces and once or twice find ourselves getting a bit emotional. It's incredible to be in a place where poetry is wild and everywhere, I don't know why I've never come to hear poetry performed before. I don't know why I didn't try to be an audience member before I was a participant.

That's not true. I do know.

If I'd come just to watch and not take part, I would never have built up the courage to change roles. I'd have convinced myself more with every visit that I wasn't good enough.

I've become so comfortable that it comes as a bit of surprise when Great Scott announces:

'Our next poet is new to Little Panther, but I'm sure she'll be great. Please give a great big warm welcome to Wendy.'

I really hope someone else here is called that.

Everyone applauds. I should get up, but it's a long, exposed walk to the stage.

'I believe,' Cats smiles warmly.

'You do?' I ask.

'I do believe,' Cat reaffirms.

I take the long walk. I step unsteadily onto the stage. I stand behind the microphone and stare down its inquisitor barrel.

I hope it doesn't screech that terrible feedback noise when I speak, like how it happens in movies. I hope my voice doesn't come out as a squeak. Cat smiles broadly and encouragingly from our table. Everyone else looks on with polite low expectation.

'Isn't it sad?' I start. My mouth is too dry; I can't.

A presence in me pipes up.

'Let me drive,' says homunculus Wendy, my tiny hidden true self. 'I've been waiting for this moment.'

I hand over the reins. I start to speak. Over the course of the poem I even start to perform. Homunculus Wendy is in her element. The more the audience seem to listen the better she – the better I – feel.

This is what I say:

'Isn't it sad that dreams have a deadline?
Imagination is fine if you're young
and can't understand
that what takes off has to land.
You want to believe you can stay up forever.
You'll never fit that star-shaped fantasy
into the square hole of reality.
Why are we told
to put our imaginations on hold
when we grow up?
Told we have to toss them in an imaginary box
sealed with practical locks?
Even if abstract thoughts or plans
help us understand
the world, we have to hand
them over to pragmatism.
A tree is a tree.
A bird is a bird.
It doesn't matter what you see,
or the message you've heard

In their songs.
Money has to be made.
Life has to be lived.
And you have to give
in to the fact that you
can't expect to be able to fly.
If you want to keep your head held high
The only way to do that is to grow up.
Art is fine for kids,
Adults have to wear ties.
You need to try.
Begin to fit in or
they'll grimly
put your head on a block.
Time for daydreams to stop.
You're bound by the tick and the tock
of the crocodile clock.
I remember my guidance teacher
and all of the stress,
on her face when I took my place
in her room and filled in a test,
To determine what job suited me best
in my future.
Which career path would be brighter.
When the response came back it said 'writer'.
I was absolutely delighted.
All I wanted,
all I ever wanted,
was to tell stories.
Now that we'd hunted
I felt glorious.

Somehow, some algorithm
had seen my dreams
and agreed with them.
Maybe given me the means
to start to pursue them.
I could feel myself lifting a little.
Getting closer to the sun.
I got quickly pulled back
before I reached the clear air.
She said it was a mistake.
It meant English teacher.
It can't mean writer.
There's no money in writing.
No life to be lived.
I've no right to write, I have to give
something more to society.
There's better uses for me.
As though there's no place in this world for fiction or poetry.
But here, right now, hope has started to bloom.
I'm looking at you all, I can see a room
of people who know there's no difference
between words and wings.
That's what makes us what we are.
A whole room, a whole tribe, a whole sky
of aeronauts, blinking like stars.
Every one of us dreamers,
who confuse and upset guidance counsellors.
Realists with clippers
try to strip us
of those hopes.
They try to tether our feathers

with rope.
They warn us that if we fly too close to the sun,
we'll fall.
I want to fly anyway. I need that heat.
It feeds me, grows me, shows me,
that I can show them,
That life isn't a game where we have to compete.
A salary isn't a high score to be beat.
I don't need to play to feel complete.
A cat doesn't know it can land on its feet,
if it's afraid to take a leap.
It's true. Some of us will find,
that when we put our soul on the line,
we'll reach for the sublime and we'll fall.
But if you're drowning in the brine of the sea,
While frowning critics say your crime is trying to be
a conduit for beauty,
but lacking the talent to perform that duty,
you just need to relax.
Firstly: because the wax in your wings only melted
because you were so close to where you want to be.
Secondly: it'll help you float.
Swim back to shore.
Craft wings of stronger words.
Fly a little higher.
Fall a little further.
Dream about the day you'll soar.
If growing up means giving up,
Never grow up. Never give up.
Fight back, don't look back, take a stand.
Like a never bird over never trees,

You and me.

We.

We never land.'

I complete the poem and stand like a gladiator awaiting Nero's *pollice verso*. That's a word from my notepad. It means that thing where they give a thumbs up or thumbs down to show whether the gladiator lives or dies. Cat looks around with nervous expectation. I can tell she's eager, desperate even, to start the applause, but knows that if she does then it will mean less. She wants me to have the affirmation that comes from the approval of strangers. The dead air is tense.

All at once, the room erupts into applause. I think it's the biggest ovation I've heard all night, even though really that's probably the endorphins skewing my perception. It could be that the crowd are extra generous because they know I'm a newcomer. It may even be that a piece about how noble and important it is to be a creative in a room full of poets was always going to be a winner. I don't care what the reason is, it's…

It's transcendental.

Cat shakes a victorious fist. She looks so proud.

'Great.' Great Scott bellows between claps. 'Absolutely great.'

The applause reverberates off the black gloss walls and bounces back transformed into waves of acceptance and belonging. The small space fills with it.

This must be what it feels like to start a revolution.

27

Speaking to the Stars

I'm still buzzing from my performance at Little Panther and Cat has taken us out for dinner to celebrate. Of course because it's late, and because we don't really have any money, 'out for dinner' means we went to a drive-through and parked somewhere to eat it.

'My car's going to stink of chips now,' Cat says.

'Cat,' I say. 'You know I can see your back seat, right?'

Cat isn't the kind of selfish scumbag who would throw a bag of rubbish out of her car window, but she's also not the kind of enterprising go-getter who finishes a drive-through and then finds a bin. The back seat of her car is littered with paper cups, paper bags and little cardboard burger boxes.

'Yeah, fair play,' Cat laughs.

'This isn't very anti-capitalist of us,' I point out.

'No,' Cat agrees, 'but it tastes amazing. I'll have yours if you like?'

'Make a move and the bunny gets it.'

'Thought so,' Cat says. 'But you are right. Places like this are like the big evil face of capitalism.'

'What are we meant to do though? Not eat?' I ask, shovelling a handful of chips into my mouth just in case.

'Right? Seriously though? I don't know what the solution is. I just know there's got to be something better than' – she gestures around her – 'all this.'

'That's alright,' I say. 'You're not the first minister or prime minister or Leader of the World or whatever.'

'Not *yet*,' Cat winks.

'I'd vote for you,' I say.

'See if you knew someone that only thought people were of any worth if they were of some use to him,' Cat says, 'you'd call that guy a sociopath, wouldn't you?'

'I'd call him Kevin,' I say.

'Who's Kevin?'

'Not worth talking about. What were you saying?'

'Right, so,' Cat goes on, 'if a person only saw value in someone if they had a use you'd call them a sociopath, but when our whole social structure acts the same we think it's totally normal. We're just like "cool, no bother, lets go with that".'

Cat has driven us to a hill that overlooks the city centre of Glasgow. The idea was that we'd have a really nice view of all of the streetlights below us and all the stars above us, but Scottish weather hates to be taken for granted. Between the drive-through window and the hill it began to pour. Now, sitting in the car with the engine off, which leaves us with no wipers, all we can see is thick waves of water, like the tide is coming in on Cat's windscreen, and all we can hear apart from each other is the rumble of rain on the roof. I don't mind. In fact, I quite like it. We're in here, and the world is out there, and we don't have to worry about it.

'How's your head?' I ask.

'Ugh,' Cat winces. 'That sheep caught me an absolute belter. The bruise is under my hair but, so that's lucky. Want to see?'

'Obviously.'

Cat moves her hair aside and shows me an impressive blue-black bruise behind her ear.

'Ouch,' I say,

'Tell me about it.'

'Did you really get in lots of fights in school?' I ask, remembering what she'd said when we freed the sheep from the fence.

'I even got expelled from one school for it,' Cat nods. 'Primary school. I was, like, nine. My mum was bealin'.'

'Why were you getting into fights?' I ask, enjoying hearing about Cat's life before I met her.

'Sometimes it was because people were winding me up,' Cat admits, 'but lots of the time it's because some wee dick was picking on someone he didn't think would do anything about it. I hated that, so I'd do something for them.'

'So you'd beat them up?' I ask, keenly.

'I mean, sometimes. Lots of the time I'd just *get* beaten up,' Cat says. 'You could tell how my school week was going by checking if the bruises were on my face or my knuckles, but at least those little pricks weren't getting away with picking on someone else.'

'Hero,' I announce.

'Shut it,' Cat says, fondly. 'It wasn't like that. I just got angry. People shouldn't treat each other like that.'

Cat takes a contemplative sip of her milkshake.

'Right,' she says eventually. 'Kid on you're in an elevator.'

'Okay,' I agree.

'There's ten floors up, and ten down, and you're on the ground floor.'

'Got it.'

'All the floors going up are good feelings.'

'Happy thoughts,' I suggest.

'Yes,' Cat agrees enthusiastically. 'And all the floors going down are bad thoughts. Most people's elevators can go all the way to the…I don't know…the penthouse of happiness.'

'The penthouse of happiness?' I laugh.

'You've got poetry, I've got paintbrushes; give me a break,' Cat smiles. 'So most people's elevators can go all the way to the top or all the way to the bottom. Sometimes it feels like my elevator breaks.'

'How?'

'It won't go any higher than the first floor. Or any lower than one floor down. Sometimes it won't leave the ground at all and I just feel…' She trails off and shrugs.

'That sounds horrible,' I say.

'Then,' she adds, 'the cable snaps and the whole elevator just plummets right to the bottom.'

'Is your elevator working just now?' I say, tentatively, feeling a little silly for asking.

'Yeah,' Cat smiles. 'Everything's cool just now. Don't look so worried.'

'Tonight my elevator is on…' I consider. 'Like an eight or nine I'd say. What about you?'

'Tonight?' Cat asks. 'Hanging out with you? That's a solid three.'

'Hey,' I protest, playfully hitting her arm. I'm guessing the rule about hitting the driver only counts when the vehicle is in motion.

'Kidding on,' Cat laughs, throwing a few chips at me.

'*Now* your car *will* smell,' I point out.

'Worth it.'

I turn to look at her.

'Cat, can I tell you something?' I say, seriously.

'What is it?' Cat replies, concerned.

'I've been meaning to tell you,' I take a deep breath, 'but the time was never right.'

'Wendy, what is it?'

'It's just,' I say, 'you have blue paint on your face.'

'What?' Cat exclaims. 'Seriously?'

'Under your eye,' I confirm.

'Mortified,' Cat says, using her rear-view mirror to find the rogue paint.

'I didn't think you'd mind; you've pretty much always got paint on your fingers.'

'That's my fingers. I don't usually kick about with it on my face. Lucky your poem was that good, so nobody was looking at me, isn't it?'

'I think it suits you,' I say, trying to act cool about the compliment.

The drumming of the rain dies down as suddenly as it began, and a few final sheets of rain water cascade down the windscreen. Below us Glasgow glows from streetlights, windows and shop signs. Red brake lights and white headlights decorate the distant streets like fairy lights on a tree. Above us, through a break in the clouds, a few brave stars try to illuminate the whole sky.

'I find it really hard to sleep sometimes,' I confide. 'I feel like something is watching me.'

'We can stay here all night if you like,' Cat says.

'Thanks,' I smile. 'I actually usually sleep a lot better on days when I've seen you.'

'Aw, cheers,' Cat teases. 'I'm glad my chat puts you to sleep.'

'That's not what I mean,' I say, faux-exasperated.

'I know,' Cat says, 'I sleep better, too.'

We watch Glasgow for a while as we drink our milkshakes and finish our chips – or 'fries', I suppose; that's Americanisation for you. I have no idea what time it is, but I'm not ready to find out yet. I want to stay here for a while.

It's been a good day.

28

Runagate

Sometimes I worry my mind isn't on my side. I feel like it's lying to me. Like it hates me.

I'm scared I might be crazy.

I had to leave the café I was hiding in – the one with the ethically sourced Arabica beans – because the barista was looking at me funny. I suppose I can't blame him. I was, and still am, wearing my ramshackle disguise, and I was sitting next to what most people would automatically correctly assume was a covered-up painting. He kept on looking over like he was trying to figure out what was going on with me. I had to leave before he managed.

As well as that, my coffee was cold. I'd nursed it for too long. Cold coffee is even worse than hot coffee; it tastes like teacher's breath.

But the real reason for moving, above both the meddlesome barista and the congealed coffee, was the creeping certainty that the man in the red velvet coat was closing his net.

If the police found me, I'd see them coming. If Red Velvet's friends found me, I wouldn't know until it was too late. I doubt that Red Velvet makes his associates wear any sort of helpful uniform. I don't think keeping my eyes out for anyone wearing moth-eaten vintage clothes would have been enough to keep me safe.

Any lost child knows the best way to be found is to stay where you are, so it makes sense that the best way not to be found is to keep on moving.

I didn't want to risk public transport again – It was pretty stupid to get on a bus the first time in retrospect – though, even if I had wanted to get a bus or train, I didn't have any more change.

I also realised, belatedly, that if anyone were looking for a suspicious girl with a stolen painting then I would be on the security camera footage for the café. They'd review the tape and see me sitting there for an embarrassingly long time, and sure, they hadn't caught me there, but if they watched the footage, they'd see which way I went when I left.

I made a point of turning the wrong way when I left the café, then I doubled back on myself. I started to use backstreets and alleys to move around. I had to avoid any busy streets because the more people there were the higher the likelihood that the area would be under surveillance. I couldn't cut through any shopping centres, train stations, or even pedestrianised areas. I tried to avoid alleys that had shops backing off into them because they would probably have cameras on their back door in case anyone broke in. I tried to keep my pace leisurely and unsuspicious.

Just a girl out for a walk.

In her trench coat.

With her painting.

Surveillance is something we might be a little too nonchalant about. I once heard that the most under-surveillance country in the world is China, which isn't really relevant to my current situation, but the United Kingdom comes fourth, and that feels very relevant. Of course, most people would argue that having a lot of security cameras is a good thing because it keeps you safe. Most people aren't on the run with a stolen work of art. I realise I might not get much empathy complaining about how tough it is to be a criminal. George Orwell would be on my side though. I wish he were here now. Whatever happened to him?

Then I remembered something.

When I was in high school there were days when I couldn't face going to class – the packed corridors, the strict faculty, the chemical clashing of so many hormones all contained in one building – it was all too much, but I was lucky because I got good exam results. When I was in high school they ignored your attendance if you were helping to bring up the school average in academic achievement. But not going to school has its challenges – it's not like I could just stay at home: my gran was there and would take skipping a lot more seriously than the school itself did. And I couldn't just wander the streets. The legend, whispered in hushed tones in the school social areas, was that truancy officers prowled around during school hours. They were police officers whose sole task was to spot children of school age not at school. It would have been easy to spot me; I went to the kind of school with a strict uniform code and a predilection towards bright blazers.

I have no idea if truancy officers were even a real thing, but I'd hidden from imaginary ones plenty of times, and when I did there was a place I would go.

Between my house and my old high school there was a

garage. The guy who owned it used to have a couple of vans that he'd store there. I think he had a small business – maybe as window cleaner. Sadly, his business must have failed, but the spacious garage was still there. Either it was still his or belonged to no one at all. The door to the abandoned garage was thick and severe-looking, but never locked. Inside, there was a ladder that led up to an overhead metal walkway running along one wall near the ceiling. I don't know what the walkway was meant for, but I used it as an elevated hidey-hole.

I wish I'd thought of it earlier. I don't know why I didn't.

I made my way there. My disguise was starting to feel a bit too conspicuous. I kept on toying with the idea of dropping it all in a bin. There were a few issues with that plan, though.

The first was that without the disguise, I'd have no disguise. Obviously.

The second: I'd become strangely sentimentally attached to the trench coat.

The third: I would still be carrying a pretty incriminating piece of evidence – the actual stolen masterpiece.

I kept my gnarly eighties hat firmly on my head.

Security at the garage hadn't improved since my teens. The door was still unlocked. Rust and cobwebs gave the place an even more foreboding look than I remembered.

That's where I am now, hidden in the corner of a derelict building. It's dawning on me that this isn't really a long-term solution. Even if no one will ever find me I can't stay here forever. I can't even lie low here for long enough for this whole thing to blow over. The police aren't the kind of people who get bored chasing someone after a few hours and lose interest, and I have a bad feeling that Red Velvet isn't either.

My left arm has swollen up into a bruise that covers

everything from elbow to shoulder. I need a plan. Any sort of plan. I wish Cat were here.

Cat meant for us to steal the painting without anyone seeing us do it or finding out who we were.

I really messed that up.

Right now, Kevin Is probably spilling his guts to detectives Davies and Llewelyn. I bet he'll have called the police himself to share his insider knowledge. He's probably telling them all about me, and how I was led astray by a girl who was bad news and now I'm essentially the love child that El Chapo and Vincenzo Peruggia never had.

They'll have taken my gran in as well. There's no way that conversation they were having with her at the front door when I snuck out the back didn't end in them taking her to the station for more questions. If they find out I was home, they might think she's an accomplice. They better not be horrible to her.

She's there because of me. In an interrogation room, probably. For the first time in her life, as far as I know. All because of me.

Okay. I've been mulling it over as I write. I've come up with a short-term solution. After I finish writing this confession, the plan is this: I'm going to write a series of anonymous tips – all in different handwriting if I can. I'm going to send them to the police station. They'll probably suspect that they're hoaxes, but they won't know for sure. They'll absolutely have to check up on them – all of them. How embarrassing would it be if the media ever found out that the police were given a tip-off they could have used to catch a notorious art thief but assumed it was a prank? If I can inundate them with fake leads, they'll spend all their resources chasing those leads and not chasing me. They'll be looking for the truth among all the lies but there won't be any truth, and while they are all redirected across the city, looking for me in all the wrong places, I'll go somewhere far from everywhere I've sent them.

Now I just have to work on a way to evade Red Velvet and his crew.

Also, I can't afford envelopes.

Or stamps.

Or the risk of going to a post office.

And I don't know how postmarks work but if the police receive a bunch of letters all sent from the exact same location, they would probably just go there first and start searching in that area. They'd probably start their search by looking in likely hiding places, like abandoned buildings.

I'm in trouble. I really am. I'm in trouble.

I could just turn myself in. They might be lenient. I just have to hope that none of those people were seriously hurt.

They might be seriously hurt. I might have seriously hurt them.

No, turning myself in isn't an option. If you knew the whole story, you'd know that I can't let Red Velvet have this painting. I don't think Cat would ever forgive me.

You don't know the whole story yet, though.

You will, soon.

Okay. Deep breath. Here's how I got here.

29

Pedestal

There's a small black cloud slithering around, hiding in corners or flattened against the ceiling. Once every few hours or so, when I least expect it, it launches a sneak attack. It engulfs my head in a microclimate thunderstorm; the lightning bolts electrically trace the name 'Kevin'.

I'm still so angry. Worse, I'm angry that I can't stop being angry. I ought to be able to just feel good right now, but I can't. The echo of the words he used must have a half-life as long as plutonium because they've been bouncing around here since the second he said them.

'Grow up.'

'Crazy.'

'Bitch.'

It's words. It always has been. Words are the problem.

I'm making my way over to Cat's flat. We've been texting back and forth all day, like we do most days. We haven't seen each other in person since Little Panther, and that was about a week ago.

I'm still checking my emails regularly and unnecessarily. Nothing ever comes through except for the occasional promotional mailshot from companies I've bought something from in the past – reminders that at some point I wasn't canny enough to click or un-click a box asking them not to email me every few days for the rest of time. I know I could unsubscribe, but I don't. When I refresh my mailbox and the notifications pop up telling me I have new messages I get a minuscule jolt of endorphins that just slightly outweighs the disappointment of finding out it's all spam. Earlier this evening, though, it wasn't all spam. I had three legitimate emails. What a momentous occasion.

The first was a rejection letter for the first job I'd applied to. It was generic and unhelpful. Generalised rejection.

The second email was from the second job I'd applied to. It told me they had had a high standard of applicants and the choice had been extremely hard. It was a standard email so the same message was obviously sent to every failed applicant, which was a bit patronising, we can't all have sent in great applications; some of them must have been shit. I think I preferred the first rejection. This one felt like it was trying to coddle me and kick me at the same time.

The dark figure in the corner of my eye came along with the emails. He grinned his predatory grin, and this time it was so wide it split his face in two. Like a snake with an unhinged jaw he opened his maw, sizing me up, almost ready to consume me. I heard the hiss and gurgle of his expanding gullet as I read.

Tick-tock, tick-tock.

The third email was from an address I didn't recognise. It was from Great Scott at the Little Panther. Turns out his name is actually Tony, which spoils my fun a little. It was a courtesy email, I guess. It just said that they'd really liked meeting me, thought I was a great poet and my poem was exceptional. He said they'd be delighted if I came back another time to read again.

I'm trying really hard to be totally upfront with you, and I don't think I exaggerated the response I got at Little Panther, but it was really nice to see, in writing, that even if I'd made it more in my head than it really was, they at least definitely enjoyed it a bit.

'Exceptional,' it said.

But, even better than that, it said I was a 'poet'.

I said earlier that you can't just crown yourself a poet; it's a title someone else has to give you. Now someone had.

That's when I'd told Cat I would like to see her. It was a small win, but it felt like progress. I was really excited by that stupid little email; I needed to share it.

I'm on my way to share it with Cat now. The streets are quiet tonight. Occasionally cars pass. You can hear the trundle of their tyres along the road from much further away than usual because there's no other noise pollution. It's been a nice day. People have tired themselves out enjoying the sun while it shone. Now the warm afternoon has given way to a chilly, clear-skied night. Park loungers, day drinkers, barbecue-grill gods, and fun runners have all retreated inside to hide until the sun comes again.

I remember, when I was young, all the streetlamps used to be orange. They used sodium, which only needs a small amount of electricity for it to glow. It made streets look otherworldly. Every passer-by looked jaundiced, every turn foreboding. I think it was cheap, though, and would save on local council's electricity bills.

I'm glad that now they're white, but the bright LEDs have their own problems. Everything feels too real. In the bright white lights, anyone I pass looks ghostly. Their pupils are all too wide, they're zombified by the pallor the streetlamps paint on them.

I turn a corner and Cat's block of tenements comes into view. So does she. I must be instinctively looking up at her window as I walk onto her street. Maybe I'm expecting her to be standing at it.

She isn't standing at it.

Cat is sitting on her narrow windowsill. She's leaning her back against the window frame. One of her feet is propped up on the sill, her other leg dangles in space. Her arms rest on the bent knee of the leg that's still supported by the plastic ledge of the window. She's holding on to nothing, just like she held onto nothing when we were in the tree, but in the tree, we were ten feet up, at most. Cat's fifth floor flat is at least five times as high.

Though she's high up, I can see that Cat isn't wearing anything.

I can't understand what I'm seeing. I notice I'm not alone on her street. There are two men standing below Cat, pointing up at her. They're my age, or younger.

A ball of anger bursts in my temple. I know it's impossible, but in my mind these are the same boys from the car who screamed at us, all purple-faced and entitled. I don't know what Cat is doing, but I do know that something's wrong. I know that she's not there for these men to look at. I begin marching towards them. At flipbook speed, scenarios play out in my mind, alternative-universe versions of what I'll say and what I'll do when I get close enough to confront them. I mentally roll up my sleeves. I'm ready for a fight, an actual physical fight. I can't remember ever being ready for a fight before in my life, but these men are taking advantage of Cat when she's vulnerable. I won't let them.

Then one of the men shouts up to her.

'Hey,' his yell is loud but uncertain. 'Are you okay?'

I stop in my tracks. I wasn't expecting him to be concerned about her; I thought they were opportunist voyeurs. Cat doesn't flinch. She doesn't look down; she doesn't acknowledge him at all.

'Excuse me,' the other man joins in. 'Do you need help?'

Her eyelids don't even flicker.

I've stopped close enough to them to overhear the rest of their conversation.

'What should we do?' asks the first man.

'I don't know,' the second replies.

There's an edge to their voices. They're afraid. At first, I think they're afraid *for* her.

'What's she staring at?' the first man says in a hushed tone.

'Nothing,' the second looks around uncomfortably. 'There's nothing out there.'

I realise that they're not afraid *for* her; they're afraid *of* her. I look up at Cat again. This time I see what they see.

She doesn't look vulnerable in the least. The three of us on ground level are washed in the headache glow of the LED streetlights. We're luminous and exposed; she's high above them. She's lit by the stars and moon shining in the cloudless sky. It gives her a blue tint.

She doesn't seem to be affected by the cold. She doesn't shiver, she doesn't huddle, she doesn't budge.

Her eyes are fixed into the distance. She's a catatonic lunatic, mesmerised by the moon. Only, maybe *not* the moon. It seems like she's looking further – past the moon, past space, past anything any of us have ever considered or dreamed. She blinks so irregularly that her eyes take on the glassy sheen of the taxidermised.

Cat is there, on her narrow windowsill, in body. In spirit she's far away – in the countryside again, maybe, or in that perfect place of real solitude where no people walk that I daydreamed of that first time I came here, or maybe somewhere entirely different. Somewhere near the stars of the Milky Way. A place that she won't be able to enter until sunrise.

Why wouldn't the men be scared of her? She doesn't care that they're looking at her; they're irrelevant. She doesn't care what they think of her. She doesn't care that they think at all. She looks as though she's painted in oils. She looks ethereal. They're right to be scared of her.

'Come on,' the second man pulls the collar of his coat up and shivers, brushed by a gust of cold wind that never happened. 'Let's go.'

'Okay,' the first man says. 'Okay. You're right. Let's go.'

They stumble on in a daze, both look sporadically over their shoulder, back towards Cat. Their expressions are troubled.

Now it's just me and her.

I have to help her.

I want to shout something to her to stop her falling, but I'm afraid if I do something wrong, I'll startle her and make her fall. Just now she's balanced, I don't want to throw that balance off.

I feel a tinnitus-like ringing begin in my ears as I look up at Cat. It's building to a crescendo too quickly. I can't swither or agonise over the consequences any longer. I have to do something.

'Cat,' I bellow.

She blinks. Humanity begins gradually to return to her face, but she keeps her eyes fixed on the distant sky. With the underwater speed and rubberised limbs of a sleepwalker she folds herself back through her window. It's not until her feet are inside once again that the trance seems to fully lift. She looks down at last. She sees me. Realisation dawns on her. She darts deeper into her flat.

I stop holding my breath.

What do I do now? What have I just witnessed? Should I still go inside? Will she want me to? Should I try to, even if she doesn't want me to? I stand directionless on the street, still staring meaninglessly at her window.

My phone vibrates. I have a text message.

'Sorry. Didn't see you. 'Mon up,' Cat's text says.

30

Non-fatal Terminal Velocity

By the time I get up to Cat's flat she's wearing clothes and a sheepish expression.

'Sorry,' Cat says.

'What were you doing?' I ask.

'I got out of the shower,' Cat says, 'then I just...I don't know...spaced out.'

'Are you high?' I ask, without condemnation.

'Yeah, five storeys,' Cat smiles wryly.

'That's not what I mean,' I say.

'I'm not,' Cat reassures me. Then, like a switch has been flicked, her expression changes. 'That was really stupid.'

'Are you okay?' I ask.

'Nothing could survive falling that far,' Cat says. It's like she's still on the windowsill as we speak.

'A cat could,' I say to distract her, to change the track of her train of thought.

'What?' she asks. 'No it couldn't.'

'A real cat I mean, not someone called Cat,' I clarify. 'But yeah, an actual cat could survive that fall.'

'How?'

'You know the old saying about cats always landing on their feet?' I ask.

'Aye, because people are comedians and they like to say it to me all the time.'

'Because of your name.'

'Because of my name.'

'So, you'll also know that it's totally true. Cats do always land on their feet. Well, almost always. They have to be high enough up so that they can turn around. If you hold a cat upside down an inch from the floor and drop it then it'll land on its back.'

'That'd be a bit cruel,' Cat notes.

'Yeah,' I agree.

'Funny, but,' she adds.

'Yeah,' I agree.

'It's because they have gyroscopic inner ears. They flip around to the right way up automatically because their ears tell them to,' I say. 'You'll also know the saying that cats have nine lives, right?'

'We can probably just assume I know all the things people say about cats, to be honest.'

'So that comes from the first skyscrapers in New York. They were the tallest buildings ever built at the time and the people living there were, I guess, just ludicrously bad at making sure their windows were kept closed when they had cats wandering around.'

'Oh no,' she joins the dots.

'Oh yes,' I say. 'There was a spate of cases of cats falling or jumping out of windows. Some of them were literally one hundred storeys high, but almost all the cats survived, and nearly none of the surviving cats needed any medical attention.'

'So people decided that cats just reincarnate as soon as they die,' Cat says, 'Fair enough. But, how were they actually not dying?'

'I'm glad you asked. I love this,' I grin. 'As well as gyroscopic inner ears, when cats are falling they do this thing where their legs all splay out in different directions. You know terminal velocity?' I ask.

'Is that another action movie?' Cat teases.

'I mean…yes. It is. And we should watch it.'

'It's when the air resistance pushing up on something is the same as the force of gravity pushing down on it. It's top speed for falling,' Cat says.

'Yes.' I love that she knows that. 'Cats are light compared to their surface area when they're spread out like that, so they become like little furry parachutes. The air resistance pushing up on them slows them down to a survivable speed.'

'Is that why when people are wrecked they survive falling off bridges and things and just walk it off even though it would have killed them sober? They just spread out and float down like a wee drunk hand glider?'

'Kind of,' I reply.

'Piss off,' Cat laughs. 'Really?'

'It's about tension,' I say, 'If your muscles are relaxed the impact of hitting the ground is less damaging than if you're all tensed up and panicking.'

'I get it. If you're drunk you might hit the ground before

you know you're falling,' Cat fills in.

'So you don't have the chance to tense up, exactly,' I say, 'and cats do that too. When a falling cat realises that it's not actually falling very quickly, it begins to relax and just enjoy the scenery. It's called non-fatal terminal velocity.'

'That's pretty cool,' Cat admits.

'There's a caveat,' I say, taking the chance to use a word from my notepad. 'The cat has to have time to go through all three stages. It needs to be high enough to let its ear gyroscope turn it around, to spread its legs, and to relax. Otherwise it'll die.'

'So, a cat jumping from a fifth storey window has more chance of living than one jumping from a third storey window?' Cat asks.

'Go big or go home,' I say.

'Wendy, you're quirky,' Cat says warmly. 'I love it.'

Cat seems to be back to herself again. The colour is back in her cheeks.

'Is all that true?' she asks.

'I wouldn't lie to you,' I say with mock indignance. Then I feel guilty. 'I mean, except the stories about what happened to my parents.'

'Hang on,' Cat feigns surprise. 'Those weren't true?'

'Uh-oh. I guess the cat is out of the bag.'

'Okay, enough cat sayings now.'

'Do you mind,' I ask earnestly, 'that I make stupid stuff up like that, sometimes?'

'Wendy,' Cat says, 'I love when you tell stories.'

'Good,' I smile.

We sit down together, comfortable in each other's company. 'You don't have to answer if you don't want to,' she says, 'but what *did* happen to your parents?'

I look at my hands, wishing I'd written the best reply to her question there.

'They just left,' I say. 'Simple as that.'

I sigh. I take a deep breath.

'When I was still a baby, they asked their neighbour to watch me for a few hours because they both had to go to an appointment or something. They never came back,' I say.

'That's awful,' Cat says.

'I guess they thought the neighbour would let the police take me away, and I'd get put into the care system, but the neighbour was an older lady who had always wanted children, so she adopted me.'

'So your gran...?'

'...Isn't actually my gran,' I complete. 'People can be really insensitive when they see a woman her age with a new-born baby, so she called herself my gran to shield me from all of that.'

'People are such arseholes,' Cat says.

'They are,' I say. 'So that's it. That's the truth. They just left me and I'll never know why.'

There's silence for a few seconds and I'm worried I've made Cat uncomfortable.

'Your parents had the chance to know you and they didn't take it,' Cat says. 'I'm sorry, but your parents are bloody idiots.'

'They are?' I ask.

'Total idiots,' Cat says.

'Massive idiots,' I say. It's cathartic. 'Sorry, that was a bit of a downer, the made-up stories are much more exciting.'

'Did telling the real story make you feel better?' Cat asks.

'It did.'

'Then I like the real story even more than the made-up ones,' Cat says.

I cosy contentedly into the couch.

'While we're talking about parents,' Cat says, 'I'm sorry about that day with my mum. I'm such a fraud.'

'What?'

'I'm always going on about how capitalism is evil and stuff, but I can only afford to because someone is giving me money.'

'That doesn't make you a fraud. We all have to play even if we hate the game. That's what makes the whole thing so shit.'

'Woah,' Cat looks impressed. 'The student has become the master.'

I bow, sagely.

'What did you want to show me?' Cat asks.

I open up the email from Great Tony and hand Cat my phone. I'm terrified she won't get why it's a big deal. I sit nervously as she reads.

'This is amazing.' She's so enthusiastic I think my heart will burst. 'Wendy, the poet.'

'Shut up,' I say, blushing happily. 'They liked it. They actually really did like it.'

'Of *course* they did.' She wraps me up in a hug.

I can't handle the focus being on me for too long, so I change the subject. 'Have you heard from Lily Caplan?'

'I have,' Cat says, 'but I don't want to be a thunder-stealing dick head.'

'Well now you *have* to tell me.'

'Alright, alright. So she's having this big charity auction thing at her gallery, but a wee bit of the money raised on each painting goes to the artist as well because every painting is by what she calls "up-and-coming talent". Anyway, she's got lots of really influential – and absolutely loaded – friends who really like to show off how philanthropic they are, and lots of them are important in the art scene. So…' she trails off.

'So?' I almost scream with the pent-up excitement.

'Oh,' Cat says, realising she's buried the lead. 'She wants to auction one of my paintings.'

Cat's neighbours probably hear how happy I am. Cat's neighbours' neighbours too.

'What painting?' I ask. 'One of these?'

Cat shakes her head. 'It's a new one. I've been working on it non-stop. Literally. I've done so many all-nighters – can't even remember the last time I really slept.'

'Can I see it?' I blurt.

'I really wish you could,' Cat says regretfully. 'They came and got it off me a few hours ago.'

'That's okay,' I shrug, 'I'll see it soon enough.'

'I think you'll like it.'

'I know I will. I believe.'

Cat offers her hand and we give each other another cool low five.

'I know this is coming out of nowhere,' Cat says, 'but I would tell you everything about me, if there was time. There isn't. But I would.'

'It would probably take a while to tell me absolutely everything,' I admit.

'Yeah,' Cat says sadly.

'I suppose we'd better get started then.'

'What?' Cat asks in trepidation. 'Am I about to be interrogated?'

'You asked for it,' I say. 'So, what would I like to know about the enigmatic Cat?'

We while away the hours swapping stories about ourselves. We tell stories whose specifics I won't remember, but I will remember the feeling of belonging that came from sharing them. I'll remember laughing with her until my ribs hurt.

Everything feels right, the world is in balance. We've both taken a step towards our dreams, and even though it's a tiny step, it's one that so many other people never get to take. We're flying. We're daedalists.

I don't know that tomorrow Cat will be dead.

31

Never

I leave Cat's building and step back onto the street. I see the two men as a ghostly echo image in my mind's eye. They're walking away with fear and concern on their faces. She'd explained she'd been at the window because she'd just spaced out, and I'd accepted it. I was trying so hard to just make things normal again that I hadn't pushed it.

She was fine, wasn't she? We'd just had a really wonderful night. She was happy; we both were.

I walk down the street a little. I can't shake this worry that I can't find a source for. Cat had said something else, hadn't she? Something that had struck me as strange on a subconscious level, but that I hadn't really registered.

'I would tell you everything about myself. If there was time. There isn't,' comes a whispered memory of Cat's voice.

She meant there wasn't time tonight, didn't she?

Didn't she?

Everything is alright. It has to be, so why do I feel apprehension weighing on me like a wool coat saturated with rain?

I walk a little further down the street. I stop. I walk a little further. I stop. I turn around.

I'll buzz up to her flat, she'll answer, I'll pop up and see her, I'll tell her I was just struck by this bad feeling, we'll laugh about how I thought I was psychic. That's how it'll go. I might look a little silly, but it'll put my mind at ease. I don't mind looking a little silly in front of Cat, anyway.

I buzz her flat. There's no response.

I wait as long as I can bear to, then I buzz again. She still doesn't answer.

I begin to text her, then realise that if I can't wait for the response to a buzzer then I can't wait for a response to a text message. I call Cat's number.

It rings out. A friendly robotic voice tells me the number I'm calling can't come to the phone right now. I try again; the same happens. A third time; no reply.

I try to rationalise it. She could be asleep? No, I don't believe she's fallen so deeply asleep that her buzzer and phone can't wake her, and she can't have fallen asleep in the time it took me to walk down the stairs and up the road a little. She could be listening to music? No, if she were listening to music loud enough to drown out those other noises I'd be able to hear it from here. She might be listening on headphones? No, I didn't see any retro cd players or anything like that. If she were listening to music it would be on her phone, and a call would have interrupted it.

What do I do?

I dial 999. I ask to be put through to the ambulance service.

'I think my friend might be trying to kill herself,' I say when I get through. I don't have time to think of a euphemism. Saying it out loud is terrible.

The call handler I speak to seems professional, but unconcerned. She probably gets calls like these all the time. Young people, in a panic, sure that something awful is happening. I let her know that neither Cat nor I have been drinking or taking drugs. I tell her where I am. I try to keep my voice level and calm and serious. I'm terrified she's going to think I'm a prank caller. She doesn't seem impressed when I tell her my worries are based on a feeling, and that I have no evidence at all. There's an edge of incredulity in her voice; I can tell she thinks it's ridiculous I would call emergency services just because my friend won't answer her phone. Nonetheless, she assures me an ambulance is on the way.

I pace for the entire time I wait for the ambulance to arrive. I try the buzzer again and again. I phone Cat over and over. I just want her to answer. I want to magic her phone into ringing louder. I know that if this is all just a mistake then soon there will be a very annoyed ambulance crew looking for answers. I'm sure we'll laugh about that later. Just now I just need to hear her voice. I've no idea how long it takes for the ambulance to arrive; it feels like forever.

When the paramedics do arrive they are comforting and calm. I tell them what's happening as succinctly and clearly as I can. One of the crew has some sort of skeleton key to the building, he buzzes once and when there's no answer within a few seconds he uses it. When we reach the door to Cat's flat on the fifth floor he knocks authoritatively. He shouts Cat's name. She doesn't reply.

'She's definitely in there?' he asks.

'Yes, she hasn't left. I was here with her.'

'She can't be in the shower or anything?'

'No.' I shake my head. 'She showered before I got here. She wouldn't be.'

'Do you have a key?'

I want to scream at him that if I had a key I'd already be in there. I shake my head.

'Break it down,' I say. 'Please. I'll pay for it. Just break it down.'

He looks reluctant.

'Please,' I beg, 'she could be dying.'

They break the door down.

When they do, their attitude changes immediately. The man I've been speaking to orders another paramedic to take me downstairs. I see the body language of the crew become professional, efficient, and urgent. As I'm led away, I see Cat through the open door. She's lying on the floor. I catch a glimpse of a packet of something by her hand.

They let me go with Cat in the ambulance. Her breathing is so shallow. I talk to her. I quietly tell her stories. I know she can't answer, but I know she likes stories.

When we arrive at the hospital, I'm ushered to a waiting room. I wait.

In the early hours of the morning, Cat dies. Her heart stops. She dies for three and a half minutes.

They bring her back. Like Lazarus. Like the phoenix. They revive her.

A member of hospital staff brings me the news and all the tension and terror comes out of me as tears.

She's alive. Cat is alive.

They tell me she's stable and asleep. She won't be able to

talk to me for a while. They tell me to go home, get some rest, and come back tomorrow to see her.

I do. I dream about what would have happened if I hadn't turned back to check on her. The important thing is she's okay.

When I visit, I find Cat sitting on her hospital bed. She's hugging her knees, curled defensively. She doesn't look at me.

'I'm so glad you're okay,' I say. I want to hold on to her and never let her go in case she evaporates.

She doesn't look up.

I feel awkward. I don't know where to go from this point. I don't know what I'd expected her to be like when I saw her, but I hadn't been ready for this.

'How are you feeling?' I ask, weakly.

'Why did you stop me?' Cat mutters.

I don't know what to say. I stand there, petrified to the spot. The gossip magazine I bought as an ironic joke gift hangs limply in my hand.

'I didn't want to be saved,' Cat says. 'I wanted to die.'

I can't respond. I don't know how.

'You should go,' Cat says.

I leave. I tell myself I have to be alright with the fact that Cat is angry with me. I have to be alright with it, even if she's angry with me forever. If losing Cat from my life is the price I have to pay for Cat to still have a life, it's more than worth it.

I tell myself that we might never speak again, and that I have to accept it.

A few days later, she texts me.

'I didn't mean what I said,' it reads.

'Can I visit?' I reply.

'I'd love that,' Cat writes back.

Her bedside table in her corner of the hospital ward

is covered in the standard gifts a person gets in hospital: chocolate, diluting juice, fruit destined to go untouched into the bin.

'I'm sorry I put you through that,' Cat says.

'You don't have to apologise to me,' I say. 'Or anyone. I wish I'd realised you weren't alright.'

'They won't let me have anything sharp,' Cat says.

'Well,' I say, gently. 'Good.'

We both laugh.

'They're going to have me talk to a psychiatrist. They say they might put me on some drugs,' Cat says.

'I bet that'll be good stuff,' I say, with a playful smirk.

'I'm going to be so bloody high,' Cat replies, a light-hearted twinkle returning to her eye after a sabbatical of a few days.

'Cat,' I say, 'I'm glad you're alive.'

'Me too,' Cat says, her voice cracking.

'Everything is going to be okay, isn't it?' I try not to let the desperation seep into my voice.

'They'll help me,' Cat says, 'they'll teach me how to fight this. I'm a pretty good fighter.'

'I'm shocked.'

'Are you, aye?'

'Can I do anything for you?' I ask, then I add, 'I'd do anything for you, you know that?'

'Everything's going to be okay,' Cat says, comforting me even from her own hospital bed. 'Just think of all of the amazing things we're going to do together.'

'Together,' I say.

I'm so grateful for the future I can imagine us having. I'm so relieved we'll get to share it.

It might never have happened.

32

*

Reality

None of the last chapter was true.

I wish it were. Every second of every day I wish it were.

I didn't go back to Cat's flat. I didn't notice anything was wrong at all. I didn't save Cat's life.

I just went home. I went to sleep. I looked forward to texting Cat in the morning.

The next day my gran goes out to the shops. I offer to come with her and help her carry things, but she waves me away. She has a sprawling network of friends whose schedules are all aligned so they meet regularly when they are out and about. They might not give her all the gossip if I'm there.

I send Cat a few messages, she doesn't reply, I assume she's still asleep. She could easily have started painting after I left. I know she works best at night, when all the distractions are tucked up in bed.

I haunt the house all morning, moving cups and glasses

from one room to another like a poltergeist, spiriting away snacks from cupboards like a fairy, occasionally half-heartedly cleaning things like a bored brownie.

The doorbell rings. When I open it a man and woman show me their badges.

'Good morning. I'm detective Davies,' says the man. 'This is detective Llewelyn. Are you Wendy?'

I'm sure they're here about the lunch we stole from Pixie Cove. I bite my tongue and manage to stop myself from blurting out that we went back and paid. These aren't standard police officers; these are detectives. They must consider running out on the meal to be a more serious crime than I thought. Unless they know about the drugs as well?

'Yes,' I say.

'May we come in?' asks Detective Davies.

I lead them to the living room. I ask if they'd like coffee or tea, but they both turn me down. We all take a seat at the living room table. I hope they'll be gentle with me because it's my first offence.

'How can I help?' I say, as innocently as I can.

'Wendy,' says Detective Davies gently, 'were you at your friend Cat's last night?'

'Yes.' They must know we did it together. I hope that admitting I was with her hasn't somehow landed her in trouble too.

'Wendy,' says Detective Davies again, with calm compassion, 'Cat is dead.'

My face turns cold, the floor and walls of the living room fall away. I hold on to the table to stop myself plummeting into the void with them. The three of us drift and rotate slowly and sickeningly in space.

'No,' I manage. I know what he's saying isn't true. I saw her just a few hours ago, she was fine.

'I'm so sorry,' Detective Davies says genuinely.

'How?' I ask, incapable of more than one syllable.

'Suicide,' Detective Davies tells me.

'Suicide,' I repeat. The word feels alien. Meaningless.

'We'd like to ask you a few questions, is that okay?' Detective Davies asks. Why can't he see my house has turned into an empty swirling abyss?

'At the police station?' I manage, despite a creeping numbness in my lips.

'We can do it here,' Detective Davies says with a small smile, both sad and sympathetic.

I tell Detectives Davies and Llewelyn everything I can think to tell them. I can hear my own voice echoing inside my head. It's like I'm listening to someone that sounds exactly like me, speaking inside a huge empty school gymnasium.

I rummage through my memories and dissect anything Cat said. I tell them that months ago she said she had thought about crashing her car, but I didn't think she was serious; I thought it was because we were high. I tell them about her sitting on her windowsill, but that I'd believed her story about having just come out of the shower. I tell them about running from Pixie Cove, jumping out of a tree, racing on quiet country roads. I don't see how any of it can have any meaning, but I tell them anyway. I'm not really in control of my mouth any more. I hadn't seen this coming. I hadn't expected this.

I don't realise until I look back on our conversation later that I confessed to all of the crimes I was worried they were there to arrest me for. I don't care. They don't seem to care either. None of that matters any more.

After I've finished telling them all I can, I hear myself ask, 'What happened?'

Detective Davies replies in a measured tone, laying out facts without making any inferences. I can tell, despite how disconnected everything seems from reality, that he's being gentle with my feelings.

In the late hours of last night, or the early hours of this morning, Cat got in her car.

She drove north, into the countryside.

She abandoned her car by the side of the road, near the start of a walk that goes to the peak of a mountain.

She walked the route in the dark, probably by the light of the torch on her phone, since no other light source was found.

It seems as though she reached the summit. She was found dead on rocks that weren't anywhere near any trails. She can't have been climbing, because she wasn't found with any climbing gear, so it was likely she got to the otherwise inaccessible area by jumping from the top.

'Why?' I ask.

Detectives Davies and Llewelyn just look at me. Their eyes are kind, but they don't have any answers.

Detective Llewelyn gives me two phone numbers. One is to call if I think of anything else; another is a line to call if I feel I need counselling or emotional support. They apologise for my loss and they show themselves out. I find a notch in the wood of the tabletop and dig away at it with my eyes as my mind races further and further away.

I have so many questions. As she was driving did she listen to old pop songs like we had? Did she sing along? Did she know, when she took the long walk up the mountain, why she was there? Did she tell herself she was just out for some air?

Was she just looking for somewhere quiet that was away from all the noise and confusion of the city? What did she think about as she put one foot in front of the other again and again on the steep climb to the top? Did she think about her family? Her art? Did she think about me? Was she afraid of the dark when she was out there alone? Did the light of her torch light up the slopes and fields and the rocky trail enough that the rustling of the wind-blown grass didn't make her jump? Did she put enough fuel in her car to come home, or did she know it was a one-way trip?

I can't make myself understand foreverness. I want to ask Cat all these questions, but I know that I can't talk to her. It only feels as though I won't be able to talk to her for a very long time, though, not that I won't ever. I can't understand the idea of never. I can cope with weeks, months, years, decades, but never is too much. It's impossible that I won't be able to see her again ever. That's not fair.

I can press the reset button, I can reload, I can use an eraser or the delete key, I can skip back to the start of the episode, I can open the book on the first page again, I can apologise, I can make amends, I can repair the break, I can renew the licence, I can pay the fine, I can serve the time for my crimes; everything is fixable. It can't be forever. There is no forever.

I'll see Cat again. Of course I will. She'll be gone for a while and then I'll see her again.

She wouldn't leave me.

I killed her. I killed her by not noticing the signs. I killed her with my idiotic talk of non-fatal terminal velocity. I killed her because she said that If she were to feel truly genuinely happy, then she'd kill herself. Maybe I made her happy and that's why she did it. I did this. It was me.

I want to call the detectives back and tell them I'm a murderer. I want to fall at their feet and ask them to lock me up forever and let Cat off the hook. It wasn't her fault, so just let her off with it. Let her not be dead any more, and I'll go to jail for the rest of my life. It's a fair trade. She didn't mean it.

My gran comes home. I don't know how long it's been since Detective Davies and Detective Llewelyn left: she might have met them on the garden path, or they might have been here hours ago. I only know it's the same day, because my gran wouldn't have been out for longer than that. The notch on the table hasn't gotten any deeper despite how long I've stared at it.

I can tell by her expression just how terrible I must look.

'What's the matter, darling?' my gran asks.

'Nana,' I say, 'my friend is dead.'

She has lived to see so many friends die, and the end of so many stories. She's seen so many people leave, had so many final conversations, said so many last goodbyes. She has adapted to the world so many times as the landscape warped following the deaths of people who were its bedrock. She looks at me in a way she never has before. I'm part of a terrible club now, one that everyone joins at some point if they're lucky enough to live a long life. She walks over to me and puts her arms around me without saying anything.

Then I cry. It's strange that it took so long for me to start crying. It wasn't real before. Now it is. If my gran is hugging me this tight, then it must be real.

I cry endlessly and she never lets go, or even loosens her tight grip. I cry until it feels as though the tears are vinegar, the sobs in my throat are razorblades, and the deep gasps of air filling my lungs are full of ball bearings. I want to focus on the actual physical pain of crying. I think pain will be better than sadness. If I can just hold on to the pain, then I might be able to stop the tears. But the sadness keeps attacking me. It sends wave after wave.

Eventually the sadness seeps into the centre of my heart. I stop crying then. I haven't cried since.

33

Dragon

I stagger through mists of dysphoria. They block out all the light and almost all the sensation. The next time I start paying attention to myself, or to anything going on around me, I'm at Cat's funeral.

A celebrant is giving Cat's eulogy. It all seems generic. They say she was so full of promise, so young, had so much ahead of her. They say she was loved and brought light into everyone's life.

They make her sound so boring.

They take a life so inimitable and rare and make it sound so flat. They don't understand that talking to her was like finding a clear radio station when all the rest of the time all you could hear was static, or that just being with her made the whole world make sense.

I watch the celebrant read, squashing my three-dimensional memories of Cat onto a few two-dimensional pieces of paper.

An application form is a terrible way to sum up a life; a eulogy is far worse.

Cat's mum says a few words. She talks about how Trini would have become a lawyer one day, and how Trini hadn't had the opportunity to put her law degree into use before she was stolen away. She doesn't mention art once. I resent her for that. She had Cat's entire life to get to know her, but still didn't know how important art was.

I only got months with her. Not long enough. If I'd known, I would have made sure I saw her every day. I never would have left her flat.

Cat's mum keeps calling her Trini.

'Her name was Cat,' I shout.

I don't really though.

You know that by now.

Cat's mum never looks up from the script she's written for herself or strays from what's on the page. She doesn't trust herself to speak from the heart without breaking down, you see. She wants to finish her goodbye to her daughter.

I haven't been totally honest with you; you know that by now too. I left some bits out earlier when I told you about Cat's mum coming to her flat. I didn't tell you about how desperate she seemed, like she was scared for Cat but didn't know what else to do. I didn't tell you that when she took the painting she didn't destroy it or anything, she just said she was keeping it so Cat would focus on finding a job; then she'd give it back. I didn't tell you that before she left, she told Cat she loved her.

I need someone to blame, so I missed those bits out so you'd be on my side. I wanted her to be the source of some really awful trauma, the answer to the question of why Cat did what she did. She isn't.

I don't like her, but she isn't the monster I need her to be.

I let the rest of the service wash over me. I don't focus on what people say. I relive my own memories of Cat quietly in my head instead.

The funeral ends. I ought to offer my condolences to Cat's mum, but I can't bring myself to go near her. What would I say?

'Hi, remember me? Well, If I'd paid more attention to Cat I'd have noticed she wasn't okay, and she'd still be alive today.'

Or, maybe, 'You say you loved her, but you never accepted her. You tried to steer her away from her dreams and told her to do something with her life. Well now she can't do anything with her life. She's dead and it's your fault.'

I can't speak to her. I know she's not a monster, but I still think I might hate her.

I begin to walk towards the door. A lady comes towards me on an intercept course. Short of running away there's not much chance I can avoid her. She doesn't look like Cat or any of Cat's family. I don't think she's related.

'Are you Wendy?' she asks, as the gap between us closes.

'Yes,' I say, resigned to a difficult conversation filled with platitudes about how sad and tragic what happened was. I don't know that I can take it. I can't make small talk with a stranger about my dead friend.

'I'm Lily,' says the lady.

'Lily Caplan?' I ask.

'That's right.' She shakes my hand. 'Cat spoke about you a lot.'

'She did?' It means so much. My heart flexes and skips.

'All the time,' Lily says. 'I know a strange woman stopping you from leaving Cat's funeral isn't what you want just now, but I saw you and I didn't want to let you go before asking you something I think Cat would want me to ask.'

'What?' I say.

'How are you feeling?' Lily says. I'm so disappointed, I thought she might have asked me something that would help me understand.

'It's tragic, what happened,' I say, hollowly.

Lily examines me.

'Wendy, you don't know me,' she says, 'but you should know that I don't ask questions I don't want the answer to. I know how important you were to Cat and I'm sure Cat was just as important to you, so, how are you feeling? How are you actually feeling?'

'Angry,' I say, suddenly. I surprise even myself.

Lily doesn't recoil. She doesn't even twitch an eyebrow.

'That's reasonable,' she says.

'It's not,' I yell at her. How dare she be understanding. She can't understand; no one can. She barely reacts to my outburst at all.

'I'm not going to ask why you're angry,' Lily says. 'I know why you're angry, but I'm going to ask you to say it out loud. Will you do that?'

'No,' I say.

'You won't?' Lily asks.

I realise I'm breathing heavily, like I'm being chased.

'Because she left me,' I burst out, 'without any explanation. Now I want to blame myself, or her mum, or just anyone. I'm furious that she did that to me. I trusted her so much but she didn't trust me enough to tell me what was happening to her. She abandoned me, and I can't even ask her why. I can't believe she was that selfish. I'm just so angry.'

It's the most awful thing I've ever said, and I've said it to a complete stranger. How can I be angry at Cat for dying? How can I think she is selfish, when I'm so hung up on my own feelings I can't even cry about her being dead? I wait for Lily to tell me how disgusting I am. I want her to; I'm abhorrent.

'Good,' says Lily. 'Look, the world is still turning. You weren't dragged to hell for your sins. Your feelings are valid. No one can tell you how to feel.'

If Doctor Jekyll had taken his serum and then hadn't mutated into Hyde, or if a werewolf had seen the full moon and hadn't transformed, they would have felt like I do now. Not a monster, just a confused, lost, human.

'Here's a fact that might help you,' Lily says, 'from someone who knows.'

I nod wordlessly.

'Cat jumped – that's true and there's nothing we can say to change that – but she was also pushed. She was thrown by the thing that whispered the seeds of her ideation into her ear,' Lily says. 'A demon, a spectre, call it what you will.'

'A dragon,' I say.

'A dragon,' Lily agrees. 'If a knight were to try to fight a dragon and they got killed, we wouldn't blame the knight.'

'We'd blame the dragon,' I complete.

'Cat didn't commit suicide, Wendy,' Lily tells me. 'Don't let anyone tell you she did. She was a victim of suicide.'

'It's not selfish to be a victim,' I say, understanding.

Lily places a hand on my shoulder, the contact grounds me. It makes our meeting feel real. It makes me feel less alone.

Misery really does love company.

'What's "ideation"?' Even though I'm heartbroken, I still hear the unfamiliar word and want to collect it.

'It means to have ideas,' Lily says. 'Usually it's only used for the bad ones. It's a psychology term.'

'How do you know it?' I say, before realising it's rude to ask. All I know about Lily is that she owns a gallery, so I'm curious.

'Because not everyone who stands at the top of the mountain falls,' Lily tells me softly, 'but when people think they might, it's important they get help. Don't you agree?'

The memory of Kevin's voice taunts me: 'You're insane. Look at you. You're crazy.'

'I don't know,' I say to Lily, defensively.

'It was lovely to meet you at last, Wendy,' Lily says, 'I'm sorry it wasn't under happier circumstances.'

'Thank you,' I say, dropping my shields again. 'Thank you for talking to me.'

Lily smiles and turns to walk away.

'The painting,' I say, and Lily turns back to me. 'Will the auction still happen?'

'Do you think she'd want it to?' Lily asks.

'I think it would be really, incredibly important to her that it does,' I reply.

'I agree,' Lily says. 'I plan to push the event back a little, as a mark of respect, and her mum will have to give permission as well of course, but yes, if I have a say in it, the auction will go ahead.'

'I'll be there,' I say.

'I know you will,' Lily says.

'You're really nice,' I say. 'When I pictured you, Lily Caplan the big successful gallery owner, I thought you'd be…'

'A bitch?' Lily asks.

'Umm. Yes. Yeah, I guess so.'

'Well, that would depend who you ask,' Lily says warmly,

then she's gone.

I'll never know for sure what happened to Cat. What I do know is how she'd like me to picture it. I know that she liked my stories.

I see her, a knight, dressed in resplendent armour, her sword keen and ornate.

She climbs the mountain. It's so steep the trees themselves lean forward to keep their balance, their moss-covered roots erupt from the precipitously tilted ground like exposed veins.

The rain comes, angered that soon it will be forced to wash away the evidence of a fierce battle. It falls in heavy sheets. From Cat's armour emanates a cacophony as each drop hits the metal.

She pushes on to the summit. She won't be slowed.

Finally, she reaches her destination. Forked lighting cracks and her silhouette is exposed onto the night sky like film. She's not alone up there. Red eyes open, each as big as her. Black scales glisten. Standing stone teeth adorn a cavernous maw. Canvas wings beat in slow motion, sloshing torrents of rainwater with every extension. Fire burns in a colossal gullet.

Cat isn't frightened by the dragon's fierce visage. She's met it many times before.

With mercurial speed, and pinpoint accuracy, she thrusts towards the beast. She knows there is a weak spot between two of its gargantuan scales.

Her sword finds its mark; the creature howls.

The dragon falls from the sky. As it plummets a serpentine tail flicks with a vicious bullwhip crack. Cat, hit with such force that her thick armour is useless, is thrown from the peak. A bold and brave knight who fought to the very last second.

Cat falls.

She didn't jump. She was pushed.

I'm not angry with her any more. I'm proud. Not that she fell, but that she did all the incredible things she did in her life while the whole time fighting a dragon that no one else could see. I'm proud of everything she was, before the dragon made her its victim. She faced it every day and won every single battle. Every battle except the last.

She was brave.

No knight could have been braver.

34

Forgiveness

I wake up every morning and I think 'I can do something today.'

Then a voice in my head tells me, 'No, you can't. Today you'll do nothing.'

I give in to it, every time. It's right. It's too soon for me to do anything. I don't know if it will ever have been long enough.

I wander around the house feeling itchy, as though there's somewhere I ought to be even though there isn't. After a few hours I start to worry that the way I'm stalking the halls of our little home is annoying my gran, though she'd never say so, so I let her know I'm going to go for a walk. She wants to ask if I'm alright. I can see the words huddled behind her teeth trying to force their way out, but she knows that I'm not, so she's holding them back. She wants to make everything better, but she can't, and I feel so guilty for that. Instead she says, 'Take care, darling.'

There's a chill in the air but it's a nice day. I resent it. It's cruel of the world to continue like normal.

I see Cat walking ahead of me. I recognise her hair just like I did when I saw her through the shop window. But it's not her. I see her again and again, but it's never her, and it never will be. I can't stand the hundred little hopes and heartbreaks so I put my head down and don't look at anyone. It's one straight road from my house into town and I don't remember a single step of it when I tune back in forty minutes later walking up Jamaica street.

There's a building on Jamaica street made mostly from glass. It was an architectural landmark when it was built way back in the eighteen hundreds, but now it's a sad, soulless chain pub. There's a man standing outside the front door.

Kevin.

He's dressed smartly, which I guess must mean today is a weekday. He's scrolling his phone in one hand, and with the other he's taking a draw from a cigarette.

'Isn't it addictive?' I remember him saying to me.

I stop, hearing my shoe squeak like a basketball player who's suddenly changed direction. I want to cross the road but it's too busy, and I didn't spot him until I was so close that all he has to do is look up and…

'Wendy?'

Shit.

'I didn't know you smoked,' I say with all the venom I can muster. I'm surprised to hear my words come out more hollow than confrontational.

'Well, my manager does so…' Kevin says, as though it explains everything. I suppose, in a way, it does.

'Yeah,' I say, with my hands deep in my pockets.

'So, how're things, how're you and your friend? Cat, was it?'

'Fine,' I lie. There's nothing Kevin has to say about Cat that I want to hear. I don't want his sympathy or his insincerity. He doesn't get to know. He doesn't get to know anything about me any more.

'Did you ever find a job?' he asks.

On days like today the pub puts tables outside so people can enjoy the weather. I pick up a pint glass, dregs of lager sloshing at the bottom, and I smash it directly into Kevin's eye.

No.

I don't.

'Not yet,' I say.

'Look, I wanted to say...' Kevin begins, but he's interrupted by someone calling his name.

'You're a totally new kind of social smoker, aren't you? One who smokes alone,' she says, not seeing me at first. 'Nice of you to tell me you were going out for one.'

Freya. Of course Freya's here. Until recently, I'd always thought that Kevin was the one who made university bearable when Freya was making it terrible, that he was the one who had my back. Now all I can picture is him and Freya in bed together, laughing.

'Oh. Wendy,' she says, noticing me. She seems uncomfortable. Good.

'So,' I say, 'do you work together now? Is Freya your new "colleague"?'

If Kevin gave me the application form then he gave it to Freya too; he'd have hedged his bets. As it turns out, he was always hedging his bets.

'I didn't actually get the job,' Freya replies. 'Some guy did.'

'Well, that's shit, isn't it?' I say, without sympathy.

'Yeah, it is,' she says. 'I'm sure you'd have done much better. Only, my mistake, didn't you apply too?'

'Nope.'

'Listen to you two, getting along," Kevin says.

I grab his lapels. He's stronger than me, but I've surprised him and he's off balance. I push as hard as I can and he stumbles into the road directly in the path of the number 38 bus.

No.

I don't.

Stop it.

'There'll be other openings,' Kevin has the audacity to comfort Freya in front of me. 'You'll come out on top.'

'You won't,' I say. 'You can't. There's no winning. Either you do what makes you happy and die of starvation, or you forget your dreams and make money so you can enjoy life when you're eighty and you can't remember the thing that made you happy in the first place.'

Maybe I'm over simplifying, or being cynical, but I'm not in the mood for nuance just now.

'Wow,' says Freya. 'I can see you're still fun at parties, Wendy.'

'Parties? You mean sad binge-drinking sessions where you try to forget your shitty lives?'

'Christ almighty, Wendy,' Kevin says, positioning himself between me and Freya as though he thinks I'm Chloe and I'm about to punch her.

'Sorry – bad form,' I say, and Kevin's expression sours, hearing me use the phrase he'd banned.

'My life isn't shitty,' Freya says, quietly. She's not the same as she was. She looks as though the world is a bad joke told at her expense. I feel a twang of guilt.

'Maybe it's not,' I concede.

In first year Freya was horrible, but it was manageable – it was just a mean comment here and there. Second year, when Kevin and I started getting together, is when it all got out of control.

'Freya,' I ask, 'did you know that Kevin was sleeping with me from second year?'

'Wendy, for God's sake, do we have to do this here?' Kevin demands.

I completely ignore him and focus on Freya.

'I didn't know for sure,' says Freya, 'but I suspected.'

'I didn't know about you,' I admit. 'I didn't even suspect until about fourth year.'

'Right. Enough.' Kevin puts his foot down. 'I won't have my personal life discussed in the middle of the bloody street, thanks.'

'Let's go inside then,' I say, and I kick him in the centre of his chest. He falls backwards through the nineteenth-century glass front of the pub, landing bleeding on a bed of sharp shards and generic beer-stained carpet.

No.

Tell the truth.

'What were you about to say, Kevin?' I ask.

'When? I wasn't about to say anything.'

'Just before Freya came outside, you started to say something.'

'It's not important,' Kevin says.

'It sounded like it was,' I press. 'You said, "Listen, I wanted to say…" So? What did you want to say?'

Kevin sighs.

'Sorry. Okay? I was going to say I was sorry.' It's a top

contender for worst apology of the year.

'For what?' I ask, pointedly.

'The things I said.'

'What things?'

'You know, the names I called you.'

'What names?'

Kevin falls silent.

'What's the matter? You're too polite to say them now?' I ask.

'I'm sorry for how I treated you,' would be a perfectly reasonable thing for Kevin to say, but to my surprise it's Freya who says it.

'Exactly,' Kevin says lamely, like someone who didn't buy a gift but wants to put their name on the card.

They've apologised. Both of them. I never thought they would. This could be closure. This could be a fresh start.

'So?' says Kevin, awkwardly.

Without another word I start to walk away. They owed me an apology. That doesn't mean I owe them forgiveness.

'Classy – you're just going to walk away without saying anything?' Kevin shouts after me.

Fine. If he wants me to say something, I will. But not to him.

'Freya,' I say, turning around, 'we never would have been friends, but we didn't have to be enemies. Kevin gaslit us, played with our insecurities, and made us hate each other. *He* did it. I don't like you, but you can do so much better than this prick.'

I don't wait for either of them to answer, I turn and walk away again with my heart racing.

Bitch. That's what he'd called me.

I guess that would depend who you ask.

35

Tigerlily Arts

I'm relieved when Cat's mum gives her permission for the auction to go ahead. I was worried she'd decide it wasn't appropriate. I appreciate Lily so much; she delays the whole event for weeks so that Cat's art can be part of it.

Lily's gallery is called Tigerlily Arts, and it's in the West End, tucked away in the warren of streets that act as short cuts between Byres Road and Great Western Road. As a Strathclyde uni alumna I feel like an undercover spy. This is Glasgow University turf. When I arrive at the gallery Lily is stage-managing a crew of constantly disappearing and reappearing staff, giving them new jobs as soon as they pass into her line of sight, which they hurry off to complete without complaining. She gives me an efficient wave when she sees me.

It was hard to come here alone. It's a place I've never been, full of people I've never met, doing a thing I've never done before. I spent days building up the courage, and at least fifteen minutes on the bus here trying to come up with a plan about where I would stand during the auction, and another fifteen rehearsing conversations in case anyone spoke to me. Even though it scares me, there was no question whether I was coming. Nothing would have kept me away.

The auction hasn't started yet. Everyone is milling around looking at the art displayed on walls and plinths. Sleeping Beauty, the security guard, sleeps at his small desk by the front door with his hat tipped over his eyes. Immaculately dressed staff with trays offer complimentary wine and canapés. There are a few people in groups of two or three quietly talking. The hushed purr of polite conversations sounds like dry leaves pushed across a path by the wind.

I amble slowly around the gallery, passing time. I don't know anything about feng shui, but I feel like this gallery has *good flow*. It's basically just a big empty room. Without good guidance it would be overwhelming, but I'm aware I'm being gently guided around a circuit by unassuming freestanding divider walls. They don't force you down a set route – it's not Ikea – but they suggest what order to look at things in. Smaller less heavy works of art like charcoal or pencil drawings are hung on the moveable divider walls, so they aren't just crowd control but part of the exhibition in their own right.

I examine paintings, getting lost in the huge number of different art styles that modern day artists can choose from. Some are disturbing, some provocative, some beautiful. These walls are covered in captured human emotions. For every feeling I've ever had there's a painting here that seems to say 'I've felt it too; don't worry'.

There's mystery as well: each work of art has a secret hidden in it somewhere that only the artist will ever really understand, but that you can sense, like a name on the tip of your tongue.

Being here, in a place Cat loved, and surrounded by the thing she loved, feels like a better way to remember her than her funeral did.

At the far end of the gallery are the paintings that are going to be auctioned today. It's a very savvy strategy – making people walk the whole length of your collection before being able to see the art that they're there to bid on. The crowd is a bit thicker here. Lots of the paintings have tight clusters of people grouped around them, scrutinising the items they might soon be trying to win, or flicking through catalogues that give more information about each lot. I squeeze through as politely as possible to get my first glimpse at Cat's painting.

I don't need the small plaque on the frame to tell me which one is hers, or even to tell me what the painting is called. I recognise Cat's painting immediately, because it's a painting from my own imagination. It feels as though it's singing to me.

In a lagoon that at high tide opens out to a sea of a thousand islands, two figures bask, marooned on a rock. Their scaled tails refract the light of the sun prismatically, making their whole lower halves radiate rainbows. On the tidal shore behind them the skeletal remains of ships rot in the sun, their broken bows looking forlornly towards the clear, cloudless sky. The figures' eyes follow me, inviting me in, irresistibly, insisting that they are true and the real world only a dream. Their mouths, slightly ajar, are the source of their soundless arias. I can hear them, though they are nothing more than an arrangement of pigments. I can feel them beckon me, even though they're only a deliberately placed series of blemishes on a canvas. In the corner of the image there is a small shape against the sun, almost imperceptible. A winged man, hidden like an Easter egg.

'The Mermaids,' I gasp out loud, startling the people on either side of me.

'I think you'll like it,' Cat's memory echoes from our final night.

'You were right,' I say, quietly.

Cat has taken a silly bit of plot from a dumb story I made up and made it real. It's exactly like I'd imagined it. I feel like I'm Mr Huge. *The Mermaids* is one of the most beautiful things I've ever seen.

I see her signature in the bottom corner and I have a sudden need to touch it. I want to trace the letters, but I resist. I don't want to be thrown out before the auction begins.

A white cover flaps over the painting. I jump in surprise.

'Sorry,' a small lady in Tigerlily Art's chic uniform says. Her name badge tells me she's called Maimie. 'I didn't mean to scare you. We're covering up the pieces because the auction is starting soon. There was an announcement.'

'No, no, don't apologise,' I say. 'I didn't hear – I was a million miles away.'

'You like this one?' Maimie asks.

'I love it,' I say.

'Do you think you'll buy it?'

'Oh no,' I shake my head. 'It's worth a lot more than I can afford. I'm just here to see it go to a good home.'

'Friend of the artist?'

'That's right.'

'Well, they're very talented,' Maimie says, covering up the remaining works.

'Thank you,' I say.

'You better go find a seat. They'll be starting soon, and I think your friend's one is up first.'

The narrow divider walls have been cunningly rearranged into a temporary room. Inside the pop-up auction house, foldout chairs have been put in rows pointing towards a raised stage. On the stage there is a podium, an empty easel, and a man I guess must be the bid caller fussing with his suit.

Some people are taking their seats. They must be observers like me, because the people who want to bid on lots are registering with a stern-looking gentleman at a desk who hands them paddles with numbers on them.

I did some reading, and usually new art is commissioned for a set price or put on sale with a specific price tag. This auction is set up to draw out people who have money to spend and are willing to fight with each other over who gets to spend the most, all in aid of a charity. It's a way for rich people to show off how much richer they are than their friends, while also feeling virtuous. It's smart.

Little Panther's tribe like wearing black and hiding in basements. The Tigerlily Arts tribe at the auction are as far from them as you could imagine. The bidders, holding their paddles like duelling gloves, are dressed in bright coats, silk clothes, and expensive jewellery. It's not so much that everyone is very fashionable; it's more that everyone is very noticeable. They're shamelessly eccentric. They let their expressions talk a lot louder than most people would. Mouths pucker in distaste or eyes roll at the sight of anyone they don't like. I feel like I've stepped into a period drama. Cat would have loved this.

They say money can't buy happiness and, based on the faces of most of the people here, it seems they're right.

One man in particular has really made some striking choices. It's hard to say how old this guy is for sure. His slicked-back hair is such a dark black that, where the light hits it, it looks almost blue. He has a carefully styled Salvador Dalí moustache twisted at the ends. His face is a toolbox: gimlet eyes, chisel jaw, scalpel-sharp cheekbones. His mouth looks like it's never formed a smile. His shirt is fashionably baggy, and tucked into his trousers, which are too tight. His boots have been left carefully unbuckled.

He has quite a lot of people with him. Each of them sometimes acts like a trusted grand vizier or, a few seconds later, like a simpering sycophantic henchman. I wonder if some of them are personal security guards, but I can't figure out why he'd need security here.

The thing that brings his whole outfit together is a tattered, vintage, floor-length coat. I've never seen a coat of that length made from such a bright fabric.

Who would come to an auction wearing a coat made of red velvet?

36

Dark and Sinister Man

'Honoured guests, welcome to Tigerlily Arts,' the bid caller begins. He tells us about how the auction will work. It sounds like it's going to go exactly like people imagine an auction should go, which, in reality, probably isn't how *real* auctions run but is likely to be exciting, and what better way to separate rich people from their money? It's all for a good cause.

He also tells us what the good cause is. It's a suicide prevention charity. This must have meant a lot to Cat. She was fighting so hard.

'Lot number one,' the bid caller announces, after his introduction, 'is the first piece painted by a promising young artist...'

He goes on with the introduction to Cat's painting, but he keeps talking about her like she's still alive. Does he even know? It's the reason the auction was postponed – surely he *has to* know? I look around for Lily, but she must be off gracefully fighting a fire. Cat isn't promising; her promise was stolen. These people need to know that this was the last thing she ever did, and how important it is. I'm wound up by his incompetence. My hackles rise.

The Mermaids is brought to the easel and unveiled.

'I have a commission bid at five hundred pounds,' the bid caller says. I'm not sure what a commission bid is, but five hundred pounds is way too low. It's insulting.

Calm down Wendy.

It's only the first bid.

'Will anyone make an advancement on five hundred pounds?' the bid caller asks.

A paddle comes up a few rows ahead of me.

'Seven hundred and fifty with the lady in the fifth row,' the caller acknowledges.

Almost immediately another paddle goes up.

'One thousand pounds with the gentleman on my left,' the caller says.

I realise that it's like a game of cards. The man who quickly jumped in with a bid of one thousand has a bad poker face. Now everyone can just sit back and wait for him to bid until he hits his limit, then they can either swoop in or decide not to. There's no risk to them as long as these two are upping the ante between them.

If the bids are only going up two hundred and fifty pounds at a go it's going to take a very long time before anyone reaches a figure even close to what *The Mermaids* is worth. I wonder if the auction is rigged so that eventually someone will burst through the door (or in this case, burst through the gap between the temporary walls) and make a huge bid, while people gasp and faint, and their monocles fall out.

The lady who lifted her paddle first comes back and increases the number to one thousand two hundred and fifty. The man who seemed too keen counters, which brings us up to one thousand five hundred. First Paddle retaliates, Keen Man doesn't back down. Now we're at two thousand.

First Paddle bows out.

I look scornfully at the back of her head. If she was going to drop out at just two thousand then why did she bother to get involved in the first place? Did she honestly believe she'd be able to take Cat's painting home for so little?

I'm getting a bit carried away. Two thousand pounds is a stupidly large amount of money – way more than I could afford. Five hundred was way more than I could afford, but it's all about context, isn't it? One hundred pounds for a packet of crisps is too much. One hundred thousand pounds for a work of art that will become the next *Red Vineyards Near Arles* is a bargain.

Keen Man looks smug and the caller fiddles with his gavel, pretending that he thinks two grand is the winning bid. As Keen Man leans backwards, resting on his laurels, I see another paddle smoothly rise a few rows behind him. One uncommitted bidder has been taken out of the game already. Now the sharks start to circle.

Speaking of sharks, the lady who made the latest bid has a really interesting poker face. Most people try to stay neutral and hide every little micro-expression. This lady has decided to pick one strong emotion and stick with it. She grins an unsettling sharky grin.

'Two Thousand, two hundred and fifty now,' announces the caller, 'with the lady near the back.'

Keen Man never saw it coming. He's snatched defeat from

the jaws of victory. He has the guile to take a quick look over his shoulder, which even I can tell isn't appropriate.

'Sir?' asks the bid caller.

'Yes, yes,' Keen Man replies irritably, raising his paddle.

'Two thousand five hundred,' the caller confirms. 'Madam?'

Shark Smile flicks her paddle like an itchy fin, her lips never covering her gums.

'Two thousand seven hundred and fifty,' the caller notes. 'Sir?'

Keen Man is livid. He gives Shark Smile a snarky glare before shaking his head at the bid caller.

Shark Smile thinks she's won. That's when a gentleman in a tartan flat cap proves her wrong with a confidently displayed paddle.

My pulse is racing. It's like when Cat and I ran away from Pixie Cove. I'm exhilarated. I don't think I could be more nervous, even if it were my own painting.

The caller refers back to Shark Smile, but before she can raise her bid, she's interrupted by the introduction of a new paddle.

'A new bidder. We're on three thousand two hundred and fifty with the man in the red coat,' the caller updates.

It's Red Velvet. His little entourage scowl around the room. There's a dip in the mood. The wind has been taken out of the sails of all the other bidders. It's not like they're frightened of him exactly. It's more like he's the kid in the park who owns the football and he's going home, even if that means everyone else's fun is over. I get the impression that Red Velvet might have so much wealth, power, influence – or a combination of the three – that everyone knows bidding against him is pointless.

'Any advance on three thousand, two hundred and fifty pounds?' the bid caller asks, but he knows it's all over. 'No? Going once…'

I don't think anyone is going to burst through the door after all. Soon Red Velvet will own *The Mermaids*.

For only three thousand, two hundred and fifty pounds.

He'll own more than a painting, though. He'll own countless hours of practice and self-doubt and learning. He'll own bouts of hopelessness and heights of ecstasy. He'll own a snippet of a dream and a snapshot of a mind. He'll own her sleepless nights, her fingernails covered in crusted paint, and her hands too tired to bend. A masterpiece, a swan song, everything that's left of her. He's behaving as though all he's paying for is the canvas. What he's buying is a life.

'Folk don't think about that stuff,' Cat's memory reminds me.

'Going twice,' the bid caller's gavel is raised.

'It's not enough,' I say out loud.

Red Velvet's head snaps around. He fixes his eyes on me and, with a voice rich with threat, he says, 'Bad form.'

If he'd said I was being rude, he may have shamed me into silence. He didn't. He used that cute little two-word reprimand I trot out much too often to remind myself to be seen and not heard. I've always tried my best to live my life without upsetting people, but now I realise that some people deserve to be upset.

'Fair warning,' the bid caller goes through the motions.

I'm sure that Red Velvet knows *The Mermaids* is priceless. He knows that his clout will let him buy it for a pittance and sell it on for a fortune. He wants to undervalue her for his own benefit. He wants to steal her. He's a thief. He's a pirate. He's a bully.

'Sold, to the man in the red coat for three thousand, two hundred and fifty pounds,' the bid caller says, rapping his gavel.

Felicia Malcolm was a bully, Lindsay at Chay Turley was too, and Freya, the boys in the car, and so many others. I hate bullies. Cat wouldn't have needed me to stand up for her – Cat could stand up for herself – but Cat isn't here.

Before I talk myself out of it I'm not just on my feet, but standing on the chair.

Despite all the words I've tried to learn, all jotted down in my notepad. Now I use one of the simplest, one of the first words any baby learns. It may not be the most flowery, but it's the purest. As loud as I can I shout:

'No!'

37

The Heist

I sprint down the aisle between the rows of seats. The bid caller stumbles backwards in a panic. To him I'm not a girl, I'm a bear. I jump onto the stage, knocking over his silly podium as I pass. I grab *The Mermaids*. It's heavier than I'd expected.

Everyone is still. No one is sure whether this is meant to be happening.

'Stop her,' the caller shouts in exasperation. He's the closest to me but must still be afraid I'll bite.

The auction erupts into movement. People in the front rows start coming towards me. People near the back start taking out their phones, either to call the police or to film it all for social media. Red Velvet's crew get to their feet and start advancing threateningly. Any one of them could probably lift me up with one arm. Red Velvet himself stays in his seat, glowering at me with undisguised hatred.

I jump from the stage holding *The Mermaids* in a death grip.

I run towards the gap between the walls that acts as a door. Gallery staff and auction goers realise there's only one way out and huddle in front of it, blocking my way. I dart and dodge and then change direction. If I can't use the door, then I'll have to make one.

I run full-speed directly towards one of the freestanding divider walls. I hope they're less sturdy than they look. I want to hit it with as much force and momentum as possible, so when my brain starts screaming to me to slow down, I do the opposite. I jump into the air, and I hit the wall with the full force of my flying body. The whole thing collapses.

My left arm takes most of impact. It hurts like hell. I'm sure I'll have a very impressive bruise.

I remember Cat and I standing on the concert hall steps releasing balloons and me telling Cat that it was technically littering.

'Add it to the rap sheet,' Cat had said.

I start to tally up the rap sheet.

Littering: a fine of up to one hundred and fifty pounds.

Cannabis possession: up to five years in prison.

Running off without paying at a restaurant: up to two years in prison and a fine up to one thousand pounds.

All of that is small potatoes next to the consequences of stealing a priceless work of art. For that I'm looking at up to eight years in prison and a fine of about seven hundred thousand pounds.

It's adding up really fast. I'm not even out of the gallery yet.

I pick myself up and start to run again, the horde at my heels.

I can't just run outside with the painting uncovered, I'd be too conspicuous. Leading the pack behind me in a wide loop

I circle back towards the area where the lots were displayed before the auction. I see the lots that haven't been called are still on the table. I snatch a dust cover from one of the waiting paintings. As the artwork underneath is revealed an out-of-body part of myself thinks, 'that's pretty'.

Petty theft of a dust cover: up to six months in prison.

I veer in the direction of the front door, which is still the entire length of the gallery away from me. I'm bundling *The Mermaids* in the dust cover as I go. I run as fast as I can, but I can hear people gaining on me. I move close to one of the freestanding walls, grab the edge, and tip it over. It falls into the group who were directly behind me. It's not heavy enough to do any real harm, but it slows them down. Drawings scatter across the floor.

About six counts of assault: up to three years in prison.

Vandalism: up to three months in prison or a two-and-a-half-thousand-pound fine.

With the seconds I've bought myself I'm brave enough to look around me. I'm trying to find an escape route.

To my right I see Lily Caplan standing at a door, dumbstruck by the scene in front of her. Behind me, past the crowd chasing me, stands Red Velvet, adjusting the cuff of his hideous coat without taking his eyes off me. To the left nothing but a wall – a real brick wall; not one of the collapsible kind.

Still running full-pelt through the gallery, I turn my eyes forward again. Sleeping Beauty, the security guard, has woken up. Now that the time comes to do his job, he's ready to act. I shouldn't have doubted his professionalism. I've noticed him too late and I've built up too much momentum, I careen into him before I can stop myself. My lip impacts with the radio on his lapel and it bursts open. Blood sprays everywhere, but that's the least of my worries. Sleeping Beauty has tumbled backwards down the marble staircase that leads to the gallery's exit.

As he tumbles, I update the rap sheet in terror.

Manslaughter: a life sentence in prison, and a life sentence haunted by guilt.

He lands. He gets up. He brushes himself off, wincing.

Oh, thank God; just another assault charge. Six months. I barrel past him and out into the street.

Most of the people still chasing me are distracted by the injured security guard. I manage to outrun the others once we get outside. I wipe the blood from my lip with the back of my hand, it doesn't stop my lip bleeding, but now I also have a bloody hand. I see a police car coming towards me with its sirens wailing. I slow to a walk.

'Real casual like,' says Cat's memory in a cowboy drawl.

The car whizzes past me.

Evading arrest: is that a crime here? I don't think it is, but I'm not sure. That's Americanisation for you.

Oh, I'm in trouble. I really am. I'm in trouble.

I have to get as far from here as possible. I stop at a cash machine and withdraw twenty pounds. I'm about to wave down a taxi when I see a man a few feet behind me that I think I recognise.

He's not chasing me. He's acting completely casually. He's wearing shades of beige. Didn't I see him in the gallery?

I'm not sure.

I think so. I think I did.

If he was there why isn't he chasing me? Unless he's following me?

The gallery staff wouldn't follow me; they'd catch me and

stop me. The police wouldn't follow me; they'd arrest me. If I'm being followed it's not just by someone who wants to catch me, it's by someone who wants to find out where I'm going so they can get their revenge and get the painting without being seen.

He's one of Red Velvet's men. He must be.

I have to be sure. I walk away at a brisk pace. I make the first left turn. When I glance over my shoulder, he's taken the same turn as I have. I turn right, so does he. I make another left, he turns the corner a few seconds after me. I walk faster, so does he. I slow down, so does he.

I wonder if this is how Cat felt when I followed her. I remember how she'd confronted me, waiting around a corner for me to turn it.

I try to move unexpectedly. I break into a run, hoping it will catch him off guard.

As I run down the street, with the painting in my arms and blood on my face, I can see that dark creature in the corner of my eye run along beside me on spindly legs. It's shadowy head has unhinged at the jaw; the top half bounces and lolls as it runs, while its throat gurgles with laughter.

I run to the next turn in the road. Around the corner I find there's a small bin waiting by the kerb – the kind you use to put food waste in. I lift it up. It's heavy, probably filled with moulding onion skins and pepper cores.

I expect him to come running after me, scared that he's lost me, but he's just walking. As he turns the corner, I swing the bin filled with rotting leftovers.

It impacts with his nose with a hollow thump. He falls to the ground. He's nose is bleeding. I drop the bin. I pick up *The Mermaids* from the wall I'd leaned it against, and I start running before he can get back to his feet.

When I got a proper look at him, lying on the ground with blood streaming from his nose, he didn't look that familiar at all.

I can't deal with that right now.

Another assault: another six months in prison.

That brings my total up to just short of twenty years, and a fine of seven hundred thousand pounds and change.

I wave down a taxi.

'You alright, hen?' the driver asks. 'You're bleeding a bit.'

I laugh brightly.

'I know, I'm so clumsy. It's this thing.' I lift the painting. 'It's so awkward. I tripped carrying it and did *this* to myself. That's when I decided I should probably get a lift.'

'You've made the right choice there, hen,' the driver says. 'Want me to stick it in the boot for you.'

'No,' I reply, trying not to bark the word. 'I'll keep it with me.'

'You're the boss,' he says with raised hands.

I step hastily into the back of the taxi.

'So, where to, doll?' the driver asks, then with a hearty laugh suggests, 'I'll drop you at the hospital. They can fix your broken face?'

'No, thank you.' I don't think it's very funny.

'I'm just kidding on; you look great. Honestly. Beautiful. You'd hardly notice it,' he goes on. He's looking at me too much. I'm worried he'll remember me if the police track him down – or worse, if Red Velvet tracks him down. I think about getting out.

Out of the front windscreen I see the man in beige jog along the street looking around in dazed confusion. He's looking for me.

I give the driver my gran's address.

'Right you are, hen,' he agrees.

I sink down in my seat as the taxi pulls out – the heist Cat and I always daydreamed about now a horrible reality.

38

To Fight and to Fly

All of the last chapter was true.

I actually did those things. I can hardly believe it myself.

There are things I regret. I didn't want to hurt anyone – not Beige Man, Sleeping Beauty, or any of the people caught in the wake of my rampage. I didn't want to disappoint anyone – not Lily Caplan, Detectives Davies or Llewelyn, or my gran.

I regret hitting that wall so hard with my left arm. I'm beginning to wonder if I've fractured it. It hurts when I move it now.

I regret not seeing the dragon Cat was fighting, grabbing a sword and shield, and fighting it with her.

Wait. What's that?

There are voices outside. I can hear men talking. They've found me.

I'm still in the old abandoned garage that I decided to hide in. I'm on the overhead walkway I told you about. I've pulled the ladder part of the way up. I'm huddled under a bundle of old sheets. They smell of damp and mildew.

There's no reason anyone would be interested in this run-down old building. The only reason anyone would be here is to catch me. How did they track me down? I worked really hard on not being followed. They won't take long to find me once they come in. I don't have much time.

Tick-tock, tick-tock.

Look there are lots of things I regret, but there are some I don't.

I don't regret stealing the painting; Red Velvet didn't deserve it. I don't regret standing up for myself and standing up for Cat.

Mostly, I don't regret meeting Cat. I've never been so sad, I've never been so angry, and I've never felt so lost, I'm in agony because she's gone, but if I could trade the pain of losing Cat and instead never have known her, I wouldn't. I wouldn't trade my time with Cat for anything.

I wish I could cry for her. I wish I could cry for you, Cat. My heart's broken, but I can't cry.

The door just opened. They're inside. They'll find me soon.

That's okay. Maybe I'll be arrested, but at least I got to have one last adventure with Cat. We had our heist. There wasn't any safety harness.

It was worth it.

The men are getting closer. They're moving around down in the garage below me. I thought this hiding place was so ingenious – there's only one entrance so I can easily see anyone who comes in, which I thought would be safer because there'd be no chance anyone could sneak up on me. If I'd thought it through just a little longer I would have spotted the obvious flaw: only one entrance means there's only one exit, and they're between me and it. There's no way I'd get past them unnoticed carrying a big framed painting.

Oh my God…why didn't I take the painting out of the frame? I…

I'm pretty annoyed with myself right now.

If television shows have taught me anything about being arrested and interrogated it's this: by tomorrow, I'll have told this story a hundred times, and each repeat will be more like a copy of a copy of an old VHS tape. I wanted to write this confession before I started to forget, or give into the temptation to lie about what I've done.

To lie more than I have.

The two men are directly below me now. One is asking the other why the ladder has been pulled up. The other is telling him there's a pole somewhere to pull it down with. They'll find me in minutes.

Thank you for staying with me. Thank you for reading this. I hope you don't hate me.

I have to come down to earth now.

I have to give *The Mermaids* back.

…

Do I, though? Am I caught for certain?

No.

They can't have it.

They've underestimated me. You see, there's only two of them. If they plan to take Cat away from me then they should have brought an army. I've let her be taken away from me once; I'm never letting it happen again. I'll fight if I have to. They can't have her.

It's strange to write this down as it happens, but Cat's here.

She's under this camouflage with me, or at least, her memory is. She's smiling, she's saying:

'Think happy thoughts.'

Simple as that?

'Simple as that.'

If you're reading this, then maybe I *am* already dead, but I went out in a blaze of glory, like Liberty on the barricades, like a knight, like a daedalist.

'Ready?' Cat's memory is asking.

Okay, I'm in.

Epilogue

Words

I just found this again. I was going through my things to put them in boxes and it turned up, so I've spent the last few hours reading it. At first it was just procrastination – reading this was better than packing. Then the memories drew me in. I left you on a bit of a cliff-hanger, didn't I?

I've decided I should tell you what happened. If this *is* found fossilised in the year 3020, I don't want people to think I died fighting a criminal gang. I didn't.

I've got a little bit of time just now, and a pen, and there are enough empty pages at the back of this dog-eared pad not filled up with my unusual word collection, my poems, or my confession, that I can finish the story. Let me fill you in. Let me take you back to that garage where I was trapped. Let's go back to my last stand.

The two men have found the pole. When the ladder is lowered,

I try to charge into battle. It's harder than I expect: people don't often charge down ladders and if they do, they don't do it carrying a framed picture.

The men jump back. I take a stand in front of them, wild-eyed, my head snapping back and forth as I try to look at them both at once.

'Why are you in my garage?' says one of the men.

He's not a police officer, he's not one of Red Velvet's crew, he's just the owner of the garage.

That's when I cry. At last, finally, I cry. All the adrenaline and fear and sadness is released. I drop the painting. I drop to my knees, and I sob.

'What happened? Are you alright?'

I struggle to get myself under control. After a while I manage to tell them I have to go home. The owner of the garage offers me a lift, which I turn down. He seems unsure whether he ought to let this weeping, dirty, blood-stained, ridiculously dressed girl just walk away, but he can't really stop me.

I walk back to my gran's house. When I get there, Detective Davies is sitting at the living room table. My gran is there with him. She's given him a cup of tea.

'I'm sorry,' I say as I walk through the door.

My gran hugs me like I'm a runaway teenager and not a criminal.

'There, there. It's alright, darling,' she says.

'We thought you might come back here,' Davies says, as though explaining why he has tea and biscuits.

I pull myself together as much as I can. I stand in front of Davies.

'I'd like to turn myself in, please,' I say.

Detective Davies stands.

'That's a very brave thing to do,' he says, gently.

'Don't be kind to me,' I insist.

Davies nods, agreeing not to be kind.

'Do you have the painting?' he asks.

'Yes,' I reply.

'I'll take it,' he says.

'Yes,' I reply again, quietly. 'And what about me?'

'Wendy,' Davies says, 'do you know the first thing the gallery curator said, before anything else – before she even knew the extent of the damage you may have done?'

I look at the floor. I have no idea what Lily might have said about me.

'She said, "I don't want to press charges".'

'No,' I argue. 'That's not fair. She has to.'

He doesn't understand, To let me off the hook is an insult to Cat. The people who stole *The Scream* from the Munch museum didn't just get a mild reprimand. If they finally tracked down the criminals who robbed the Isabella Stewart Gardner museum they wouldn't give them a warning and let them be on their way. If he treats this whole thing like it's not serious, then he's saying that Cat's work isn't important enough to be taken seriously. All this time I thought I was being chased, I'm scared to ask Detective Davies if I really was. If the police weren't chasing me, I'll be furious. It'll prove that they don't understand the value of Cat's work, or the value of Cat.

As well as that, I can't stop thinking about that poor man I hit in the face with a bin.

'So, you want to be punished?' Davies says.

'I deserve to be,' I reply, wilfully.

'You'll be happy to know, then,' Detective Davies replies,

'that the second thing the curator said was that she wants to talk to you in person when you turn up. So, don't think you're getting off lightly. I would rather spend a night or two in a cell than have to face her after causing such chaos in her gallery. You better start coming up with a strong apology.'

'I will.'

'Right, I'd best be off,' Davies says. 'Wendy, you'll be at the gallery at nine o'clock tomorrow morning. The curator will tell me if you aren't.'

I nod.

'Thank you, detective. It was nice chatting with you,' my gran says. Her voice is so comforting, it's good just to be around her again.

'Wendy,' Davies says as the door closes, 'I'm glad you're safe.'

I arrive at the gallery at eight in the morning. I didn't want to risk being late. I stand around dreading what's about to happen, like a kid waiting outside the headmaster's office.

Lily arrives at about half-past eight, with the keys to the gallery in her hand.

'Well,' she says, 'I suppose you'd better come in.'

Tigerlily Arts feels very empty compared to the mayhem of the last time I was here.

'I'm so sorry,' I begin.

'For all of it?' Lily interrupts, sharply. I almost agree automatically, but she's arched an eyebrow. She's reminding me that she only asks questions when she wants the truth.

'For most of it,' I say, cringing in case that's not the answer she had hoped for. I know it's another contender for worst apology of the year.

'You don't think Catriona would have liked the way the auction turned out if you hadn't intervened?' Lily asks.

'I don't think she would have wanted her last painting to be taken by that man,' I admit. I'm scared; I know Lily told me she values honesty, but saying you value honesty and actually valuing it are two different things.

Lily breathes in deeply through her nose.

'No,' she says at last. 'Nor do I.'

'You don't?' I reply, stunned.

'I've told the gentleman that he can't have the painting. Given the circumstances, he didn't have any objections. I've been wracking my brain and there's only one person I can think of that Cat would have wanted to have her last painting,' Lily goes on. 'You. She'd have wanted you to have it.'

'Me?'

'Here's my issue, Wendy,' Lily explains. 'I've paid Cat's family what they would have got from the sale of the painting, and I've made sure the charity got paid what they were owed too. I didn't think it was fair they have to wait any longer. That amounts to three thousand, two hundred and fifty pounds. So, I'm that much out of pocket. As well as that, the gentleman who bought the painting would have paid a commission price over and above that, which would have gone directly to the gallery. That would have amounted to hundreds of pounds. I can't just give you the painting. I'll need to be paid for it.'

I'm crushed.

'I can't afford that.'

'I didn't think you could,' Lily says, sternly, 'which is why I think it's only fair that I take a percentage from your wages until your debt is paid. Does that sound reasonable?'

'Yes,' I say immediately, grasping on to any chance there

may be that I could really take *The Mermaids* home with me.

But, hold on, I think I've missed something important.

'Wait, what did you say?'

'I liked Cat a great deal,' Lily says softly, 'and it's not just you that feels guilty that you didn't notice how much she was struggling. But I can see that *you* are struggling, Wendy. I might not have been smart enough, or perceptive enough, to help Cat, but I won't make the same mistake with the person who meant the most to her in the world. There's a job here for you, Wendy. If you'd like it.'

Then I cry *again*. A different kind of crying though. Tears of gratitude. Tears of hope.

Lily makes it really clear that the work will be hard. She explains that she expects a lot of her staff, and warns me not to let her down.

After a few days working there, she unveils her plans for a bare corner of the gallery. It's the spot where the auction was held, but now it stands empty. Soon it will be an exhibition of the works of a talented local artist taken from us too early. Cat's mum has already agreed. The finished paintings in Cat's flat will be displayed in Tigerlily Arts indefinitely, only to be sold at a worthy price, and to a buyer who can prove their love of them.

I start making money. My gran and I talk about things. With my earnings we can afford to move into a more modern house – one without stairs, and with the possibility of adding the odd mobility aid.

'I'm not getting any younger,' gran likes to tell me. I see the steel in her though: she's not getting any older either – not in any way that really matters.

We start looking into moving to a new house.

I write poetry on my lunch break and in the evenings. If I have performances to give or readings to do, Lily is happy to arrange my shifts around them, as long as I don't take the piss.

'Cat's mum was here,' Lily tells me one day. 'She thought this might be yours.'

Lily hands me a little, battered, creased, red notebook – the book of my poems I gave to Cat that day we sat in Queen's Park.

I remember how she'd pronounced it 'poyum'.

I don't know how I feel about it coming back to me at first; it's a reminder that she's gone. It turns out, though, that it hasn't come back to me exactly as it left. On the last page someone's written something. I'd recognise the handwriting anywhere, even though I've only seen it in one place before. It's the same as the signature in the corner of *The Mermaids*.

It's a message from Cat.

'I believe,' it says.

One last apology. This one is for you.

I know Cat's painting isn't really a priceless masterpiece. I'm sorry I let you think it was. I wasn't really lying to you though: I thought I was being honest. To me it *was* a priceless masterpiece.

To me, It still is.

A few months later I go to an appointment that I've known I ought to make for a long time.

A voice calls my name. I follow it from a neat waiting room into a private office.

As we both sit down on comfortable seats, the GP introduces

herself, 'I'm Doctor Moira; you can call me Angela. How can I help today, Wendy?'

I don't want to cause a fuss. I don't want to be overdramatic. I hesitate, and consider backing out, but I force myself to make a short, simple statement that might change my life: 'I think I might need help with my mental health.'

Angela reacts as though it's the most normal thing in the world. She asks me what's led me to feel I might need help, and asks me how my day-to-day life has been affected. She takes it all very seriously – more seriously than I'd expected, if I'm honest; I thought she'd be flippant or procedural, but she's warm, patient, and empathetic.

'Have you ever considered hurting yourself?' Angela asks.

'No, it's not like that. I don't get those feelings.'

'I hope you don't mind that I asked?'

'Not at all.'

I wish asking were more common. Asking is important.

'Am I crazy?' I say, terrified of the answer.

'No,' Angela smiles reassuringly.

'Are you *sure?*'

'I'm positive,' Angela says. 'And if anyone tells you any different you send them to me and I'll sort them out, alright?'

'Okay,' I laugh.

'It sounds to me like social anxiety for certain,' Angela says. 'And, I believe, also depression. Does that ring true?'

'It does.'

It's amazing the power a name has. The shadowy thing that has always been just out of sight can't keep hiding now that I know what its called. Social Anxiety and Depression are its names, and now I see it's not as big or as scary as I thought. When I look at it, it cowers like a scared mouse.

'So, there are a few options,' Angela tells me. 'One is medication. We can give you a thing called beta-blockers, which may help, and move on to other options from there. I think though, if you agree, the best option for you might be cognitive behavioural therapy.'

The thought of medication intimidates me, which I get is silly, because the thought of painkillers wouldn't intimidate me if I'd broken my arm.

'What's cognitive behavioural therapy?' I ask.

'I'll arrange some meetings for you, you'll talk to an expert who'll teach you some techniques for dealing with things, and that way you'll be more equipped if you have anxiety attacks or if you're just having a low day,' Angela explains.

'So, it's just talking to someone?' I say, relieved.

'That's right, and if it doesn't help you can come back to me and we can look at other options.'

'I'd like that,' I say, feeling lighter already.

It's words.

It always has been.

Words are the solution.

Thanks

I owe so much to so many people that I don't think I could cover it all here without doubling the length of this book. I'll try my best to be concise. Thank you:

To my parents, who read me bedtime stories until I decided I could write my own, and who have supported me in every possible way, constantly and unerringly, even though they knew the path I was choosing was hard. I am exceptionally lucky to have them.

To my siblings. My brother David who has spoken my words on many stages, my brother Rick who has collected everything I've ever written, my sister Lisa who has a strict rule that no one picks on her brothers (except her), and my sister's husband, my very old friend, Darren.

To my mother and father in-law who from the very start have shown limitless belief in me.

To my sister in-law Caitlin and her husband Gordon,

whose encouragement is sincere and heartfelt. To Caitlin and Gordon's sons, my nephews, Rory and Alfie who are a constant source of inspiration and joy.

To my oldest friends Neil and Charny who have always been there for me and who I will always be there for.

To my friends Karen, John, Gillian, and Alasdair who I often subject to the ragged and unfocused early drafts of the things I write and who I can always rely upon to be honest, but gentle.

To the friends who are such positive and warm influences on my life, such as: the Perfect Strangers – Ryan, Angela, and Natalie; the Old Coach House Gang – Adam, Alan, Emily, Kieran, Jen, and Robyn; Assorted Geeks and Goths of Fine Fettle – Des, Jolanta, Sophie, Euan, Ash, and Theresa; Hill Walkers, Dinner Partiers, and Rock Stars – Mika, Vaughn, Hannah, Letty, Becca, James, Alison, and Martyn; Everybody needs good neighbours – Stuart and Lindsay; and my bestie since college – Cat.

To Clare and Kirsty. The best part of a decade ago, when I first told the earliest version of this story, I wrote it as a play. Clare played Wendy in that play, and Kirsty painted the wonderful artwork that Wendy stole.

To my aunties, uncles, cousins, and other relatives who kindly follow my career.

To those of you who have helped me through the kind of mental health struggles that I write about in this book, or who have these struggles themselves. I don't want to name you all, because mental health still has such stigma attached to it, but thank you for letting me know I wasn't alone.

To Bramble, Corrie, Skye, and Molly. These are dogs, and I know dogs can't read. I'll read this out to Bramble when the book is released though, and I'd like to think that each dog's owner will do the same for them.

To the team at Lightning Books for taking on an author they'd never heard of and giving this book a chance to see the world.

To the people I admire who are more successful in the literary or creative world than I am, and who read the book and said such beautiful things about it ahead of publication.

Most importantly: to my wife Claire. She is unique in this world and her empathy is boundless. She believes in me always, and believes in me even more when I don't believe in myself. Though she'd hate for me to say she's perfect, with all the pressure and unattainable expectations that come along with that word, I can say that she's perfect *for me* and that I wouldn't be who I am without her.

And, finally, to the people I haven't thanked yet but who contributed to this book, directly or indirectly: it's a cop out to say 'you know who you are'. But *I* know who you are, and I appreciate you.

If you have enjoyed *The Tick and the Tock of the Crocodile Clock*, do please help us spread the word – by putting a review on Amazon (you don't need to have bought the book there) or Goodreads; by posting something on social media; or in the old-fashioned way by simply telling your friends or family about it.

Book publishing is a very competitive business these days, in a saturated market, and small independent publishers such as ourselves are often crowded out by the big houses. Support from readers like you can make all the difference to a book's success.

Many thanks.
Dan Hiscocks
Publisher
Lightning Books

Also published by Lightning Books

The Darlings

Angela Jackson

From the winner of the Edinburgh International Book Festival First Book Award

When Mark Darling is fifteen, he is the golden boy, admired by all who know him. Then he kills his best friend in a freak accident.

Years later, he bumps into an old schoolfriend, Ruby, who saw the accident first-hand. Mark is pulled towards her by a force stronger than logic. But can he leave behind the wife he loves? His unborn child?

The Darlings is a story about betrayal, infidelity and our own relationship to the truth.

Angela is a true writer and an extremely powerful voice
Bidisha

Eccentric...compelling...subtle... A dark, humorous novel in which a troubled man's crises have clear consequences
Foreword Reviews

It's brave to write a book that focuses on adultery, and even braver to tell it from the point of view of the adulterer but, without question, this will be one of my books of the year
Anne Williams

The Shifting Pools

Zoë Duncan

Fleeing war and the death of her family, Eve has carefully constructed a new life for herself.

Yet she is troubled by vivid, disturbing dreams, symptoms of her traumatic past, which intrude increasingly on her daily life. As she is drawn further into her dream world, she finds herself caught up in a fresh battle for survival.

The Shifting Pools is a dark, lyrical fantasy about healing and reconnecting with the full richness of the self.

A beautiful, moving story that skilfully stitches together the fragmented pieces of a brutalised and shattered soul so that it just might fly again
Emma Jane Kirby

A seriously stunning debut that took me as a reader on a haunting and spiritual journey
NB Magazine

Zoë Duncan's beautiful debut novel effortlessly moves between the internal and external reality of a deeply traumatised individual. It's as if she finds a new language to express the inexpressible
Eric Karl Anderson, the Lonesome Reader

This novel has a lyrical quality that movingly deals with loss and memory
Buzz Magazine

We Are Animals

Tim Ewins

A cow looks out to sea, dreaming of a life that involves grass.

Jan is also looking out to sea. He's in Goa, dreaming of the thief who stole his heart (and his passport) forty-six years ago. Back then, fate kept bringing them together, but lately it seems to have given up.

Jan has not. In his long search he has travelled the world, tangling with murderers and pick-pockets and accidentally holding a whole Russian town at imaginary gunpoint. Now he thinks if he just waits and does nothing, fate may find it easier to reunite them.

Featuring a menagerie of creatures, each with its own story to tell, *We Are Animals* is a comic Homeric odyssey with shades of Jonas Jonasson's Hundred-Year-Old Man. It moves and delights in equal measure.

A warm, funny and really original story. It's been one of my favourite books of 2020
Frances Quinn

Wonderful. A funny, heartwarming and craftily clever book
Matson Taylor

Tim Ewins' adventurous tale elegantly combines elements of romance, thriller and comedy while exploring long-lost loves and moving friendships
Woman's Own